THE DARK BROTHERS: BOOK 2

TRAPPED TO TAME

KYRA ALESSY

Copyright 2022 by Dark Realms Press

All rights reserved.

No part of this book may be reproduced in any form or by any electronic or mechanical means, including information storage and retrieval systems, without written permission from the author, except for the use of brief quotations in book reviews.

This work of fiction licensed for your enjoyment only. The story is the property of the author, in all media, both physical and digital, and no one except the author may copy or publish either all or part of this novel without the express permission of the author.

Cover by Deranged Doctor Designs

IF YOU ARE IN ANY WAY RELATED TO ME

Seriously, I feel the need to put this in every book I write. If you are a part of my family, put this book down. Don't read it. Burn it and forget about it. It'll be better for everyone.

Granny, if you're reading this … Ok, fine! But I did warn you, old woman.

To everyone else who's related to me:

Especially you, mom, because I KNOW Granny told you my pen name even though I told her not to, the evil old hag! (Don't worry, I love you anyway, Granny. xx)

If you do not heed this page, never ever speak of it to me. I don't want to hear anything about this book from your lips.

I don't want to hear that you're surprised that I'd write dark romance, or about orgies, and creative ways to use a knife handle and I definitely don't want to you ask me if I write this stuff because mommy and daddy got divorced when I was 8. (SPOILER: It's not. I just like it!)

ALSO BY KYRA ALESSY

Sold to Serve:

Book 1 of the Dark Brothers Series

www.kyraalessy.com/sold2serve

One woman enslaved. Three callous masters. Secrets that could destroy them all …

Bought to Break:

Book 2 of the Dark Brothers Series

www.kyraalessy.com/bought2break

A woman freed from chains. Three ruthless mercenaries redeemed. Intense attraction that won't be denied – no matter the cost.

Kept to Kill:

Book 3 of the Dark Brothers Series

www.kyraalessy.com/kept2kill

A girl in captivity, cursed. Three elite mercenaries, lost. Will forbidden love conquer … or will it kill?

Caught to Conjure:

Book 4 of the Dark Brothers Series

www.kyraalessy.com/caught2conjure

A powerful witch who escaped a life of cruelty. Three Dark Brothers who have a score to settle with her. Will they band together to stop the destruction of their world, or is their hatred stronger than any love?

Seized to Sacrifice:

Book 6 of the Dark Brothers Series

(coming Feb 2022)

www.kyraalessy.com/seized2sacrifice

She has no memory of her past. They remember her crimes far too well. Can love save them, or will everything they care about be destroyed?

For more details on these and the other forthcoming series, please visit Kyra's website:

https://www.kyraalessy.com/bookstore/

CHAPTER 1

EVE

She crept along the forest floor, her eyes peering through the undergrowth, her bow at the ready. The sun shone through the leafy canopy, its rays gathering into little pools of golden light. Sensing movement, she let the arrow fly, striking a deer through its heart some distance away.

She started towards it, but found herself in its place, the bolt protruding from her own chest instead. A man she didn't recognize knelt next to her. He didn't look at her but, with a grim resignation, he began to pull it from her flesh. She screamed, trying to fight, but she was too weak.

Eve woke gasping, clawing at the air above her head, but there was nothing there. She was alone in her freezing room.

She collapsed back onto the thin pallet that barely protected her from the cold floor, letting out a harsh breath. She'd been having the same dream for months, the man in it changed, but it was always one of three. She didn't recognize them, but she'd found herself starting to study the spectators in the crowds while she fought in the ring, almost hoping to see one of them. Gods only knew why. Did she hope they'd save her? She almost smiled at that foolish thought. More likely, she'd get herself killed while she wasn't focusing on her opponent.

Sitting up, she rubbed the sleep from her face and listened to the sounds of the men outside the tiny hovel at the edge of the fighting rings where she lived. The fights had already begun for the day which must mean it was late evening. It would be her turn soon.

The main attraction.

Glancing around her small room, Eve noted that there was no food on the table next to her worn, leather jerkin. Her heart sank. That was Jays' way of telling her that she was meant to lose tonight. Her body didn't need food if she wasn't exerting it to win, and her keeper never spent money when he didn't have to.

Heart thudding hard, she padded across the dirt floor, the iron chain attached to her ankle clanking. She ignored the evidence of the rats that ran rampant down here in the poorer part of town. She was used to them. So long as they didn't try to steal what was hers, she didn't bother with them much. Well, except to talk to them when she was feeling lonely, pathetic as that was.

While donning her red leather armor – and she used that term loosely, for the jerkin was much too small, affording her very little in the way of protection and only real purpose being to show off her small chest advantageously for men to ogle during the fights, she tried to calm herself, not think about later. It would soon be time, and she needed a clear head even if she would be beaten by the Bull tonight.

Swallowing hard, Eve thought about the last time she'd fought him. She'd been given a bowl of thin stew. That meant she was to win. At the time, she'd been glad of the respite, but now her comeuppance was here. The Bull didn't like to lose, no matter how strong his opponent was, no matter what he was told to do. He'd take it out on her later when he returned for his payment – for it wasn't coin he'd take, it was her body.

How much time would Jays allow him after the fight this time? Sometimes it was just enough for him to bend her over and plow her into the table, others he spent hours making her cry and beg for him to stop before Jays finally opened the door and told him to fuck off.

She heard Jays' footsteps outside her room and her stomach leapt into her chest.

It was time.

Taking a long breath, Eve pushed back her shoulders, drawing herself up and ensuring her eyes weren't on the floor. She didn't want to meet their gazes, see the excitement in their faces at the prospect of her humiliating defeat in the rings, but looking down was showing fear and showing fear was like throwing oil on a fire to the Bull. He reveled in her panic even more than her pain.

She put on her old, holey boots and opened the door, masking how the onslaught of sound made her want to cower; men roaring and chanting for the Bull, hoping he'd win tonight and strip her bare in front of the crowd while she hung her head in shame because she was too much of a coward to disobey, showing everyone the trophy he'd won like he had the last time while the town's soldiers turned a blind eye.

Eve was a prize no one else had attained, after all. She was strong; stronger than all the men here, which was a blessing in that she'd only ever lost to the Bull because they told her to, and a curse because her remarkable strength was what had made Talik choose this as the way she must pay her dues.

If she could go back in time, she'd never have joined him officially. She'd have found another way, but street children who didn't ally themselves with a gang died early and Talik was the logical choice. His gang was strong, and he'd looked out for her as long as she could remember. She'd been lucky he'd taken her in, truth be told. She'd never have survived once her unnatural strength made itself known if she hadn't already been one of them.

She watched the Bull, already in the ring and staring at her with a sneer on his face. He knew by now that she'd been told to let him defeat her. He didn't care that it wasn't real so long as everyone else did and he could play with her body after. Feeling sick, she resisted the urge to retch in the dirt. She could practically hear the guffaws from the men around her at *that* sign of weakness.

Money began to change hands as she was assessed. Bets were called, and she knew that more than one man would lose too much coin tonight and find himself in over his head when his debts were called in with Talik tomorrow.

Eve knew how she looked; thin and ill. That was another reason she wasn't fed much. She was strong enough to beat all the men she fought regardless, and it was all part of the hustle – when she was meant to win anyway. Making her lose to the Bull was just another way of Jays and Talik reminding her of her place.

Jays came forward and unlocked the manacle around her ankle, freeing her for the first time since her last fight three days ago. They knew by now that that was all the time she needed to heal from injuries sustained in the ring as well as whatever the Bull did to her after, so that was her only reprieve.

She began to stroll unhurriedly through the throng, smelling unwashed bodies intermingled with the perfumed ones of the monied. Talik would be happy she was drawing the attentions of the wealthier freefolk, that was for certain.

Eve stepped into the pit and, at the Bull's lingering gaze, made herself meet his eyes.

She could hear comments behind her; hoping the Bull would win, put the bitch down, what he'd done last time to make her scream and what her body looked like.

Bile rose.

She couldn't take whatever the Bull had planned today, she just couldn't. She made up her mind in that moment that she would not be losing. She might be fatigued from lack of food and shuddering with real fear, but she would not let him touch her despite the punishment she would undoubtedly receive from Jays later.

Drax

'I DON'T UNDERSTAND why you've dragged us to this hole of a fucking place,' Priest muttered as they picked their way down the muddy main road of yet another town that looked like every other one in this realm.

'We're here because she is here.'

Behind him, Priest snorted, brushing his dark hair away from his face. 'We should already be at the entrance to the Underhill, trying to get through. Instead, we waste time on fools' errands.'

Drax looked over his shoulder at his Brother. 'The portals are gone. That's common knowledge now. If we want to find out what happened in the Underhill, we need help to get there. We need this woman.'

Priest shook his head. 'And who is *this woman* that we're so desperate to find? All we have is vague prophecies – your dreams, Brother. Who's to say she truly exists, that she can even assist us?'

Drax scowled. 'Shut your mouth. You're not the leader here, Priest. Not any longer. She's no more a figment of my mind than you are and she's close. I can feel it.'

Priest shook his head, but didn't speak again and Drax was glad, though his Brother would probably sulk for the rest of the day now. Fie, the third of their unit, eyed them both with a tired expression, but, as usual, elected to stay silent while Drax and Priest argued.

They walked slowly down the main thoroughfare, houses and businesses lining both sides. This town was larger than some, but when the portal in this area had disappeared two years before, the surrounding lands were cut off from the profitable Dark Realm trade routes and more than one noble family had been reduced to poverty overnight. This town had clearly fallen on hard times in the wake of that catastrophe.

'Come,' he said, squelching through the thick mud where the road hadn't been repaired in some time.

There was a chill in the air. Though it wasn't yet winter, the nights were cold, and they'd already traded their thinner cloaks for their fur-lined ones in preparation for their trip north.

'This way.'

Drax walked down towards the river, noticing that the buildings became more and more broken down with casements falling off their hinges, houses without doors and rotten timbers making roofs sag.

They heard the dim roaring of the men watching the fights in the pits and he knew, without a shadow of a doubt, that this was where they would find the female they were seeking. His gift was foresight and, though at times it was maddeningly vague, some visions – as this one had been –

were so clear in his mind's eye that there was no misinterpreting them.

'There's only one manner of woman who'd be in this part of the town,' Priest muttered and, though Drax secretly agreed with him, he sent his Brother a warning look.

They approached the rings, seeing that the fights had already begun for the evening, and Drax was taken aback to see there was a tiny woman fighting a great bear of a man. He stopped to watch, and it looked as if she was holding her own though she was so much smaller than her opponent.

Interesting.

Drax stepped closer, watching her fight the man who was at least three heads taller than she and practically as broad as a building where she was a tiny, bony thing. He grabbed her around the throat, laughing as he cut off her air and she flailed.

He was playing with her, Drax thought. Perhaps that was why she wasn't lying face down in the dirt already. But she surprised him by pulling one of the great man's meaty fingers back and levering his hand from her neck. Clearly, her small stature belied a greater strength. Drax cast his eyes over her thoroughly, even more intrigued.

She was painfully thin and short with light hair that was plaited out of her way. Dull, brown eyes were vacant and showed little. In truth, she looked like every other downtrodden human woman in this realm who'd had a hard life; nothing out of the ordinary.

She pulled her arm back and struck the man in the face hard enough for him to fall over. The crowd shouted and booed, but he recovered quickly and backhanded her in kind, causing the men around them to thunder their approvals. Clearly this woman wasn't well liked.

She staggered and slipped in the mud, and her opponent approached with a jeering laugh. But she kicked out at him as soon as he was close enough, striking him in the knee. He bellowed in pain, stumbling back a step, and holding onto his leg.

He growled something, and she bared her teeth before she unstuck herself from the muck. Again, he advanced on her, arm raised to swat her as if she was a gnat to crush. She ducked, her short stature making it easy to avoid the giant as she stepped close and delivered an uppercut to the underside of his chin so hard that he flew off his feet and landed some paces away, unconscious.

The men around them jostled, deafening, in a frenzy as their favorite lost. Money was changing hands rapidly and a few men at the front looked very angry indeed. The fight had not gone their way, it seemed.

Drax watched the woman walk to the edge of the ring. A tall man dressed in rags came to stand next to her, surveying her unmoving foe and giving her a scowl that she ignored.

The announcer called for another to fight her, and no one stepped forward, the unruly crowd quieting oddly. They feared her. Drax didn't hesitate, however. He strode into the pit, passing his tunic and belt to Fie.

The woman rolled her eyes as she saw him but met him in the middle of the ring as if she was simply humoring him. He almost smiled at her arrogance. Soon she'd know what real strength looked like, felt like. She'd not find him so easy to beat as the man she had just fought.

When the fight began, Drax began by taking her measure, letting her move around him. He watched the way she darted in and out, saving her strength. She was slender and gaunt. How she'd overpowered the other man, Drax didn't know.

She was staring at him now that he was closer with an odd look on her face. He watched as she shook her head slightly, banishing whatever thoughts had been stealing her focus, and she stepped forward again.

He let her get a strike in, though he could easily have blocked her fist. Pain exploded in his jaw. She was strong for a human woman. He grinned, disconcerting her as he sprang and, quick as a snake, hit her across the face with the back of his fist. Her head snapped to the side, and she fell into the dirt with a cry, looking up at him with a mixture of fear and surprise.

'Aye,' he murmured under the sound of the men gathering closer, clambering to watch. 'No one's hit you that hard before, have they, woman?'

She got to her feet, looking a bit dazed and moving her jaw as if it pained her. Her eyes narrowed on him, truly seeing him, and treating him with respect now that she understood he was more than her equal.

He let her get two or three more hits in before he retaliated, moving in and striking her straight in the stomach, making her double over and retch in the dirt. He knelt next to her as she wheezed, trying to recover as her body cramped, and grabbed her by the throat, lifting her into the air. A trickle of blood came from her lip, and he smelled it; oddly muted ... and somehow familiar. Human *and fae*.

So that was where her strength came from. He barely subdued the growl that emanated from his throat as he realized why she smelled familiar, the bloodline she belonged to ... exactly why they'd been led to her. He knew who she was, and the smell of her catapulted him into a fury. Gods only knew why she was in such a place as this, but what mattered was that they had finally found their means of entering the Underhill and for that reason alone he wouldn't kill her. Not yet.

Holding back a cold smile as her eyes began to roll into the back of her head, he came up with a plan to use this turn of events – and her – to their advantage. He glanced at his Brothers who stood in the crowd looking bored. He stifled a snort of amusement. They looked how he felt. After all, they'd fought in the rings in more than one Dark Realm, battled beasts that would make these humans piss themselves in terror. This wasn't real combat to Priest and Fie any more than it was to him. Now that Drax knew who and what this female was, this one-sided fight was a waste of his time.

He set her down, loosening his hand, and, when her eyes opened, he watched them widen with no small amount of satisfaction as he pulled his fist back, hitting her in the jaw just once more; hard enough for her to go limp in his arms. Drax dropped the female back in the mud and ignored the shout of praise that came from the many men there. Her thin keeper approached him when he got to the edge of the small arena.

'Now or later?' was all he asked.

Drax glanced at his Brothers who both wore the same expressions of confusion. But he wasn't one to give up the higher ground, so he merely inclined his head, pretending to know what the man was talking about.

'Later.'

The man nodded. 'Come back when the moon is high.'

The woman was lifted up by her laughably scandalous clothes now covered in mud as if she were no more than a piece of luggage. After she was taken out of sight through a small door that looked half-rotten, he, Priest, and Fie turned away, walking the short distance to the local taphouse to wait for the moon to rise.

Eve

'HE'S HERE,' Jays said. He looked her up and down and pointed at her. 'Do as you're told,' he warned. 'No funny business or I won't let you eat for a week, bitch, I promise you that.'

She glowered at him, and he turned away, leaving the room. Sitting on the edge of the pallet in her long, threadbare chemise, Eve awaited her fate.

She'd been surprised when Jays had said the man who had beaten her in the ring was coming back though she shouldn't have been. She knew what men were like and he had won her, after all. That's how he would see it anyway. That was how they thought.

Still, at least he seemed cleaner and definitely more handsome than the Bull. Perhaps it wouldn't be so bad with him.

She could hear Jays talking outside the door with the winner, could see his shadow moving.

'Them too,' came a gruff voice she didn't recognize.

Jays shrugged and she tensed. *More than one?* Her mind went blank with fear. She'd only ever been with the Bull, never his friends, but Jays wouldn't care as long as there was enough of her left to heal when they were finished.

Her eyes darted around the room, looking for something, anything that she could use as a weapon to protect herself. But there was nothing. Jays had taken everything while she'd been unconscious. Even her boots were gone. Her chain clanged as she shifted. The coward had put her on her leash while she'd been out as well.

The manacle made her body feel weaker. She'd been very careful never to bring any attention to that fact, always remaining docile while she wasn't in the ring so no one would find out how vulnerable she was in here. But that meant she couldn't fight these men who'd come for her in any capacity. She'd have to let them do whatever they wanted ... just like she had to with the Bull.

She stood up as the men entered, a piteous display of strength, but it was better than nothing. Three of them.

The dark-haired one who had beaten her was in front. His face bore a scar or two, but he didn't look like a seasoned fighter. She'd noticed that before in the ring which was why she hadn't even considered that he might be a match for her. He was handsome, more so than other men she saw in this part of town where most spent what little coin they had on drink and faerie flowers to smoke.

He was dressed in a dark green tunic that brought out his eyes of the same hue. She tried not to stare at him, but, as the other two entered the room, she found it wasn't difficult to tear her eyes away. The other two were just as large as the first. One had blue eyes and long hair so fair it was almost white. It was plaited in places with braided pieces of leather and silver beads woven through it as if he took great care with it. His clothes were of tan animal skin, and his boots were tall and black. He was as handsome as the first but looked a bit younger.

The final one had dark hair like the first, but it was longer like the blonde's and plaited in parts, but with no beads. He wore a deep grey tunic and breeches of fine, dark leather that hugged his thighs and, somehow, made him look indecent.

They were all leaner than the Bull, but that wasn't saying much. Most men were. They were taller than him too and it made her feel even tinier than usual. It was yet another item in a very long list of things she didn't like about this moment.

Eve gaped at them all; their handsome faces and clean, quality clothes marking them as outsiders. She recognized them. Though she'd never seen them here before, knew them instantly. She'd seen them all for months while she slept at night. She didn't know what that meant, but she'd bet it wouldn't be good for her.

They shuffled inside, staring at her. The door closed, leaving them alone. The one who had fought her stepped forward and she raised her chin in defiance. She would not tremble before them, though, as her knees knocked together, she wished her body had gotten the message not to show fear.

'Get on with it,' the winner's dark-haired friend behind him muttered.

The winner was their leader, she supposed.

He stepped forward again and she involuntarily took a step back, feeling the wall behind her. She cursed herself. There was nowhere to go. Why was she pretending to herself that there might be any outcome other than what was going to happen now?

'I need you to open a portal to the Underhill,' he said, and, for a moment, she simply stared at him in utter disbelief, wondering if she'd heard him correctly.

Of all the things she might have expected him to say to her, that phrase was definitely not one of them.

'A portal, female,' he said, impatiently. 'Open one now!'

She gave him an incredulous look. *Open portals?* A laugh bubbled to the surface, and she covered her mouth, trying not to let it burst forth, but she failed. She practically doubled over with it; couldn't remember the last time someone had made her giggle.

He looked angry ... and something else. He thought her mind unhinged. She could see that same wariness in his eyes that were in her opponents' sometimes.

She put her hand up to stay him.

'It's been a long time since anyone made me laugh,' she said between cackles.

'I don't understand the jest,' he said, sharply.

Inwardly, she flinched at his tone, but she didn't let it show. This man did not like to joke.

'Do you think,' she asked, giving him a haughty look, 'that if I could simply open a portal, I'd be here?'

She wiggled her bare foot and the chain clanged. His attention moved down to it, and he looked confused.

'You don't know how to open a portal.'

Was he a simpleton?

'No,' she said with a roll of her eyes. 'I don't, but if I did, I'd suck you into the darkest realm there is.'

He stepped forward and she darted back, tripping on the chain, and falling onto the pallet. She scrambled away from him, pulling the chain with her so that she could curl up into the corner of the room even though she was only delaying the inevitable.

The man reached for her and this time she did flinch away, fear rushing to the fore. But instead of using the chain to pull her towards him and spreading her legs immediately as the Bull would have done, his thick fingers wound around the manacle. She noticed, with an acute awareness that swept through her, the warm skin brushing inadvertently against hers as, with brute strength, he pulled the metal apart and it practically disintegrated in his hands.

Her mouth fell open. How many times had she tried and failed to get that cursed thing off?

'Inferior iron,' was all he said as he moved away from her, giving her space.

She rubbed the red, chafed skin where the manacle had been, not taking her eyes off them while she focused on the door behind them immediately. Could she make it without one of them catching her?

Even if she did, where would she go? She'd spent all her life in this town. She had no friends anywhere and no means of supporting herself bar on her back. Perhaps in the fights, but wherever she went, her steps would be dogged for there were very few female fighters. She would always be noticed in the ring and remarked upon. Remembered. Talik would find her.

For the moment, she stayed where she was, sensing that these men were not finished with her yet. Already she trusted the man in front of her more than she did any other she'd ever met before. In that one second, he had done more for her than anyone ever had. It wasn't saying much, but it was enough to make curiosity win out over self-preservation.

CHAPTER 2

PRIEST

*P*riest stood behind his Brother. Her blood. This room reeked of it, and he knew the smell of that bloodline well, already disliking the small female in front of him for that reason alone.

'Make her do what we came here for and let's be away from this foul place,' he grumbled.

His Brother turned to him. 'She's already said that she cannot.'

Priest gestured to the door and Drax followed him out to where the woman couldn't hear them.

'Then why did you free her?' he said, his tone low. 'She doesn't even know what she is. She doesn't know how to conjure.'

'We'll take her with us.'

Priest didn't hide his disparaging grimace at Drax's ridiculous idea. 'She's useless. I say we leave without bothering with her any further.'

'No,' Drax growled. 'I'm not wrong. You can smell her too. You know who her father must be.'

'All the more reason to leave. Slay the bitch, and let's be gone.'

'I say we need her,' Drax insisted. 'I'll have my final revenge when we're finished with her.'

He left Priest standing in the doorway as he went back inside the dirty hovel, clearly finished with their discussion.

Priest followed slowly. If he was still in command here, he'd slit her throat now in the knowledge that all the fae were better off with one less branch of her family tree in existence; half-blood or no, but it wasn't his decision to make. Not anymore.

'We need you to help us,' Drax said to the female. 'If you do, we'll free you.'

Her unremarkable brown eyes narrowed as she surveyed them. She seemed slightly more intelligent than he'd first assumed, he'd give her that.

'Fine,' she said simply.

Priest didn't let the doubt show on his face, but that had been far too easy.

Even as he thought it, she darted up from her stinking pallet and ran from the room. Fie moved to stop her, but Drax stayed him with a gesture.

'We know her scent,' he said. 'She won't get far. Besides, she doesn't even seem to have any clothes. She'll freeze out there tonight if she runs from us.'

Priest heard a thud outside and the female returned a moment later, carrying a pair of boots, some trousers and the ridiculous leather jerkin that somehow made even her inadequate tits look enticing.

She began to get dressed in front of them and Priest walked out into the darkness with a shake of his head. Beside the building, he found her keeper slumped over asleep. This man had, in effect, sold her to them.

They hadn't known earlier why they'd been told to return

at this late hour, but they didn't want any trouble that would delay them, so they'd waited. From the state of the female when they'd arrived, though, it seemed that she'd been prepared to spread her legs for them.

Priest snorted. As if they'd want such a tiny, weak thing. He liked his women with a bit more substance to them, even the human ones when he was so inclined.

But even if he'd been interested, as soon as he had smelled her family's blood in that room, that would have put a stop to any feelings of ardor. One thing was for certain, once she got them to the Underhill, he would slit her throat if Drax didn't regardless of their bargain with her. The bitch should know better than to make deals with fae and expect fairness anyway. Hopefully one day soon, he'd get the chance to kill the one he really wanted as well. Her sire.

Feeling like taking his aggression out on someone, he walked briskly to the slumbering keeper, but as he neared, Priest noticed the man's head rested on his shoulders at an odd angle. God's, it had been practically twisted off. He glanced back into the room and snorted. She'd taken her own revenge quickly. He'd have to remember not to underestimate her. She was more than she seemed.

Eve

EVE DRAGGED ON HER BOOTS, ignoring the chill of the night air as it blew through the tiny room made all the smaller by the three hulking men taking up all the space. They were attractive, more so than other men who frequented the rings, but there was something about them that made her fear.

She was rarely afraid of small groups of men regardless of their size, but these ones ... they were predators and they made her instinctually feel like prey. She didn't like it, not at all.

They spoke of taking her with them, making a deal, and she couldn't stay here, not after what she just done to Jays. She didn't regret it. It had felt good to feel the bones in his neck crack under her fingers. He'd deserved that and more.

Finishing getting dressed, she looked at them expectantly, and they seemed at a loss as to what to do with her for a moment. Perhaps they'd thought she wouldn't willingly go with them.

'I'm Drax,' said the one who must be the leader. He pointed with his thumb behind him to the other dark-haired one. 'Priest.' And with the other hand. 'Fie.'

'Eve,' she said roughly.

'Eve,' the one called Fie muttered. He said her name like a caress as he looked at her.

She swallowed hard and ignored his smirk, as if he knew how he affected her.

'Come,' Priest said. 'She's killed her keeper. We need to be gone before anyone sees.'

She snorted. 'No one will notice until morning.'

Drax ignored her words, gesturing for her to follow them and they all filed through the doorway of her room.

She looked around it for the last time. She wouldn't miss this place, she thought as she stared at the uncomfortable pallet on the dirt floor and the rough, uneven table ... the fireless grate. For nigh on twenty years, she'd been alive and all she had to show for it was a pair of worn, holey boots that made her slip in the mud, and threadbare clothes that didn't keep her warm and made her look like a woman who sold her wares at night.

Eve trailed after the three men, deciding to bide her time for now. She walked past Jays and spat on his corpse. If the men noticed, they didn't give her any indication as they walked in front of her through the town to the nicer echelons; places she hadn't seen since she'd been brought to the rings that first time when she was probably only about thirteen winters. So much looked the same, yet older, more worn. Much like her, she supposed.

When they reached the main gates, the portcullis was still open. They passed under it and, though there were guards loitering around, no one interfered with their leaving, which made Eve pause. Town soldiers sat around in groups, not even looking in their direction. She was used to these so-called protectors of the innocent turning a blind eye to the horrors that happened in the town slums every day; things that they were paid not to see, but this was different. It was as if she and the men she walked with weren't even there.

'Keep up,' Drax commanded, and she scurried after them through the main gatehouse.

Dense forest lined the other side of the road and the men in front of her walked into the trees as if there was nothing to fear.

But Eve had never been outside the town wall.

Her heart seized and, just for a moment, she froze. She forced a breath into her lungs and looked back. Foolish as it was, a part of her wanted to run back into the confines of the town. She'd never been in the forest before; never even been allowed near the gates to see it.

'What's wrong with the female?' Priest asked.

She didn't need to look to know it was him. She already recognized his gravelly, condescending voice. He was angry. He didn't like her. She didn't give a fuck. It wouldn't be for long, she promised herself. They were fools of the highest degree for not ensuring she was bound in iron before they destroyed her chain.

She made herself follow them into the trees, and they

came upon a small camp with a fire burning brightly – one she hadn't smelled nor seen until they were right on top of it.

Another oddity.

There were three black horses close by; the largest she'd ever seen, munching on hay that had been left on the ground for them. Something delicious-smelling was bubbling in a pot and Eve hid a grimace as her stomach rumbled loudly. She didn't want them to think she needed them, but she hadn't been fed for two days.

The one with the blond hair, Fie, gave her a sideways look as he sat by the fire.

'Come,' he said, stirring the bubbling pot.

He ladled some out into a bowl, offering it to her and she took it gingerly, half-afraid it was a trick. But she was hungry, too hungry to give it any more thought than that as she dipped her fingers into the thick gravy, digging for the meat first though it burned her fingers and scalded her mouth. Shoveling it in as quickly as she could, she used her fingers to mop the bowl clean, and only then did she realize that all three pairs of eyes were watching her with an intensity that she found unnerving.

'Been a while since you ate?' Fie looked her up and down.

Her cheeks heated, but she held his gaze, not making an excuse.

Fie took the bowl gently from her fingers and she had to stop herself from grasping it to her and practically growling at him, wanting to lick whatever remnants there were from the bottom.

But he didn't whisk it away as she feared. Instead, he filled it up again and handed it to her. Her hands shook slightly in excitement as she accepted it. *Two* bowls? She'd never been offered more. Not ever.

She was still hungry, but this time she took the proffered spoon that he held, and sat down by the fire, taking her time to eat and enjoy the fayre she'd been given, putting the empty bowl down beside her with a sated sigh when she was finished. For the first time in a very long time, her stomach felt full.

'It's late,' Drax said from the other side of the fire.

A blanket was thrown to her, and she took it gratefully. She'd been starting to shiver despite the hearty flames in front of her. She wrapped it around herself, curled up and lay down on the cold ground, pretending to fall asleep immediately. She waited until all that was left around her were the sounds of the fire crackling, logs making hissing noises at times as it burned, and the soft snores of the men. She stayed where she was until the night was late and, in fact, was probably approaching the early hours of the morning.

Eve cracked an eye open. All three men were sound asleep. She eyed them dispassionately. She *should* kill them, but as soon as she thought it, she was repulsed by the mere idea. They needed her for something, and she had no illusions that they were friends. She knew that, really, she owed them nothing, but they hadn't been unduly cruel to her, and she would not repay that by slitting their throats like a coward while they slept.

She took the blanket with her as she left, for she was no fool and it might very well mean the difference between life and death for her over the coming nights. As she walked slowly backwards out of the camp, away from the fire's flickering light, Eve spied a bag. She picked up as she went, hoping for something useful inside, and, quietly as she could, she walked away through the trees, glad to find that her eyes were able to adjust well enough in the dark for her to see enough to avoid the many obstacles out here.

Keeping her breathing slow and even, she tried not to panic in the darkness. The terrain was as alien to her as if she were a wild boar in the center of town, but she could do this, she told herself. She had to. Going back to her life before wasn't an option. It didn't matter how much money she made for Talik and his men in the ring. He'd think of something gruesome as a lesson to all for what she'd done. At the very least, he'd take one of her hands. And she couldn't stay with these men either... not after the dreams she'd had of them pulling out her heart.

She went south, at least she thought it was south. She couldn't see by the stars because the night had grown cloudy. The air smelled like snow although she didn't think it was quite cold enough. Her feet begged to differ though, her toes already numb, but still she kept walking. She didn't exert herself, but neither did she waste time by resting.

By the time the sun began to rise, and light pierced the dense forest, she was happy with her progress. She opened the bag she'd liberated from the men, finding cheese and bread. She grinned to herself. A good haul if ever there was one.

Eve realized she needed to come up with a plan. She'd never even seen a map of their realm, but she supposed that if she kept walking, she'd at least come across a town or a village. Perhaps she could fight in the pit if they had one. Once or twice would be enough to buy some decent clothes for the cold, but she wouldn't be able to win every time. Talik would be waiting for news of such a woman. If she wanted to remain anonymous, she would have to keep travelling. Perhaps she could go to the sea, take a boat to the Islands, and get as far away from Talik and his men as possible. Perhaps she could start a family, find a place to belong. She gave a small laugh. It was a fine dream; one she'd had since she was a child when she'd realized how alone she was. She put it from her mind. Escape was all she should think about now. Her eyes had to remain only on her goal, or she would fail.

She heard the trickle of a stream and went to find it for a drink, washing her face in the cold water. She allowed herself a moment of respite.

She shouldn't have.

～

Fie

HE'D BEEN WATCHING her for quite a while and the foolish female hadn't even noticed him. She didn't even sniff the air. She seemed so human in every way that he could see. Perhaps it really was as Priest suspected, that she had no idea that she was half fae. But someone had to have known, surely, or else why chain her with iron, even bad quality iron?

Though he supposed it didn't really matter. He just hoped to the gods that they would be able to use her power. They needed to get to the Underhill. *He* needed to get there.

He stared at the little female washing her face. So oblivious. Cocking his head, he surveyed her for a moment more. Gods she was ridiculously tiny, even for a human woman. Had she really thought it would be so easy to escape them? He sniffed the air again. She'd been so easy to track. She had no idea how to hide her presence from the forest trails. Broken sticks, footprints; everything had been left in her wake including her sweet smell. It was pathetic for a fae, even a halfling. He almost felt sorry for the wench.

He jumped down from the bough that he had been standing on, having waited for the moment when she was relaxed completely just so that he could scare her the most. Splashing her, he landed directly in front of her in the ankle-high water. She jumped back with a scream, falling into the stream.

He laughed loudly at her – and not without malice. Fie hated this girl's father as much as Priest did, though perhaps not as much as Drax, and taunting her did make him feel better, petty as it was.

'Get up and come on,' he said. 'You've cost us time.'

'H–how did you find me?' she stuttered.

He rolled his eyes and grabbed her by the back of the neck, urging her forward in front of him so he didn't keep staring at her hard nipples poking through her thin shirt over that ridiculous jerkin she wore. At least they didn't have far to go to reach the others. The silly female had walked in circles all night and morning.

'How does even a human like you get to adulthood and be so incompetent?' he muttered. 'Your own kin should have killed you out of mercy before your first bloods.'

She gave him a look of confusion that turned sharp. 'I'm not incompetent.'

He snorted in response, his hand moving to her neck again to direct her.

She shook him off with a sound of anger. 'I don't need to be herded like a goat.'

'Walk then,' he ordered.

She was silent for a time as they made their way through the forest before she glanced back at him.

'What did you mean when you said "a human like me"?'

He shrugged but inwardly he grimaced. Had he really said 'human'? He pretended ignorance, as if it was normal for one human to call another such a thing. 'Foolish. Living in squalor. Fighting in the rings for money.' He took in her red jerkin. 'Doing *other things* for it.'

Her face was blank as she looked away, his intimation clear.

'We'll reach the camp soon,' he said, glad she didn't question his earlier choice of words any further and wanting to see her annoyance when she realized she'd walked around all night for no reason whatsoever.

She looked up at him. 'But I walked for so long.'

He chuckled. 'See? Foolish. No idea where you are. No sense of direction. It's as if you've never been in the forest before.'

She looked down again and said, 'I haven't' so quietly that if he wasn't fae, he'd not have heard her.

He stopped in his tracks, incredulous. 'You've never been in the forest? But you live in the middle of it ...'

She turned away from him, continuing to walk and not saying anything more. Humans were such an odd breed, but Fie found he wanted to know more if only to satisfy his own curiosity.

'How long did you live in the town for?'

She was silent and he thought perhaps she was finished talking, but then she answered him.

'All my life.'

He scoffed. He couldn't help it. 'And you never ventured into the forest? Ever?'

'No.'

'But—'

'Gods, but you're tiresome!' she blurted, stopping, and turning back. 'I'm the fool? Shall I say it plainly for you?'

Fie nodded.

'I was chained when I wasn't in the ring. How was I meant to stroll into the forest even if I had a mind to, which I didn't?'

Fie frowned. He hadn't thought ... 'How long?'

This time she didn't answer him.

Fie frowned. She clearly wasn't a slave, but if what she said was true, she had more courage than he'd given her credit for. There weren't many females who would go off by themselves, especially if they had little practical knowledge of the outside world. Though perhaps he shouldn't call it courage at all.

'Foolish woman,' he said instead, and watched as she bristled.

She didn't like that. He grinned again. It would be very simple – and quite enjoyable – to whip the tiny female into a fury.

She didn't speak anymore and neither did he, content to simply watch her walk in front of him, sliding every so often in her short, tattered boots.

He'd found that most, human and fae alike, would try to fill the silence with chatter, spilling all sorts of secrets, but she did not.

By the time they reached the Underhill, he'd know everything there was to know about this one though. That was his skill, after all, and he'd enjoy the challenge. He'd get inside her head, under her skin, understand what motivated her, how she thought. He'd be able to manipulate her into doing whatever he wished, and he wouldn't have to threaten or subdue her. She was in far above her head. The little female had no idea what she was in for.

He led her back to camp and enjoyed the look on her face when she saw how close they actually were, how the fatigue she was feeling was all for naught.

'Eat,' he told her. 'We leave very soon.' He raised a brow. 'And you're walking.'

She glowered as she looked away, grabbing a hard biscuit that was warming by the fire and breaking it apart with her fingers, shoving it into her mouth at speed as if she was afraid it would be taken.

'Gods, she's practically a beast,' Priest muttered from his horse.

Fie saw her cheeks redden slightly. She wasn't as immune to his Brother's barbs as she'd like them to believe.

Drax came back to the camp on his horse. 'I've scouted the way,' he said. 'We'll take the ferry upriver. That'll be faster until the freeze.'

He noticed Eve by the fire and scowled at her. 'I told you that we will free you when you have fulfilled your purpose,' he said coldly. 'Do not test my patience, female. Run from us again and you'll be punished.'

He didn't spare her another look, turning his horse and walking it slowly into the trees.

Priest snapped his fingers and the fire extinguished itself. The woman, already following Drax's horse, didn't even notice.

Fie would wager that the woman knew very little about the fae. Even if she did somehow realize something was odd about them, he doubted she'd have any idea that they were more than what they seemed unless they told her. He grinned as he watched her retreating form. She looked exhausted and she was shivering from falling in the stream. He doubted she had the stamina for another futile sojourn.

They journeyed for most of the day, reaching a small town where they'd catch the ferry that would take them just shy of Kitore. Priest, always preferring an inn to the cold, hard ground in winter, procured them a room at the finest establishment to be found while Drax booked their passage on the boat the following morning.

Fie was left to mind the female who was all wide eyes and naive expressions. She must be at least twenty winters and yet she had a child's excitement about the most mundane things. Perhaps she didn't realize that her face showed every emotion when it wasn't guarded.

He trudged up the stairs, her trailing after him. The inn was fine enough to have a bath already prepared so as soon as he got in the room, he took pity on the tired girl and gestured to it.

'Bathe yourself,' he said. 'You stink.'

If she took offence, she didn't show it as she kicked off her boots, not seeming to care that he was present. She unlaced the jerkin and pulled off her thin undershirt, her worn chemise underneath as dirty and unkempt as she was.

He turned away as she began to shuck her breeches though part of him wanted to watch. He was surprised that he had any chivalry left in him. He steeled himself not to look until after he heard her get into the water, but at her soft moan, he could wait no longer, and his eyes fell on the tiny, painfully thin female; her eyes closed and her head resting on the bath. She sighed deeply, able, it seemed, to completely relax in his presence. He shook his head. *Silly, silly female.*

She took a breath and dunked her head beneath the water coming up a moment later and he couldn't help but watch in fascination at the unbridled pleasure she took in something he found so commonplace.

When she began to lather the soap in her brown hair, he finally left the room, going downstairs to the small tap house to order food for them. He noted Drax in the doorway and gestured with his head that the female was upstairs in their room. His Brother trudged up and Fie ordered an ale, deciding to settle in until their food was ready.

CHAPTER 3

EVE

The bath was easily the best thing that Eve had ever felt. Sometimes she'd washed with water that she heated herself in her tiny room on the rare occasions that Jays had brought dried dung for her to burn in the tiny grate, but she'd never been so enveloped by warmth. She promised herself that once she escaped these men, she'd find a way to have one of these every single day.

After what she'd fortuitously heard people whispering about on their way through the town, she'd already decided on a course of action. It wouldn't be long now.

SHE OPENED HER EYES, realizing she must have drifted off to sleep, though only for a little while as the water was still warm. The room was empty, and she supposed it was time to think about her next step. She left the bath, letting the water sluice down her body to dry in the warmth of the room. She put on her stinking clothes, wishing she had something clean to wear, but even if there were clothes in the men's bags, it wasn't as if anything of theirs would fit her.

She'd probably need something more substantial to wear soon though. The weather was getting colder, and she had heard them mention the Ice Plains. Perhaps they'd provide her with something warmer if she wasn't successful in her bid for freedom tonight. They wouldn't want her to die before she did whatever it was they'd brought her along for, she supposed. But if they did, would they expect more in return? By the way they all looked at her, she didn't think it would be the same thing as what the Bull always wanted from her. That was a good thing, she told herself. All men knew how to do was hurt. Even the beautiful ones.

She plaited her hair anew to keep it away from her face. She should cut it, she thought. It was a hazard in the fights, but Jays had never let her, telling her that Talik said it was part of the draw. She bared her teeth at the thought of him and the others. She hoped that they didn't come looking for her. But if they did, she'd do everything in her power to send them all to their graves before she went back to that fucking room, before she let the Bull ever touch her again.

Her boots were by the bed, and she faltered as she began to slip her bare feet into them, knowing how they were going to feel against her warm toes. She grimaced as she forced them on and shivered. Cold and wet. The first thing she'd buy if she ever got the chance were new boots that didn't let in the weather, she decided. They'd be tall ones of the finest leather. Beautiful too.

She ventured outside the room, happy to find that the door was not locked. They didn't think she'd try to escape again. *Fools.* She made sure her hated jerkin was as tight as she could make it. She'd need to look the part for what she intended.

Having a thought, she darted back into their room and grabbed the same bag she'd taken before, knowing it would be refilled with food. She brought it downstairs with her and stuck it in a corner behind a large plant pot out of sight.

Eve entered the tap room. The three men were sitting at a table by the back wall; a strategic location so no one could sneak up. She approached them, taking a deep breath. It was time to escape these men properly. She couldn't afford to underestimate them again.

Fie nodded to the fourth chair. 'Sit.'

She did as Fie said. It was odd, but she liked the timbre of his voice, finding that it made her feel calm when she rarely did. She looked around, trying not to gape. She hadn't been in an inn for a very long time. Not since she was thieving as a child, in fact, before she'd joined Talik.

A plate of meat was slid across the table to her, and she began to eat the fayre slowly, trying to emulate the manners of the others lest her behavior be remarked upon again. Though she felt hungrier than ever, she didn't like them poking fun at her.

She felt Drax's eyes on her.

'Should have got her something to wear.'

Eve watched his gaze dip down to her breasts and noticed that one or two other men in the room were also watching her.

She didn't stop eating, pretending to ignore them all.

She heard Priest scoff. 'Probably for the best that we didn't waste the coin. The way she eats, she'll probably drop her dinner all down herself anyway.'

She didn't need to look up to know that his eyes were also staring at her chest. She finished her plate and then stood, resisting the urge to suck the marrow from the bones.

'I assume your generosity extends to ale,' she said to Drax, her eyes flicking to the long, wooden table behind which an assortment of gargantuan barrels lay on their sides, taps protruding from their bases.

Fie snorted, but Drax nodded, and she made her way across the room.

Knowing they watched, she pretended to look for a serving wench as she surreptitiously searched the room for her mark. A group of soldiers entered the tap room, and, as she watched them, she knew she had found the ones she wanted. From their uniforms, they were a noble house's men probably sent to the town to keep it safe at night.

One of the soldiers noticed her waiting alone and broke away from the group. She turned towards him with a smile and watched his eyes predictably move down to the skin she had on show.

'Haven't seen you here before,' he said smoothly.

Somehow curtailing the instinctual rolling of her eyes, she instead smiled demurely at him again. 'Perhaps you can help me. Those men there, the three sitting across the room. They're thieves planning to steal into a noble family's home tonight. I don't know what to do.'

Eve wrung her hands and looked worried for affect.

The soldier's eyes narrowed as he looked at the table where Drax, Priest, and Fie sat. They weren't even watching her now, oblivious to what she was doing.

The soldier didn't even ask her any more questions though she had thought up a story to explain how she knew what she'd just told him. He merely thanked her and went back to his friends. Eve turned away, pretending not to notice when he and his men stood and approached Drax and the others at their table.

She couldn't hear what was said, but as soon as swords were drawn, she moved, walking quickly and decisively from the room, but not so fast as to be noticed.

Eve found the bag she'd stowed and left the inn, grabbing a random cloak that was hung on a hook with some others. It was too long for her, but that didn't matter. She grinned as she walked down the street and out the way they'd come earlier, back towards the forest.

This time, before she did anything else, she found a stream and, after tying the cloak up around her waist, she waded into the frigid waters. Braving the cold, she walked against the current. She didn't know how to hide her tracks from them, but now she didn't have to. They wouldn't find her again.

She walked into the night until she was too tired to go any further. Only then did she leave the water, her feet so numb that she could hardly walk. She huddled under her stolen cloak beside a boulder out of the worst of the wind and tried to sleep.

The Dark Army was camped not far away. That was what she'd heard them speaking of in the town. The Dark Brothers. She thought she had some of the skills required to be a mercenary. She didn't know if they would let a woman like her join, but if they did, she would become one of them, she vowed.

In the morning, the weather had turned. It was rainy and cold, the sun hidden by dense, low cloud but still Eve pressed on, huddled in her sodden cloak. She left the stream, walking through winding animal trails and wondering how long it would take to get to the Army where it was currently camped in the east. They were close enough for the townsfolk to be nervous, so it couldn't be that far away.

She walked well into the day before she dug into the food she had stolen from the Brothers. She only ate a little bit of the bread though, trying to eke it out for as long as possible in case the Brothers had moved on or it took longer to find them.

She came across another stream, this time flowing in an opposite direction. She followed it, hoping it would lead her to something more than trees, copses, and valleys. She'd had no idea the realm was so fucking big!

She spent another night huddled in the wet cloak, cold and shivering and, the next day, the weather got even colder. Her teeth were chattering as she began her journey and, by midday, her reserves were completely depleted.

She sat and ate more than she had the day before, hunger, cold, and exhaustion gnawing at her desire to continue, but she had to keep moving or she would die out here. She had to find the Army. It was only a matter of time.

As soon as she felt that her legs could carry her once more, she stood up and began to walk.

It wasn't until the late afternoon that she finally came upon a small camp. Staying out of sight in the trees, she watched and waited, grinning when she saw three men dressed in black coming out of a large tent. This was but a small party, but the rest of the Army had to be close. It just had to be.

She was hungry and tired, but she circumvented the camp and continued on. Just as the sky was beginning to darken, she was rewarded by the twinkling of a hundred or so small fires in the valley below her. She'd found them! Feeling as if a weight had been lifted from her, she began to make her way down over the rough terrain of the hill.

At the bottom, she found that she was practically in the Camp already. She walked through an outer perimeter of small, patched tents where dangerous-looking people who reminded her of where she'd come from loitered in groups by tiny fires that gave out little light and even less heat. Her lips turned up in grim determination. Eve felt almost at home, sad as that was.

She reached a sort-of boundary. Everything past it was uniform and looked well-maintained. A guard stopped her as she began to cross over the invisible line, and she looked him in the eye.

'I wish to join the Brothers,' she said.

The soldier had the audacity to laugh in her face.

'She wants to join the Brothers,' he mocked, looking at her stature and clearly finding her wanting. He clucked her under the chin. 'You'd do better in the pleasure tents, sweet.'

She batted his hand away with a growl. 'I'll do whatever I need to,' she said, 'but I belong with the Brothers as one of them.'

'If you want to prove yourself, you do it in the rings, but you have to win your first fight.'

She grinned darkly. Now that was something she could do.

He nodded to another soldier close by.

'Take her there.'

Eve found herself following one of the other guards through the Camp; the real Camp. She could hear the sounds of fighting, a balm on her soul – also sad, but true.

They arrived at their destination, and she took in the scenes around her. All the rings were occupied with men, bloody and sweating. Some had weapons and others fought with their bare hands. In the ring closest to her, she found a man digging out another's eye, but she wasn't shocked nor sickened. She was no stranger to this world. For the first time since leaving her town, Eve was able to relax. This was a place she understood. The soldier nodded.

'In that tent there. You must win the first fight, or you'll be the Army's to do with what it will.'

'What does that mean?' Eve asked.

'It means death for a man.' He looked her over. 'But for you, the soldier's pleasure tents probably. I'll look forward to seeing you there,' he said with a wink and then he was gone.

Eve showed no emotion as she walked towards the tent,

ducking inside and feeling for the first time that something in her life was going her way.

∽

Priest

AS THEY WALKED through the Dark Army Camp, Priest wished again that they'd come directly here instead of following Drax's obscure visions to that fucking town after they'd escaped the capital, but it had not been his decision. He was no longer in command of their unit. Drax was.

At least they wouldn't have to worry about Greygor, the Commander who'd made them leave the Army for being what they were. That bastard was dead; killed by his own men. Fitting for that fae-hating cunt. Priest only hoped the new Commander was a little more open-minded than his predecessor had been.

It was an odd coincidence that the female had come here though. She couldn't know that they were tied to this place, could she? They hadn't worn their Brothers' blacks since the day they'd got the bird that told them Greygor would have them slain if they ever set foot in his camp again.

They kept their eyes open for her. Laughably, it seemed as if she'd tried to hide her tracks this time, but she didn't have the skills that they did. She was definitely here somewhere. Gods only knew what she was trying to accomplish by walking straight into the Dark Army's Camp.

'Do you really think she's here?' Fie asked from behind him.

'She's here,' Priest muttered, 'and I have an idea of where. You and Drax go see the Commander. See if he'll reinstate us. I'll find the female and bring her.'

He thought Drax might argue, put Priest in his place for

trying to give orders now that he was second-in-command, but he didn't. He simply inclined his head and he and Fie went off to the heart of the Camp where the Commander's tent would be.

Priest, on the other hand, made his way directly to the fighting rings. That was where she would be. He knew it. Humans were creatures of habit, after all. Gods help her when he found her. The days they'd wasted tracking the bitch! They could have been halfway to the Underhill by now, closer to finding out what had happened to their brethren. But, no, they were traipsing around this fucking realm looking for a foolish female who couldn't follow simple instructions.

His eyes narrowed. He'd teach her a thing or two before the day was over about doing as she was bid by her betters. He walked amongst the rings. Some men were practicing with their opponents, others were clearly fighting to the death. Soldiers, Brothers, and some Rats meandered around. It was relatively quiet, but it was still early in the evening. Crowds wouldn't come to watch until later.

His ears perked up as he heard a feminine voice and he smiled in anticipation, walking in that direction, and immediately finding the tiny female in an argument with one of the trainers.

'I shan't let you fight, woman.' the trainer rasped. 'Now, fuck off before I give you to the soldiers to entertain after their fights.'

Priest watched as Eve drew herself up, practically growling at him, but the man was as unmoved as a wolf would be when faced with a pup.

'I wish to join the Brothers. They told me this was the only way.'

The trainer guffawed loudly. 'Join the Brothers?' He

laughed again. 'None of the men here will stoop so low as to fight a—'

Priest stepped forward. 'I'll fight her,' he said casually, stepping into the ring as if this were a chance encounter.

In truth, he was anything but unconcerned by this turn of events. The foolish, unclaimed girl was about to get herself thrown into one of the pleasure tents, and there wasn't a fucking thing he'd be able to do about it once that happened. Did she not understand the risks that she had taken by coming here alone? He seethed, itching to punish the wayward woman.

'The fuck are you doing here?' she ground out low.

He didn't bother to give her an answer, just took up a stance in the ring. He glanced at the trainer to call the fight and, when he did, Priest decided to give her a chance. Well, make her think she had a chance at any rate. It would be all the sweeter when he beat the fight out of her.

But, as she began to move around him, he realized that, though her technique was rough, she had definite skill. It wasn't simply her fae side that had got her this far. If she honed her talents, she would be a formidable fighter even amongst their kind. Perhaps she still wouldn't be as strong as a full-blood, but he could teach her to make use of the strength she did have, to be strategic in the way that she fought.

He let out a breath, wondering what he was thinking of. He did not want to teach this female anything!

She came for him, and, in a moment of stupidity, he thought she was going to strike him with a fist. He blocked accordingly. So, when her boot slammed into his sternum, he staggered back a few steps, startled. There were not many who could surprise him.

He heard men on the side sniggering and just barely

stopped himself from rolling his eyes. As if he gave a fuck what those pathetic humans thought, Brothers or no.

She came close again and did try to catch him with a strike to the face. He grabbed her wrist and pulled her towards him, heaving her off balance. She gave a small cry as he turned her around and flung her to the ground. He was rough and merciless as he threw himself on top of her, grabbing her wrists and pulling them above her head, immobilizing her completely.

She only grunted though it must pain her as his much larger body crushed hers into the packed dirt of the ring. Still, she tried to get her leg out from underneath, attempted to lever herself up to throw him on his back instead. He knew her tricks, though, and she never had a chance considering her slight build. But she didn't stop, didn't give up, writhing beneath him in her endeavors to escape.

For the first time in a long time, Priest felt the stirrings of arousal. Disgusted, he pulled himself – and her – up. Why should this halfling female incite such passions in him? It was a fucking joke.

He twisted her arms around her back roughly, enjoying the sound of her stifled, pained cry. She was angry, struggling still. He grabbed her by her dirty, brown hair, using it to help keep her subdued.

The trainer looked amused. He did not speak to Eve again, instead addressing Priest.

'You won. Fair's fair. Spoils go to the tents,' he said. 'I'll leave you to decide which one.'

Priest nodded once, as if it was indeed his intention to take her to one of the pleasure tents.

She squirmed his grasp. 'Let me go!' she cried.

He pulled her plaited hair hard, yanking her head back. 'If you don't shut your fucking mouth,' he whispered low in her ear, 'you're going to end up tied to a cot in a pleasure tent while you're rutted to death by this camp's soldiers.'

She clenched her eyes closed and grimaced at his words, even one as foolish as her finally understanding what she'd done.

'Stupid female,' he snarled, hauling her along with him, making her slip and stagger, lifting her easily whenever her steps faltered, dragging her along like a stubborn mule.

When they got to the main thoroughfare of the Camp, Priest could only hope that Drax and Fie had been successful, both in having their unit reinstated and procuring them a tent to do what now had to be done.

Thankfully, his Brothers were walking down in the opposite direction at that very moment. He turned swiftly and smoothly to follow them to the edges of where the Camp proper turned into the fringes where the Rats dwelled.

Drax led them into a small tent and Priest looked around with ill-concealed disgust. Dirty furs lined the floors, the rickety table had a dark rust-colored stain in the center that could only be dried blood and there was only one brazier for heat. There weren't even any cots to sleep in.

Still holding the female by her hair, Priest's lips curled up into a sneer. 'Is this the best you could fucking do?'

Drax snorted. 'We're Brothers again, at least. We should change into our blacks as soon as possible.'

Priest quietly seethed. They'd once had one of the finest tents in the Camp and now they were reduced to one step up from how the rats lived.

'She wasn't difficult to find, then?' Drax nodded at the subdued and bedraggled looking woman.

'No, but we have a problem.'

'What is it?' Fie asked.

'The senseless woman was attempting to fight in the rings.'

'Fuck,' Fie muttered, staring daggers at Eve.

The female was looking confused, didn't even have the common sense to understand what was happening.

'She lost,' Drax surmised.

'I was the one who fought her. Of course she lost!' Priest said.

Drax shook his head at the woman, looking at her as if she was the most ridiculous creature he'd ever seen. 'You should be glad your throat wasn't slit as soon as that fight was over, you foolish wench.'

She opened her mouth to speak, but Priest put his hand over it. 'Silence or, by the gods, I will gag you. I promise you that.'

She did as she was told for once, though her eyes flashed in her fury.

Priest's lip curled. 'No wonder no one in that fucking town liked you.'

'Where is she meant to be?' Drax asked.

'I'm to take her to one of the pleasure tents.'

'Fuck!' Drax paced across the tent. 'Once she's in one of those tents, she'll never come out again.'

'What can we do?' Fie asked.

Drax flung his sword onto the table with a clang. 'There's only one thing we can do. It's too late now. We're in the Camp with an unclaimed female who just lost in the rings. She must be bound to the unit.'

'Make her a Fourth?' Fie asked, looking slightly horrified. 'There must be another way.'

'There isn't.' Drax growled at the woman. 'She's seen to that.'

He unclasped his cloak and threw it over the back of one of the wobbly chairs. 'We'll do it now before they realize Priest hasn't brought her to the tents and come looking for her.'

The female's gaze was moving from one of them to the other. She hadn't voiced her question yet and Priest wasn't going to tell her. He'd let Drax handle that, he thought with a smirk. One thing was certain, though, she wasn't going to let them do what was necessary without putting up a fight.

∼

Eve

EVE DIDN'T KNOW what the three of them were talking about, but she was afraid. She was trying to hide it but even that was almost impossible to do. She was tired. She was hungry. Her body hurt from the paces that Priest had put it through.

She wanted a good meal. She wanted to bathe.

She wanted to lie down and sleep.

She'd wanted to become a Brother, but even that was closed to her now because she was so stupidly small that no one would take her seriously.

And why were these men so fucking strong? How could they subdue her so easily?

Eve almost growled in her anger, but she knew instinctively that that would be the wrong thing to do in front of them. It would mean something she didn't intend. She didn't know how she knew that, but she did.

Priest still had her by the hair. He hadn't let it go since the fight.

'Get it,' Drax said to Fie and the blond one began looking through one of their packs.

A moment later, he held 'it' out in his gloved hand; a long, thin shining cord.

It took Eve a moment before she could work out what it was.

Iron!

'No!' she cried, all the times the Bull had bound her flashing before her eyes.

Why would they need that when they could already overpower her so easily?

She began to struggle anew, biting her lip to keep from letting the fearful whimpers free.

They ignored her, forcing her arms behind her back, and tying her wrists tightly.

Eve felt them sap her strength immediately, weakening her as soon as they met her flesh. She almost fell to her knees in fatigue except that Priest was still holding her by her fucking hair.

She looked at each man with hatred, but she didn't say anything as she was thrust into a chair and told to 'stay' like a beast.

Fie grabbed a goblet from the side and poured himself a wine. Priest stood over her, a knife in his hand. Before she could even react, he sliced her cheek and Eve couldn't keep the cry from bursting out. She looked up at him, eyes like slits in her anger.

He simply looked amused by her fight as he put the goblet beneath her jaw, catching the blood. Then he leaned down until he was face to face with her, and she refused to lean back to make any space between them. She did not cower or flinch ... until his tongue flicked out, and he licked the blood from her face.

She made a sound of angry disgust, but inwardly quaked with fear. Even the Bull had never done such a thing to her. What manner of man was Priest?

He mixed her blood into the goblet of wine with the knife and handed it to Drax. To Eve's horror, he took a drink and gave it to Fie, who did the same.

Her mouth hung open in shock. What were they doing? Was this a prelude to them eating her flesh? The mixture left in the goblet was unceremoniously poured to the floor and refilled with wine. Each of the men cut his finger and dripped a drop of his blood into it.

It was Drax who came forward, looking grim. 'Know this, female,' he said. 'We don't want this any more than you do and as soon as we are finished with each other, we will break this bond.'

He grabbed her chin, and she shook him off.

'Ah, ah, ah,' Priest tutted, coming forward.

He grabbed her hair again with one hand and pinched her nose shut with the other. 'Bottoms up,' he sneered and, as she opened her mouth to take a breath, the contents of the goblet were poured down her gullet.

She spluttered and coughed, choking as the strong wine burned on the way down. They let go of her, leaving her in the chair.

'It is done,' said Fie.

'Not quite. She still needs to be claimed our fearless leader,' Priest drawled.

Drax gave him a look. Something malicious and angry passed between them, as if they were the bitterest of rivals.

Priest pulled her up again and, as soon as she was able, she kicked him in the shin hard. He swore, raising his hand to strike her and, to her shame, she flinched.

'Enough,' said Drax.

He took her from Priest, grabbed her arm, and brought her to the table, pushing her down on it with a hand between her shoulder blades.

She opened her mouth to yell, but his hand clamped over her lips. He bent down close to her ear.

'If you scream,' he murmured, 'one of two things will happen. No one will come, or someone will. Either way,' she felt his smile at his own jest, 'you're fucked.'

He glanced at Fie and Priest. 'Hold her.'

They both pressed down on the backs of her shoulders, gripping her under her arms as well so that she could barely move at all.

She began to fight with everything she had left. She wasn't going to let this be her life anymore!

There wasn't much in her because of the iron and the past few days, but she was able to push both Fie and Priest back, darting away from them across the tent, running for the way out.

She got as far as the threshold before she heard Drax's voice tell her to stop; low and gravelly and laced with a power she didn't understand as her body ceased all movement without her willing it to. Her feet would go no further.

'Come here,' he commanded, and, to her horror, her body obeyed him.

Eve couldn't help but walk to him, could do nothing as he thrust her down on the table once more.

'How did you do that?' Fie asked. 'She's part fae.'

'The binding is incomplete, but it's there enough for Drax to compel her,' Priest murmured.

Drax ignored them, his attention solely on her.

'We didn't want this,' he growled in her ear, 'but you've forced my hand and there's no other choice now.'

She was shaking as her breeches were pulled down to her ankles and she felt Drax's hand between her legs. She tried to move, but it was no use. He didn't even need to hold her. She was frozen.

Eve's breath was coming in fits and starts. She'd given up any pretense of not being afraid. She turned her head and caught Fie's eye. The man actually looked at her and she saw his pity. She looked away from him immediately, staring at the black walls of the tent behind him. She heard Drax curse, and her boots were pulled off, her breeches with them, leaving her bare from the waist down. He kicked her legs apart and she let out a whimper that he ignored.

She felt his fingers between her legs, heard him spit into his hand and he pushed a finger into her. She winced as it began to move in her dry channel.

'Just fucking do it,' Priest, practically ordered his leader.

She didn't see the look that Drax gave him, but his voice sounded strained when he answered.

'She isn't ready.'

'Of course she's not, but who cares?' Priest growled. 'Do what must be done before they come for her.'

Eve just wished he'd stop taking his time. It had always been worse when the Bull took her leisurely. 'Just do it,' she ground out. 'Get it over with.'

She set her jaw, trying to escape this moment, hoping that he wasn't going to spend hours rutting her like the Bull sometimes did.

The finger inside of her kept moving, it's gentleness belying everything else about these men, this event. Although she was trying to think of something else, anything else except what was happening to her, her body began to feel hot under his. Drax's finger changed direction, twisted in her, did *something* that made her gasp as the oddest sensation passed through her. Her nethers tensed, the muscles in her stomach, contracting. His movements became easier.

'There,' Drax muttered. 'Almost time.'

A second finger joined the first, stretching her channel. It hurt, but the pain was different somehow, mixed with a pleasure that she'd never felt before in all the times that the Bull had taken her.

Eve found her hips straining towards Drax and, although some part of her was mortified, she didn't care. In this moment, she just wanted more of the sensations that his fingers were giving her. She was panting and gasping, trying not to let any other sounds pass her lips. Then a moan escaped, and she bit her lip to keep from making the embarrassing sound again.

She couldn't bear to meet any of their eyes. She just stared at the wall as his fingers left her. Eve found herself wishing that he would continue. What was wrong with her? She'd never wanted such a thing when the Bull touched her.

She felt Drax's staff at her entrance.

'Gods, she's tiny,' Drax groaned as he pushed into her.

This time she did let out a sound. He was much bigger than the Bull. It felt like he was splitting her in two. She clenched her eyes shut, her fingernails digging into the rough wood of the table, scratching at it. She let out a cry of pleasure and of pain as he began to move, thrusting hard, pushing her legs painfully into the table, rutting her like a beast.

She kept her eyes shut, afraid that they would see her tears. She couldn't let them see those. It was bad enough when the Bull did everything in his power to make her cry and then laughed at her. She would not let these men do the same.

Finally, with one last thrust, his fingers dug into her hips, and she felt his seed spill into her. He pulled out quickly now that it was done, and she heard him putting his clothes to rights.

Between her thighs stung and her legs shook in fatigue. She could feel his seed oozing out of her.

He finally released her from whatever power he'd used to crush her fight and she slid from the table onto the floor.

CHAPTER 4

DRAX

The female slipped to the ground. Her eyes were closed. She looked so defenseless now as she lay at his feet on the dirty tent floor. She had such a strength about her, even being able to flee when she was bound with iron...

Drax froze as he thought on what had just happened. He'd forgotten how small she was. Had he really just used his power on her?

He pretended nonchalance in front of the others, but, in truth, he felt sick. He'd hated every part of what he'd just had to do. It was somehow made worse that she had felt none of the pleasure that he had – more than he'd ever felt from a female before. What was it about this one that felt so different? Was it the bond they now shared?

The other two went about their business, ignoring the female huddled on the ground. Drax picked her up carefully and ordered Fie to get his bed roll out. He'd not leave their Fourth amongst the stinking furs on the floor. His seed oozed from her, mixed with her own arousal that she had tried so hard to contain ... and a little blood. He gritted his teeth. He hadn't meant to take her so roughly. He hadn't meant for a lot of things.

Fie laid out his bed roll, and Drax placed her upon it, covering her with a blanket. Something inside of him had woken and he knew that once with this female was not going to be enough however much he disliked her, and she him.

She would hate him after this, but it had been the only way. Better with him for a few moments than soldier after soldier, night after night until there was nothing left of her.

He grabbed a cloth – one of the only things in this fucking tent that was clean – and soaked it in some cold water.

He went back to the female and uncovered her. Between her legs was swollen and red, and she did not awaken as he washed her gently.

He hadn't wanted to do this, though if she hadn't run from them and come to this fucking place, he wouldn't have had to. He had been forced to bind her to them and to claim her this way when she was so unwilling. She was a fighter, through and through though, he'd give her that … and she was his.

His brow furrowed. Why was he feeling so possessive? It must be the bond, he decided, trying to push it from his mind. They had important things to do. He could not afford to attach himself any further to this halfling, the daughter of the fae who had destroyed him.

He untied her wrists, hissing at the pain of the iron on his full-blood skin as he forgot he was gloveless. Re-covering her, he ensured that she was as warm as possible. He stoked the brazier as well, swearing softly as he shivered himself.

'Was this really the best there was?' Priest asked, finally speaking as he gazed around the small tent in thinly veiled revulsion.

'Apparently,' Drax ground out. 'But then, we haven't paid our dues to the Army in some time.'

'Aye, because Greygor banished us. This isn't our fault. The cunt is dead and yet he's still a thorn in our sides.'

'Good riddance,' Fie muttered.

Drax caught Priest's eyes drifting to the female and couldn't help goading him.

'Do you want your chance at her, Brother? Are you wishing you were still in charge of the unit?'

Priest snorted. 'As if I want to rut a half-human with the worst of our bloodlines running through her veins,' he snapped. 'I'd sooner fuck the Commander.' Then he grinned. 'How went *that* meeting?'

Drax shrugged. 'Well enough.' His eyes narrowed at Fie, who was doing little save taking up space. 'See about getting our table stocked. Our female is thin and hasn't eaten in days.'

'Our female?' Priest cocked the brow. 'You're getting familiar. Remember whose get she is, Brother.' He snorted. 'But I'm sure I worry for nothing. She's so bothersome that by the time we've been in her company for more than a day, we'll all be chomping at the bit to slit the bitch's throat.'

Drax ignored Priest, waving his hand at Fie to go.

Fie scowled. 'I'm not your fucking servant.'

'You are today,' Drax replied, throwing the wet rag still in his hand at Fie. 'Now, fuck off and find us some food.'

Fie growled, but he left the tent.

'What else?' Priest asked, sitting hard on one of the chairs, and then looking disgusted as if it was too hard for his backside.

He chuckled at Priest. 'Perhaps during all that time we were stuck within Kitore's walls, you went soft, Brother. Can't even abide a hard chair?'

Priest grimaced, but said nothing more so, Drax continued.

'The Commander will reinstate us. He has no enemies within the fae, and he owes no one any allegiance outside this army.'

'Well, there's some good fucking news for once,' Priest muttered, 'and yet here we sit in this hovel of a fucking tent.'

'Aye. We shall not stay long, only until the female is ready for traveling.'

'She'd be ready tomorrow if I was still leader,' Priest murmured.

Drax shook his head with a snarl. 'Look at her,' he said, practically leaping across the tent and pulling the blanket from her, showing his Brother her gaunt, thin body, the bones protruding from her small frame.

Priest stared at the unconscious woman and then turned his eyes away. 'The binding has clouded your mind, Brother,' he muttered. 'She seems hail enough to ride a horse. You care too much about an enemy when you should be thinking of your own kind.'

'Perhaps,' Drax replied, absently. 'But she'll be no good to us if she expires before we can even get her to the Ice Plains.'

Priest let out a dry laugh. 'By the looks of her, I'd say she's used to worse than traveling while she's fatigued.'

'Aye,' Drax agreed. 'I didn't know the humans treated their freefolk in such a way. She didn't appear to be a slave though, not officially at any rate. What do you make of how we found her?'

'Does it matter?'

At Drax's raised brow, Priest sighed, deciding to humor his Brother for once. 'Odd set-up. She clearly likes the ring, enjoys combat, but the chain around her ankle ... It was low-grade, but there was enough iron in it to keep her weak when combined with the other deprivations. They were forcing her to fight for them.'

Drax frowned. 'And more it seemed from the way we found her after the fight.'

'I had that impression as well.' Priest looked vaguely disgusted at the prospect. 'As if any of us would ... if we didn't have to that is.'

Drax's lips moved into a thin line. The female might be tiny and frail-looking, but she wasn't unattractive. Why was Priest pretending the opposite? Perhaps he simply *wanted* her to be unappealing.

Drax and Priest didn't speak anymore. Drax sharpened his weapons while Priest went digging through their packs to see what supplies they needed before they moved on.

Not long after, Fie returned carrying a plate piled with meat, bread, and cheese. 'This is the best I could do for now. I've paid for them to bring us more tomorrow.'

Drax nodded. 'Female,' he barked. 'I know you're awake. Your breathing has changed.'

He watched her crack her eye open. She was afraid. How he knew that he wasn't sure, but she was. Their Fourth. He shook his head. A fucking Fourth! As if they needed that megrim along with everything else.

He could tell she was hungry too. He watched as she stopped herself from shrinking away from him, from what he'd done. He watched her pretend she wasn't terrified even as he felt her fear, and he hated himself even more.

But there had been no other way. Even if they'd tried to escape the Camp with her before she'd been claimed, they'd have been hunted down and she'd have been taken from them anyway ... after he, Priest, and Fie had been hanged by their necks from the nearest tall tree.

'It's finished, female,' he said. 'You're bound to us for now.' He decided to make it clear. 'If you run from us, we'll be able to find you no matter how you cover your tracks. There's no hiding from us.'

'Is that true,' Fie asked.

Drax nodded. 'Not usually for the human Brothers, but for faefolk, the bond is more ... *complex*.'

'I don't feel any different,' Fie muttered.

Drax cast an eye to Priest.

'We haven't claimed her ourselves,' Priest said, 'Think, Brother.'

She sat up and winced, Drax practically able to feel her pain.

'You heal quickly?' he asked.

She looked at him, her face mulish, her anger and resentment plain.

'It was unavoidable,' he said, not tempering his tone.

She looked away and nodded her acceptance. Drax's brow furrowed, knowing that she couldn't really be acquiescing this easily.

'Come,' he said.

She stood on wobbly legs, not bothering to cover herself from the waist down. He picked up her breeches and threw them at her.

'Get dressed.'

Without a word, she donned her clothes.

He picked up her boots and then thrust them aside when he saw the state of them. They were useless.

'Sit.'

She sat at the table. Drax felt her need for food as if he himself was hungry as he cut her some bread, cheese, and meat, putting it in front of her, not allowing her to have a knife just in case she tried anything. She shouldn't be able to hurt them badly because of the bond, but they'd never had a Fourth before. That wasn't something he wanted to be wrong about while she had a weapon.

She fell upon the food like a ravenous animal, tearing at the bread with her teeth and stuffing it in her mouth, practically choking on it.

He poured her a cup of wine and watched as she took it from him, gulping it down and then grimacing at the taste of it.

'Gods, she's practically an animal,' Priest muttered audibly.

Drax could feel the barest smidgen of embarrassment from her, but she ostensibly ignored Priest, continuing to eat everything Drax had put on the plate and then reaching out to grab more.

Priest looked aghast.

Drax hid a grin. Out of all of them, Priest was the one that enjoyed his luxuries the most. Drax and Fie could do without when necessary, but Priest took it as a personal affront if he was forced to bathe in cold water, don clothes that were dirty or ill-fitting unless they were on a campaign. If they were, the first thing Priest usually did when he got back was have a long, hot bath, dress himself in his finest clothes and eat the finest delicacies he could buy while he imbibed the most expensive wines.

She thrust the almost empty cup of wine away from her with another grimace and Drax replaced it with one filled with water.

He watched her, his expression grim. He shouldn't but he wanted to know more about her. The bond was wreaking havoc on him, he thought. He knew the humans didn't feel like this with their Fourths but, as with many things fae, it would be more tangible than it was with other units, he expected, as the Brothers' blood rite reacted with their natural magicks.

He felt when she was sated, and it was an odd feeling to understand her needs almost better than his own. She was tired as well. He went to her, and she tensed. With a sigh, he turned away, looking at Fie.

'See if there's a bathing tent nearby,' he commanded Fie.

'Why me?' his Brother complained.

'For fuck's sake,' Priest exploded, 'I'll go!'

He exited the tent, leaving Fie and Drax with the female.

'I'll not harm you, Fourth,' he said, 'so long as you do as you are bid. No more running off. You'll do as you're told, or you'll be punished as a Fourth.'

'What does that mean?' she asked, clearly not one to mince words.

'We'll cross that bridge when we come to it. Get some rest. It's been a long few days.'

Keeping her eyes on both of them, she went back to his bedroll and lay down upon it. It was a testament to how tired she must be that she simply did as she was told and didn't try to fight.

Her nose wrinkled. 'It smells like you.'

'Aye, it's my bed,' Drax replied, amused, and wondering if she was finally beginning to use her fae senses. 'You're safe enough here.'

His promise seemed to calm her, and he was struck by the idea that she took his words at face value. Trusting little thing.

She closed her eyes, promptly falling asleep and Drax rubbed his forehead. How were they going to proceed? They'd wanted to get to the Underhill as soon as possible, but it had been months since the portals had collapsed. Realistically, what was a few more days' delay? They didn't need to travel at a break-neck pace with her ... But they shouldn't stay at the Camp any longer than necessary. They'd be safe enough now, as should their Fourth, but one never knew for certain here. It was a camp of mercenaries, after all.

Eve

Eve woke again later unsure of the time of day. A light, cold breeze ruffled the flaps of the tent where it didn't fit together properly, and, from the outside light, it looked to be dusk or dawn. She looked around the tent with trepidation, but none of the men ... the *Brothers* were there.

She'd heard them talking. She knew what they were. Dark Brothers. Members of the Dark Army.

Sitting up, she checked her person, ensuring all her clothes were still on, and was thankful to find they hadn't done anything more to her while she slept. She padded across the tent, feet bare and toes cold on the worn dirt floor. There was food on the table; nuts and meats, other things she'd never seen before. Too ravenous to bother with a plate, she grabbed two handfuls from the nearest bowl, stuffing bits of something she didn't even recognize in her mouth and was pleasantly surprised at the meaty taste.

She'd learned long ago to take what she could, when she could because she never knew when the next meal would come, but she'd never felt so hungry. She grasped the jug on the table to pour some water into the goblet and wrinkled her nose in distaste when she smelled it was wine. How could they drink that nasty stuff?

Finding some water, she drank two cups of it in quick succession to sate her thirst. She peered through the gap in the tent flaps and wondered if she should venture outside the tent, but after what had already happened in this Camp ... she hung her head. She'd never be a Brother now and Drax had said they could even more easily track her as well.

There was no point in running. There was no escape if they could just follow her forever, wherever she went. She'd expend valuable energy. They had told her at the beginning that if she helped them, they would free her. Did that bargain still stand even after she had tried to escape twice?

There was an ewer of water on another table by the wall of the tent, as well as a chamber pot. Keeping an eye on the entrance to the tent, she quickly squatted over the pot to relieve herself, wincing as her nethers burned at the same time. She grabbed the cloth, dipping it into the water and washing herself. There was very little in the way of mess. One of them had cleaned her. She shuddered at the invasion, stupid as that was. Men did this to women. That was a fact of life.

She'd learned something more as well that she hadn't realized having only ever been taken by the Bull before. Cocks weren't all the same. Drax's was longer than the Bull's. Thicker too. She shivered at the memory, wondering why it wasn't as abhorrent as it should be. Why couldn't she think of him with the same disgust as she did the Bull? What had they done to her?

She heard someone approaching the tent from the outside, boots crunching in the frozen dirt. She pulled up her trousers quickly, turning to meet her foes. As soon as Drax entered alone, she ambushed him.

'What did you do to me?' she practically shrieked.

He looked unperturbed. He'd expected the question. 'Claimed you as a Fourth. The only recourse after you lost to Priest in the ring. It was either that or have you taken as spoils of the Camp ... to the pleasure tents.'

She let out a breath. That had been her fault.

'But Priest could have let me win,' she pointed out.

He threw back his head and laughed. 'No, female, he couldn't. You'll learn that about Priest soon enough. Besides, you're in the Brothers' Camp now. This place is not like the little town you came from.'

'Fat lot you know,' she said quietly, not believing for a moment that the Brothers here were worse than the Bull or Jays or Talik.

Deciding to eat more from the table, she took one of the wooden plates from the pile, but then she sat in the chair too hard and winced, scowling as he gave her a knowing look. He tossed a small pot to her, and she caught it, looking at it curiously.

'Salve,' he said, gesturing with a nod to her down below region. 'It'll help you heal faster.'

Suddenly embarrassed, Eve put it on the table. 'I'll be healed in two days,' she muttered. 'I don't need it.'

He gave her an assessing look. 'It wasn't your first time.'

It was almost a question, but not quite. He was fishing.

'No,' she said defensively, but his eyes narrowed as if he thought there was something she wasn't telling him. It seemed as if he wanted to ask something, but he wasn't sure of the words to say. Instead, he closed his mouth.

'The bargain you made with me...,' she trailed off.

'Yes?'

'Does it ... does it still stand even after ...'

'After all the trouble that you've been? Aye, female, it still stands. You help us. We'll let you go.'

'And this ... this thing that you've done to me, this binding, it can be undone?'

He nodded once.

'So, I do this thing that you need me to do, and you let me go. I have your word?'

'You have my word as a fae,' he said.

Her eyes widened. 'Fae?'

He looked surprised, assessing again. 'You didn't know.'

'I've never met a fae,' she admitted quietly. 'I thought you'd look different from a human.'

He walked closer to her, and his face changed abruptly.

His eyes became violet. His ears, pointed. His teeth, sharper. He looked slightly taller too, and broader.

She was at least able to stifle the gasp that came from her. 'Is that all?'

'Aye. The fae aren't too different from humans.'

She nodded stupidly, not sure what to say.

'Fie will come for you in a bit. He'll take you to bathe.'

She nodded again, ridiculously excited about the prospect of another bath.

His features changed back to human.

'Does it hurt?' she blurted out and then wondered if she shouldn't ask. Maybe she shouldn't find out too much about them.

'Does what hurt? To change my face?' He barked a laugh. 'It's just a glamor to keep us from being noticed here. There are many who do not like the fae in this realm. Donning it and taking it off is as easy as breathing, walking, eating.'

His gaze moved over her body, and she tensed. Would he use her again so soon? The Bull was usually made to wait except when she'd displeased Talik in some way. But perhaps these men – these fae – would not give her the same consideration.

She took a step back, thought better of it and took a step forward again. She would not let them see her fear. Drax still stood in front of her. He hadn't moved, but he looked like he was trying to understand something. Perhaps he enjoyed her discomfort. Perhaps he could tell that she was afraid, though she hoped not.

'What is it? Ask your question,' he said.

'What else can the fae do?'

He shrugged. 'Some have magick they can use to conjure. Some don't. Some have gifts. Visions. Sometimes, I can see the future or the past. I saw you. That was how we found you.'

She looked up at him quickly and then looked away. 'I dreamed of you as well,' she admitted.

'Of me?' he looked surprised.

'And the other two sometimes,' she said, not sure why she was telling him.

'What did you dream?' he asked.

'I shot a deer in the forest and when I went to remove the bolt from its heart, I was the deer and you were cutting my heart from me,' she said quietly. 'Sometimes it was the others. What does it mean?'

He looked grim. 'Don't know,' he said.

She didn't ask him anything more. She knew when she was being lied to. That was one of the advantages of growing up in the streets. As a child she had learned quickly who would deceive her.

He stayed in the tent with her for a while longer and the atmosphere was tense. Eve was confused by her reaction to him. Was he using fae tricks to make her feel things she didn't usually feel? She found herself watching him while his back was turned, thinking about how he'd touched her. She'd never enjoyed such things before and a part of her yearned for more. How could she want that from him again? She'd never longed for the Bull's hands on her. Why was Drax so different?

He ignored her for the most part before leaving the tent, telling her that the others would return soon.

She breathed a sigh of relief when he was gone but was soon bored of waiting for the two other Brothers. She'd rarely left her room except to fight. She wanted to see more of the Camp. Surely, she'd be safe now as a Fourth.

She threw on her still damp boots and ventured from the tent. It was still quite early, and she could hear the sounds of the rings. There wouldn't be any fights yet, but there would likely be some training.

Eve made her way towards the sounds and found the fighting pits not far away where Priest had beaten her the night before. She eyed the fighters. Some were large men, but not all. There were plenty of combatants on the smaller side practicing with weapons. They were all sizing each other up, probably in preparation for tonight's fights.

She felt someone behind her and turned to find Priest looking angry.

'Were you not told to stay in the tent?' he asked.

'No,' she said. 'I wasn't.'

A deep, growling noise emanated from his throat, but he was looking past her, and Eve realized that another man had approached.

'Wasn't this one meant for the pleasure tents?' he asked, and she recognized him as the trainer from yestereve.

'She's my Fourth now,' Priest said, his tone threatening.

The trainer looked her over, his unblinking eyes and the expression on his face making Eve shiver. 'Pity. I like 'em small.'

His hand darted out and she recoiled, feeling Priest at her back, and deciding that she'd rather have him touching her than this other man.

But Priest moved around her, and the trainer was suddenly on his knees in the dirt before her, howling about his hand which was clearly broken.

Priest's hand settled around the back of her neck, squeezing slightly as he guided her gently, yet forcefully the short distance back to the tent despite the fact that she was passively going with him.

As soon as they were inside the tent, however, the Brother turned her roughly to face him. Fearing the worst, she lashed out as soon as she was able, catching him in the cheek with a loud crack hard enough to whip his head to the side.

His expression turned even more thunderous but then he grinned nastily, and Eve understood that she'd never seen this man angry; not really.

He made a grab for her, but she danced out of his way, avoiding him easily. He was very quick, but she was smaller, lighter and she made use of that, keeping away from him as he followed her in circles around the tent.

She could escape him for now, flee into the Camp, but she found, as her lips turned up into a grin she couldn't help, that she was enjoying this. He may not see this as sparring, but all of her losing fights had led to time with the Bull. Knowing that whatever happened, this one would not, Eve found herself reveling in the fight. She might dislike this prick, but he was good, and he could move.

He finally feigned left and caught her and she let out an oomph as she was thrown down to the furs, Priest on top of her, breathing as heavily as she was.

His anger seemed to have been replaced by confusion and, as she felt his cock growing hard between her legs, arousal. She tried not to go rigid beneath him but knew that she had failed when his eyes caught hers and his glamor disappeared. Her breath caught. His violet eyes were feral, and his expression was wild as he leant forward, grinding himself against her.

'Do you yield?' he growled.

Before she could even think of an answer, his lips were on hers and she startled. No one had ever done this before. She closed her eyes, a part of her screaming that she should be struggling while another was telling her to acquiesce, to let him do what he willed because, like Drax, he would ensure that she enjoyed it at least a little.

Then he pulled back and sneered. 'Human females are all the same,' he said, shaking his head. 'All it takes is a hard cock between your legs and you mewl like beasts in heat.'

Her eyes widened and then narrowed as she took in his words. He was playing with her, but she didn't understand why.

She threw her head forwards, her forehead striking his nose hard enough to make her dizzy, but the crunch and his cry of pain made the headache she was going to have worth it as he scrambled to his feet. She did the same, standing toe to toe with him.

'You ever touch me again and I'll do worse than break your fucking nose,' she hissed.

Just then, Fie entered the tent, glancing between them in question. Neither of them said anything, Priest turning away to put himself to rights.

Fie looked at her as if he hated her and yet also wanted to ensure that she was well. Peculiar creatures, these fae.

'Come, female,' Fie beckoned. 'The bathing tent is free. We'll take you there.'

SHE FOLLOWED CLOSELY behind Fie and Priest as they walked through the Camp amongst the tents to the main thoroughfare. It was still early morning, and the frost was thick. She tried not to show how cold she was despite the fact that her feet were frozen in her boots, and she had no cloak.

Teeth chattering, she heard Fie swear and looked up to see a long line of people waiting outside the bathing tent.

'Thought you said it was free,' Priest said.

Eve gazed at the queue of men, soldiers and Brothers alike. She found it odd that these gruff fighting men would brave the cold simply to be clean. Gods knew none of the men she'd known in town washed themselves much except on feast days.

'She can't wait out here. It's fucking freezing cold,' Priest ground out, seeming to examine her lack of appropriate clothing properly for the first time.

He made a noise of anger and she glanced up at him, eyes narrowing and was gratified that his nose looked bruised despite his faster healing.

'What!' she said vehemently.

'Where the fuck is your cloak, female.'

She shrugged. 'It was left at the rings last night.'

'Gods, can you not even take care of your own basic needs? How you have survived all these years to your age, I cannot fathom.'

She looked away. It was hardly her fault that he'd whisked her away so quickly last night that she couldn't retrieve it from where she'd left it by the side lines. What did she care if he thought her a simpleton? He didn't know her. She pushed away the embarrassment she felt at what he'd said and done in the tent ... of how she'd reacted to him.

Fie said something she couldn't hear, and Priest made a sound of frustration.

'The female can hardly keep herself alive,' he muttered.

She opened her mouth to offer a retort, but then closed it again. She *didn't care* what they thought. What were they to her? *Your Brothers*, a traitorous thought entered her mind. She pushed it away. They were not hers. They'd only made her a Fourth out of necessity. That had been her fault and she couldn't say she blamed Drax for what he'd done. Better him than the pleasure tents. She had been a fool to come into the Camp, thinking she could fight her way in.

But for her that was what life had been. She fought for food, fought for clothes, fought to stay alive, fought to pay her dues to Talik so his men didn't kill her for being different. But it didn't seem as if the rest of the world worked quite the same. She needed to learn more, or she doubted she'd survive once the Brothers let her go.

Fie and Priest were muttering angrily to each other, gesturing at the line, blaming each other quietly as if they didn't want anyone else to know they were having an argument. She noticed a woman dressed in Brothers' blacks leave a tent nearby. Her hair was long and dark, plaited down her back tightly. She was watching them with an interested look on her face.

Eve watched as she approached them, taking in her lack of suitable attire. She gave the Brothers a sneer as if she blamed them personally.

'My name is Maeve,' she said quietly to Eve, ignoring the Brothers completely. 'It is my guess that you're wishing that you came out earlier this morning. Is this your unit?' she asked, giving Fie and Priest scathing looks.

Eve wasn't sure what to say. She was used to other women in the town giving her a wide berth, talking about her amongst themselves, quietly whispering, pointing, sometimes giving her pitying looks. No one had ever approached her and spoken to her as an equal before.

'She's *our* Fourth,' Priest said, stepping closer to Maeve, trying to intimidate the female.

The woman barked a small laugh. 'Careful, Brother,' she warned just as another man came from her tent, walking swiftly over to them.

She gave him an amused look as he got closer, coming to stand next to her. She brushed against his chest in intimate affection.

'No need for you to get involved, Callan,' she said. 'You know I can look after myself.'

He leaned in close, whispering something into her ear and tugging the end of her plaited hair gently. She gave him a smile in return as he turned back to their tent, leaving them.

She twisted back to Eve, practically baring her teeth in animosity at Priest and Fie. 'Your Fourth is not being looked after,' she said plainly to them and then to Eve, 'This bathing tent is not for us. There's one for women down the way, but if you don't want to wait, come with me.'

Maeve set off and Eve followed, not caring if the two Brothers did or not. Her feet were now numb, and she was glad of it, for they had been aching before with the cold, but she wanted so much to be warm after the past days.

'Wait here,' Maeve said, entering a very large tent.

Eve glanced behind her to see both Fie and Priest appearing anxious and wondered whose tent this belonged to. Maeve came back out a moment later.

'Come,' she said, taking Eve's hand and drawing her in. The woman looked past her. 'You two may enter as well but stay in the main room.'

Without a backward glance, she pulled Eve in gently. Inside, the tent was cavernous with a large, mahogany desk and soft furs over the floors. Opulent. Beautiful. Eve realized why her Brothers – no, not *her* Brothers, she corrected, the men she was bound to – did not like their tent if they were used to places such as this.

She was taken through the main room, down a small hallway made with hanging canvas, and through a thick curtain into a chamber area with a large bed and a steaming bath. A blond-haired woman met her with a smile.

'My name is Lily,' she said. 'Maeve tells me you have been made a Fourth.'

Eve nodded. 'I believe so,' she said, realizing she sounded so foolish, having no idea what had happened to her, that these women seem to know more about her than she did.

Lily gestured to the bath. 'If you're all right with my leavings,' she said with a chuckle, 'the water is still clean and hot.'

Eve nodded immediately, shucking her clothes quickly in case Fie and Priest decided to drag her out. She got into the bath with a moan that she couldn't quite keep back, and Lily grinned at her.

'Sounds like that's just what you needed.'

Eve nodded. 'Thank you,' she said, wondering why these women were being so kind to her.

'Her *unit* await her in the front room,' Maeve drawled, making it obvious what she thought of them.

Lily cocked her head. 'I will talk to them,' she said simply, disappearing through the thick curtains.

A moment later, Eve heard her new friend exclaim from the front of the tent.

'You!'

～

Priest

'You!' said the blonde female stalking towards him. He recognized her immediately and drew his knife.

Fie got in front of him, putting a hand on his shoulder. 'What are you doing?' he murmured. 'That's the Commander's Fourth.'

'Do you not recognize her, Brother?' Priest whispered urgently. 'That is the human bitch that tried to murder us in Kitore. The one who can kill by touch. Stay back!'

His eyes narrowed. Why was she working for the Commander?

'Put your knife away before someone sees you,' Fie hissed.

With a sound of anger, Priest re-sheathed his dagger and they both turned towards the blonde woman who was now standing in front of them but making no move to use her terrible power.

'I was beaten and almost killed because of you,' she

accused, pointing at them, jabbing Priest in the chest with her *ungloved* finger.

Despite the fact that she could kill him with that finger, with the merest brush of it on his bare flesh, Priest was almost amused. Aye, this woman was a Fourth all right. He couldn't help taking a step back though, afraid she would begin flailing like a trapped bird and accidentally kill him.

'Why were you working for the Library if you're a member of the Army?' he ground out.

'I *wasn't*, you fool!'

At that moment, Quin, the Commander, strolled into his tent, flanked by his unit, Bastian and Mad Mal. He looked from Lily to Priest, his eyes homing in on Priest and Fie.

'Why are you in my tent?'

Lily jabbed him in the chest again. 'These are the *fae* you were sent to kill in Kitore.'

Quin and his unit shared a look, Mad Mal drawing his own blade.

'What trickery is this?' he said, looking at their Brothers' blacks.

'It's not a trick,' Fie replied. 'Greygor cut us out of the Army for being fae, put a price on our heads. We went to Kitore and got stuck inside the city's wards until recently.'

Quin snorted. 'Someone wanted you dead badly to risk the ire of the entire Dark Army.'

Priest shrugged. 'We made powerful enemies in the city while we were working towards our own ends. The First Scholar was one of them. We thought this female was sent by him to kill us.'

He didn't bother telling the Commander who they now suspected was truly behind the attack. When they finally gained entrance to the Underhill, they'd have the proof they needed to take the bastard down. Revenge would be theirs in every way possible then.

'You gave our Fourth to Nixus! You put her in danger,' Bastian boomed, looking furious.

'An oversight,' Fie murmured, putting his hands up in supplication. 'We didn't know who she was. She never said.'

Lily turned to Quin. 'Neither did they. We didn't know who each other were. It's no matter now. It ended well,' she said. 'You have just made this unit Brothers again after all.'

She gave him a look and the Commander listened to his Fourth. Clearly the female had some sway over him for he backed down and Mad Mal put his blade away.

'What are you doing in my tent?' Quin asked again. 'Are your accommodations not to your liking?'

He smirked and Priest barely stopped himself from growling aloud at the inconveniences they had suffered since being at the Camp.

'Our Fourth,' Priest began, but Lily interrupted.

'Maeve brought their Fourth to me. She looks a little worse for wear,' she said, clearly blaming Fie and Priest for Eve's lack of clothes, cleanliness and appropriate boots.

Priest rolled his eyes. 'Eve has had an arduous journey without us and has been unable to take care of herself,' he muttered, trying not to think back to the tent when he'd had the halfling under him and all he'd wanted to do was fuck her senseless then and there on the floor after their skirmish. She was a better fighter than he'd given her credit for. His nose still pained him. He'd not expected that strike.

Maeve let out a scoff from behind Lily. 'Perhaps you cannot take care of your Fourth,' she said in challenge.

'Do not test me, woman,' Priest growled, turning his attentions back to this other infuriating female, 'or I'll see you in the rings.'

But the female did not back away or cower as he'd expected. Instead, she sneered at him.

'I'll meet you in the rings whenever you like, you faerie cunt,' she spat.

'Enough!' Quin said, 'You'll not be fighting my steward in the rings today, Brother. Maeve, you have work to do.'

'Aye, Commander,' Maeve said, turning away with a flick of her hair, her deference to the Commander just shy of mocking. She went back to that mammoth desk and began sorting documents into piles.

'Is our Fourth almost finished?' Priest drawled.

Lily's gaze flicked to him for a moment. 'I'll see.'

Giving her unit a look that said she didn't want to hear any more arguments, Quin's Fourth disappeared back into their chamber and Priest barely stopped himself from rolling his eyes again.

'Wait outside,' Mad Mal commanded, turning away as soon as he'd uttered the edict, not bothering to see if they obeyed.

'Fuck,' Fie said as he and Priest traipsed from the tent, out into the cold. 'What they said is true. She doesn't look taken care of. We need to find her some actual fucking clothes, a cloak, some boots that fit her and aren't full of holes.'

'Aye,' Priest muttered. 'Come.'

They began to walk in the direction of the main thoroughfare where all the businesses were. It wasn't far away as the Commander's tent was in a prime location at the center of the Camp.

'I don't feel anything different from the binding,' Fie commented.

Priest nodded. 'Drax will be taking on the brunt of it. He'll have a noticeable link to her now.'

'Is that normal?'

Priest shrugged. 'For fae Fourths or so I've heard.'

Fie stopped in his tracks, his expression unreadable. 'I'm going to try what Drax did.'

Priest closed his eyes for a moment in exasperation. 'What do you mean?' he asked, trying not to sound as bored as he felt.

'You know ... when he used his magick upon her.'

'That wasn't magick,' Priest scoffed. 'Most fae have none that they can use.'

'Well, regardless, I'm going to try it.'

'It won't work unless you complete the bond with her yourself,' Priest told him.

'But Drax—'

'Drax is in command of the unit. It's different for him,' Priest said, pretending that he hadn't been surprised when Drax had stopped their Fourth from leaving the tent even though he hadn't yet claimed her.

Priest had already decided to try it himself as well when he had the chance. He looked forward to putting their little halfling Fourth in her place. She seemed the type who would need constant reminders that she was at the bottom of the unit hierarchy.

They bought her a thick cloak, Priest sparing no expense. She *was* one of them, after all. He would not have her walking around in rags. Fie chose her some boots, the smallest size he could find. In truth, Priest found it laughable that such a tiny female was their Fourth. No one would ever take her seriously. They'd have to ensure they weren't tainted by association in the Camp and that meant no more arguments outside their tent. Dissention within the unit meant weakness.

They returned to Quin's tent. Maeve came out a few moments later, barely looking at them.

Fie stepped forward. 'These are for our Fourth,' he said, holding the new clothes out to her.

She let out a breath. 'Very well.'

She practically snatched them from him and walked back

into the tent without another word. Priest and Fie waited outside the tent again. It was now late morning, and the female showed no signs of emerging.

'How long does it take that female to bathe?' Priest couldn't help but lament aloud just as the flap opened and out stepped their Fourth.

Priest's eyes travelled over her. Her cloak was swept behind her shoulders. Her trousers were black, the tall boots ending past her knees, but the tunic was red leather.

'Where are your blacks? he asked, his eyes trailing down her body before he could stop them. He tore his gaze away, focusing on her face instead.

'They had little that would fit me,' she said. 'The Commander's Fourth gave me this as its too small for her.'

Priest let out a grunt in response, turned on his heel, and began to walk, not looking back to see if she and Fie were following and not liking that the female was looking more attractive to him by the day. He couldn't afford distractions. Not even if it was simply because he needed to visit the pleasure tents.

CHAPTER 5

FIE

Her hair was neatly plaited back and Fie could see that Eve's ears, although not pointed like theirs were without their glamors, still tapered up to soft peaks that to anyone else wouldn't be remarked upon, but to them, made it obvious that she was half fae.

She was lucky no others of their kind had happened upon her before he and his Brothers had, or she would have been whisked away to the Dark Realms to be some high lord's halfling brood mare these days.

They walked the short distance back to their dirty tent that Fie was now sure that the Commander had given to them on purpose. Fucking prick. At least he hadn't had them killed when he found out they had been the ones to give Lily to the First Scholar, Fie supposed.

They walked into the tent and found Drax packing their supplies.

'Where the fuck have you been?' he asked. 'How long does it take a female to bathe?'

He looked pointedly at Eve and then Fie watched Drax's his eyes follow the contours of the female's leather armor.

'New clothes?'

'Aye,' Priest muttered. 'The female is more trouble than she's worth. We found ourselves in the Commander's tent. His Fourth is none other than the woman who tried to kill us in Kitore. Remember, it was you who suggested we give her to the Library, Brother? We just almost got our throats slit. Thank you for that.'

Drax shrugged. 'You were the leader then. You didn't have to follow my counsel. It's your own fault, Brother, as was losing your command.'

Fie watched Priest stare at Drax and wondered, not for the first time, how long it would be before their unit fractured.

'Not here,' Fie snarled, losing patience. 'Bad enough that Priest and I were arguing in the fucking street. We show no more weakness despite our small Fourth. When do we leave?'

'Soon,' said Drax, looking at Eve. 'Eat your fill now, woman. We will not be stopping until late tonight when we get to the next town.'

'Where are we going,' she asked almost timidly.

'To the Ice Plains.'

Her eyes widened at Drax's admission. 'Why?'

'That's not your concern, Fourth. Be silent. Eat. Ready yourself. We leave within the hour.'

Fie got to work, stowing the rest of their supplies, and ensuring they had everything they needed for the journey into the far north. He included some salve for the female as Drax had mentioned she was not as fast at healing as they were.

Priest had gone to get the horses ready and by the time he returned, everything was packed up and Eve had eaten practically half the contents of the table, stuffing food into her mouth as if there was no tomorrow.

They met Priest outside and saw that he'd procured a

fourth horse. Eve stared at it and, as all three of them climbed onto their mounts' backs, she simply stood in the mud beside them like a lost child.

'Let's go, Fourth,' Drax said, not hiding his impatience to be gone.

She glared at Drax. 'I can't ride.'

'You can't ride?' Priest echoed disparagingly. 'Of course you can't. Fucking useless female.'

Her cheeks reddened and Fie reached his hand down to her before he could think better of it.

'You can ride with me.'

Hesitantly, she took his wrist and he gripped hers, pulling her up behind him. She straddled the horse and grasped his waist as hard as she could, squeezing him.

Amused, he glanced behind him. 'Don't worry,' he said, 'I won't let you fall off.'

She was shaking slightly, and he realized that this was the perfect opportunity to learn more about her.

'How many times have you fought in the rings,' he asked her in a low tone just for her ears.

'Hundreds,' she replied.

'What manner of men? Dangerous? Murderous? Lecherous?'

She inclined her head absently, looking down at the ground as if she stood at the edge of a cliff.

He caught her eye. 'This is just a ride on a horse,' he said meaningfully, trying to make her understand that this was nothing to fear, nowhere near so dangerous as the men she had fought.

She nodded stiffly, swallowing hard.

How could she have done all she had and still be afraid of a little ride? He caught himself grinning and frowned. He was not really her friend, he reminded himself. She was their enemy. He had to remember that. He thought about his deep hatred for her father instead, stamping out any softness he felt for her.

He glanced back again; this time eying her coldly when she wasn't looking at him. He'd find out what he could about her and relay it to his Brothers as needed, but that was all.

They began to plod along through the Camp, reaching the outskirts quickly as their tent had been so close.

'Good riddance,' Priest muttered, not looking back. 'Next time we have to come to this place, be sure we've paid our dues, Brother,' he said to Drax, who pointedly ignored him.

They did not stop for an afternoon meal, nor when the sun set. By the time they reached the walled town they had been making for, Fie was half frozen. The weather had surely turned these past few days. It was definitely full winter now.

They left their horses at the stable, Fie dismounting and helping the female down. He thought she might collapse to the ground. Not used to riding, her legs might be weak, but, of course, she was used to the fights. Her body was stronger than it looked.

They passed the first two inns that were not to Priest's liking and Fie wished his Brother would lower his impossible standards before he fucking froze to death. They finally reached one on a respectable street and went in.

Although the hour was late, they had the coin to rouse the cook who set about making them something for supper. They crowded into a small private dining area and Fie stoked the fire. They all sat around the fine, clothed table and a serving girl came in, pouring them all a cup of wine.

Without a word, Drax replaced the female's with water and Fie watched curiously, wondering if he was denying the wench, but Eve simply nodded her thanks and drank from the cup thirstily.

'How is it, female,' Priest began, 'that you cannot ride a horse?'

Their Fourth drew into herself just a tiny bit before she answered. 'I never needed to learn.'

'So, by what means did you travel? On foot?' he barked a laugh. 'By cart like a beast to market?'

She levelled her gaze at him. 'I never went anywhere.'

He looked incredulous. 'Not anywhere?'

'No.'

They lapsed into silence as a hearty venison stew with potatoes and bread was brought. Eve, of course, ate as quickly as possible, using the bread to mop her earthenware bowl clean and then looking at the door longingly, as if she wanted more already.

'Do you have no regard for those around you?' Priest muttered.

She locked eyes with him. 'If you have a problem with me, break this bond or whatever it is and leave me here.'

Priest took a long drink of his wine, eyeing her before he spoke again. 'I have no problem save that we have been forced to ally ourselves with a *human* who eats like a pig and has the deportment of a wraith.'

He stared her down and she looked away, appearing confused rather than angry.

'Enough,' ordered Drax. 'Leave the female be.'

Eve stared into her empty bowl with a small sigh as if it might refill by magick.

'Why the Ice Plains?' she asked, as if the question had just come to her.

'Because that is where one of the entrances to the Underhill is,' Drax answered.

She looked up in surprise. 'The Underhill?'

'You've heard of it?' Fie asked.

She nodded slowly. 'The fae realm.'

Drax picked up his cup. 'The fae can be found in many of the Dark Realms; this realm as well, but the Underhill is something else. There are no other realms like it as far as we know. It's a tiny place; a fold within this realm. There were only three portals to get to it. Two of them opened here into the Light Realm and a third in one of the Dark Realms, which made it a much more secure realm than any other.'

He took a long drink, setting his cup down on the table a moment later. 'The Underhill is where our children are kept secure. Most of them stay there with their mother or a guardian until they are old enough. The Dark Realms are dangerous places.'

Eve leaned forward, focused completely on Drax.

'Our problem is that all three portals to the Underhill collapsed.'

'So, there are fae trapped there?' she asked.

'We don't know,' Fie said, looking down at his bowl, his appetite disappearing.

For the first time, she looked empathetic to their plight. 'Do you have children of your own there?'

'No,' said Drax, 'but both Fie and Priest have siblings that we need to find.'

She glanced at them. 'I'm sorry.'

Priest stood up. 'I don't need your fucking pity. What I need is an open portal so we can get there and find out what has happened to our kin.' He put his goblet down on the table hard. 'I'll see about our accommodation for the night.'

He left the room, the door banging closed behind him.

'But I don't understand what you need me for.'

'We already told you,' Drax said, regarding her, 'but we'll talk about that when we get closer. We're still more than a week out, and the land between here and the Ice Plains is treacherous at this time of year.'

'More so with everything else that's happening,' Fie murmured and Drax shot him a warning look.

His Brother clearly didn't want their Fourth to know

about all the Dark Realm creatures that were spilling into this world if she didn't already.

'Shouldn't you be trying to get there as quickly as possible?' Eve asked.

Drax shrugged. 'It's been months. A few more days won't matter.'

Spoken like a true leader, Fie thought, his lip curling as he stood up.

'Months? But why has it taken you so long to—'

'We were prisoners,' Fie blurted out, turning to her in frustration. 'We got stuck in Kitore. The city's fucking wards wouldn't let us out. We were there for months until the First Scholar died, and the ward key was passed to someone else, but don't worry your tiny human brain about it,' Fie said. 'Let your betters sort it out. You just be ready to do what we need you to do when the time is right.'

'But I don't know what you need me to do,' she said, staring at him with those wide eyes of hers. She didn't look like a fighter now. She looked like a naive girl. The thought made him angry. He stood up, the chair screeching as it dragged along the floor, and left without a word, finding Priest on his way up the stone steps to a long corridor of rooms.

'How many do we have?' he asked, catching his Brother up. 'Only one. Fucking place. Fuck this realm. Fuck Drax and fuck that fucking little female as well.'

Fie chuckled. 'Perhaps you should.'

At Priest's venomous look, Fie took a step back. 'I jest.'

Priest's eyes narrowed. 'Don't forget who she is, who her father is. After what he's done, we should send him her head in a box once we're finished with her.'

Fie shrugged.

'She is a blood enemy,' he continued. 'Her father is the

reason for all of this, would that we could prove it. Regardless, I aim to get my revenge any way I can.'

Fie nodded. 'And I. She acquiesced too easily down there, and she asks questions to learn more about us. This could all be a trick, a trap for us. At the very least, I wouldn't be surprised if she tries to run again.'

'Agreed. Get close to her. Drax is feeling the bond. He won't realize that she's treacherous until it's too late. And she must be treacherous with his blood flowing through her veins. Anything she shows us that is innocent or kind we must treat as a ruse. Do not let your guard down. We'll try to keep that fucking fool Drax safe as well.'

Priest turned away and Fie wondered how much longer it would be before he challenged Drax for the leadership of the unit. He almost wished they'd get it over with, but those two would never get along while one was above the other. Another challenge for command between the two of them wouldn't do their unit any good either. They'd all lose in the end unless his Brothers sorted out whatever remained of their friendship after their months in Kitore.

～

Eve

SHE TRIED NOT to make it obvious that she'd never been in such a fine establishment before as her wide eyes darted around, taking in the colors on the muraled walls, the sanded floorboards, and the flattened glass fitted into the casements.

She shoved something else in her mouth. She didn't even look down to see what it was. She didn't care. She was hungry all the time now, and it was beginning to worry her. Gods knew she'd had little enough to sustain her during her time with Talik, but Eve had never felt like this before.

At least Priest and Fie had left for now. They clearly couldn't stand being in the same room as her. She wasn't sure exactly where their animosity stemmed from. Perhaps it was because she was human or maybe because she was a woman. Most men didn't like her, but she'd thought that was because she could win against them so easily in the rings. Priest had beaten her and Fie probably could too what with them being fae and all.

She swallowed and stuffed yet more food in her mouth, belatedly noticing that Drax was staring at her, amusement lurking in the depths of his eyes, which she bristled at. She didn't like being mocked, but she didn't say a word, just stared back until finally he looked away and she regained a tiny bit of her confidence.

But then he got up and she tensed, sure he was going to throw her over the table and take from her what he willed.

Oddly, that thought didn't fill her with the disgust and abhorrence that it should. She didn't want him to do it, did she? Between Eve's legs fluttered and she frowned. What had he done to her to make her think of such a thing being at all pleasurable?

He didn't come any closer, thankfully. Instead, he poured himself more wine and raised the jug at her, asking silently if she wanted any.

She shook her head between mouthfuls. 'No, thank you.'

'It's better than that swill they brought us in the Camp. Are you sure you don't want to try it?' he asked in that quiet way he had about him that, annoyingly, put her at ease.

A wolf in sheep's clothing. She almost laughed out loud at that. More like a Dark Realm beast in wolf's clothing. A giggle erupted from her, and she slapped her hand over her mouth to stop it. It sounded so odd to her ears.

She glanced at Drax who was now looking at her with a

peculiar sentimentality that made her uncomfortable. What was going on between them?

Eve stood up abruptly. 'I'm tired.'

He raised a brow but didn't say anything as he gestured to the door, opened it, and let her go first in a display of chivalry that confused her. She didn't like him being behind her either. She turned her head to watch him as they walked across what was now a crowded tap room.

Eve walked with confidence as she always did when she was moving through throngs of men. She didn't shy away from any eyes, though plenty were looking her way, and she wondered why. They weren't in the rings now and she wasn't wearing the jerkin that displayed her body. Usually, she was assessed like an animal for her fighting abilities, to see if she would win and make money and that was all. Well, except for the Bull.

Eve's lip curled at the thought of him. She was beginning to lament the fact that she had been able to kill Jays, but not him nor Talik. After all they had done to her, they deserved it as well.

Drax was still on her heels, staying close in an almost protective gesture which wasn't needed considering she could kill any of these men easily.

She walked up the steps in front of him. Stone. The whole place was stone. Old, unlike the town she had come from where everything was made of timber and not nearly so timeless as this place was.

'Third door,' she heard Drax say, and she opened the one he said, stepping inside a spacious room.

Her mouth dropped open. There were two beds with quilted coverlets, a small, polished table with a jug of wine in the center and matching chairs around it. There was a fire in a small grate, rugs on the stone floor, and intricate tapestries hung along the walls that ensured the room was warm. Eve found her eyes captivated by the intricate patterns and colors.

She was nudged from behind and she realized she'd stopped in the doorway. She moved into the room to let Drax pass, her gaze still riveted. She'd never seen anything so beautiful before. Drax went to the table, pouring himself a goblet and shucking his cloak and tunic. He dropped his glamor as well, and she could now see his violet eyes, slightly longer fingernails that were a bit like claws, she thought. His teeth were sharper too, making him look just a little bit more menacing.

She wrinkled her nose, hating that she was so tiny as she took off her own cloak, and put it on the peg next to the door, following what Drax had done. She took off her tunic in the warmth of the room as well, leaving herself in just the chemise that Maeve had procured for her. It was long as it was meant to go under a gown, so she'd bunched it up to fit into her trousers.

Her hand stroked the soft leather of the supple, red tunic, she'd been given. She hadn't thanked Lily, though she belatedly realized she should have. In truth, she'd been uncomfortable by the kindnesses she'd been shown, wondering what they'd ask of her in return. But they hadn't requested anything. They probably would in the future, she decided. If she ever met them again, they'd take their favors from her.

Drax sat at the table.

'Where are the others?' she asked.

He shrugged. 'Entertaining themselves at the brothel. Perhaps at the fights.'

Fights? Her ears perked up, and his eyes narrowed as if he knew the direction of her thoughts.

'We don't need the extra attention,' he said, his voice hard. 'You won't be fighting in the ring.'

The panic that welled up in her shocked her. It was the

likes of which she'd never felt before. She felt afraid. She wasn't their slave. He couldn't forbid her, could he?

'You can't stop me,' she said, challenging him before she could think the better of it.

His expression shuttered, turning almost cruel as he watched her, but she didn't care what he did to her. She would not do as he said.

Eve bit her lip to keep it from quivering, but it wasn't fear she felt. She began to move, pacing around the room with a nervous energy that made her shiver.

'You enjoy it.' He sounded surprised.

She nodded. 'I need it.'

He stood up and approached her and she knew she must look like a prey animal ready to bolt, but all he did was put his hand on her shoulder and suddenly she felt more relaxed, her alarm subsiding.

She looked up at him. What was he doing? He was doing something to her. She could feel it, same as he had in the Camp before he'd ... She twisted away with a cry.

'Don't!' she hissed.

Again, he looked surprised, but he put his hands up in supplication.

'I was merely trying to calm you,' he said, his eyes watching her reactions. 'I won't do it again, and I won't forbid you to fight in the rings, but I urge you not to here. We're too close to where we found you and someone will be looking for you after what you did to your keeper.'

She nodded slowly, the relief that she felt was instant.

'If you need the release of the fight, we can spar with you. It won't be the same, but ... perhaps it's something else you need?'

She canted her head at him in question, not sure what he was talking about.

He stepped closer, using one finger to lift her chin. 'Is it a different sort of release that you crave, female?' he asked softly, his voice taking on a sensual quality that somehow made her knees feel weak.

She shook her head, her heart beating faster, but she didn't step away, staring into his eyes as she felt his hand unbuckle her belt.

It fell to the floor with a thud, and he unbuttoned her breeches very slowly, giving her ample time to stop him. This was not like it had been in the Camp and he clearly wanted her to know it. She should step away, break this connection but, for reasons she didn't understand, she simply watched him, felt what he was doing.

Part of her was afraid from the things the Bull had done. What if he hurt her? Was she strong enough to fight him off?

He pushed her gently to the nearest bed and down upon it, pulling her breeches down as far as he could with her tall boots still on.

She gasped as she felt his hand at the apex of her thighs, his short claws scraping against her mound. His fingers teased her there for a moment before parting her, making her move her knees further apart. And then he bent down and put his tongue on her!

She squeaked in surprise and, though her mind was confused, her body seemed not to be, her hips beginning to move closer, wanting more as he licked her, thrust his tongue in and out of her.

She gave a low whine, her mouth opening on a stuttered breath as he worked her harder, the sounds of him lapping at her making him chuckle where she was mortified. She cried out, pressure building in her that she'd never felt before but grasped for, needing whatever it was. It burst over her in a wave, and she screamed with it, her body going weak. Her back bowed and she shuddered, his ministrations gentling as her hips undulated erratically.

After the feeling had waned, she was left oddly sated, as if she truly had just fought in the rings, she opened her eyes to find him licking his lips. At her confused and shocked expression, his countenance darkened considerably.

'You said in the Camp that it wasn't your first time,' he said accusingly, still holding her.

She was acutely aware that she was still practically beneath this fae with her breeches around her ankles and her core in his face.

'I didn't lie,' she said, the words coming out as a croak.

Eve wondered what the problem was and took a shuddering breath as her nethers clenched again at the thought of what he'd done.

He put her on her feet, made sure she could stand, and she pulled up her breeches, cheeks crimson.

'Take one of the beds,' he ordered. 'You're tired. Sleep.'

Not understanding what had just happened nor why he was now angry with her, Eve turned without a word and sat on the bed. She took off her beautiful, new boots and put them neatly on the floor beside her, almost afraid someone was going to take them while she slept.

She lay in the bed over the coverlet on her back, staring at the ceiling. She thought that sleep might be long in coming, but it wasn't, and she dreamed of Drax, of lying in a forest while he cut out her heart.

～

Priest

IT WAS LATE when Priest stumbled into their room; a room that smelled of sex. He saw Drax asleep on one of the beds, and his eyes darted around. Where was the female? He spied her on the other bed, the quilt wrapped around her slight frame. She looked so tiny under the covers that he'd almost missed her.

Eyes narrowing, he cast his eyes over to Drax who was still asleep, wondering if his Brother had rutted the female again. He took a deep breath in through his nose and smelled her in the air. Only her. Smirking, he wondered if the little female had pleasured herself while Drax slumbered. His cock sprang to life, and he swallowed a curse. What was it about this woman that made him unable to control himself?

He laid down on the bed next to Drax, kicking his boots off. He'd lost track of Fie during the fights. Gods only knew where his Brother was now; probably in the bed of some willing maid if he knew the younger male.

He was surprised a moment later when said Brother came through the door. He gave Priest a nod, not speaking as he hung up his cloak, poured himself a goblet of wine from the table, and drank it. Priest followed Fie's eyes as he noted the female in the bed, but he didn't look over at her again as he lay next to her and fell asleep, beginning to snore softly.

Priest's eyes meandered around the room, finding their way back to Eve and he had to admit that she looked … not quite so murderous in her sleep. He watched her for a time, her lashes fanned against her pale cheeks, which looked a bit fuller. He snorted. Well, she certainly fucking ate enough.

THE NEXT MORNING, they got up early, finding that the female was already dressed and ready to go. She seemed nervous, full of energy and Priest looked to Drax who was watching her from the corner of his eye.

Finally, Priest could take it no longer.

'Gods, female, would you sit down and be calm?'

She looked startled for a moment at his outburst and then

she ignored him, continuing to flit about the room as if he'd never said anything.

'Fie, take her down and teach her to ride,' Priest ordered his Brother, 'lest she fall and break her neck the first time she mounts her own horse.'

Fie looked annoyed, but he did as he was told, gesturing with his head for her to follow him. She looked apprehensive but went with him. As soon as they were gone, Drax stood.

'You forget your place,' he ground out.

'Not at all, Brother,' Priest said through clenched teeth, 'but you weren't doing anything about the female, so I did. It's hardly my fault that Fie lets me order him about. Perhaps you should assert your authority more with him and then he wouldn't jump to obey *my* every command.'

Priest stifled a smile as his Brother turned away with a curse.

'Go through the packs,' Drax ordered.

Priest gave him a mocking salute, knowing that Drax was only telling him to do it to annoy him, but he would go through the packs, and he wouldn't complain. Fuck Drax. It was only a matter of time. Sooner or later, Drax would make a mistake and Priest would fight him for leadership of the unit ... and he would win.

He smiled at the thought. He would command this unit again by the time they were finished with the female, and then he'd break this farce of a bond and get rid of her, he vowed.

Priest proceeded to do as Drax had ordered, unpacking and repacking their supplies, ensuring they had all they needed for the journey. When he was finished, he took their bags outside to the yard, watching from under the eaves as Fie tried to instruct the hapless female in the basics of riding a horse.

He rolled his eyes. How did someone get to be her age

and have no idea how to do the easiest of things? Perhaps she *was* a simpleton. Perhaps all she could do was fight in the ring.

He watched her on the horse's back, grasping the reins as tightly as she could, her knuckles white with how hard she was holding them. Fie was telling her to grip with her knees, and to give the horse its head, only pulling gently on the reins to show the beast where she wanted him to go.

Priest shook his head as she jerked too hard and caused the horse to turn swiftly. The foolish girl fell off, landing in the mud with a cry. She ignored Fie's outstretched hand, getting up herself and frowning at the mud that was now all over her boots, breeches, and leather tunic.

Fie told her to get back up and she looked at him petulantly, taking the reins and leading her mount towards him.

'Unpredictable beast,' she said under her breath and Priest almost grinned.

'You need to bond with her,' Fie said. 'She needs to know that you are her friend. One day she may save your life.'

Eve gave him a dry look. 'I'm bound to more than enough creatures already.'

Fie barked a laugh, looking surprised at her wit, but he wasn't deterred. He offered her an apple.

'Give her treats,' he said. 'Make her your friend.'

Eve snatched the apple from his outstretched palm and Priest wondered if she was going to consume it, as she seemed unable to stop herself from devouring any and all food in her path. But, instead, she hesitantly held it out to the mare that he had found for her in the Camp.

'Hand level,' Fie reminded her and she flattened her hand out immediately, appearing anxious, as if she thought the horse would suddenly bite off her fingers.

But, as it gently picked the apple from her, Eve looked in wonder at the animal.

Fie murmured encouragements, telling her to stroke the horse's cheek, rub her behind her ears. He showed her how to do it, and when the horse took a step forward and nudged her, she grinned.

Priest scowled, turning away.

'It's time to go,' Drax said, saving Priest from his bewildering thoughts.

They all mounted their horses, Eve now on her own, though she still looked uncomfortable as she rode between Drax and Fie, Priest following behind. They'd make the Ice Plains soon enough.

He tried not to let his gaze stray to the female but was unable to stop his thoughts and his eyes from tending in her direction. He needed to begin her training, try to harness her magick so that she could do what they needed her to. He needed to understand what triggered her power. As with a fae child, the ability to conjure needed to be unlocked, which meant he needed to learn more about her. Fie had had little luck thus far and, though it was still early in their journey, there wasn't much time.

Priest wondered if he could make her speak to him by using his power on her. He needed to try compelling her; see if he could make her do what he wanted as Drax had been able to in the Camp. He smiled nastily at her back. He'd enjoy seeing the look on her face as her body was made to do his bidding while her mind railed against him.

CHAPTER 6

DRAX

They travelled for the whole morning, stopping for an afternoon meal only, and the female ate as much as she possibly could, shoveling it all into her mouth at speed as if she was afraid it would be taken from her.

Drax frowned at her, wondering again at her life in that town before they met her. He and the others had been blessed with childhoods in the Underhill, but he'd wager her experiences had been a far cry from theirs.

'Why do you eat so much?' Priest asked in that cold way of his.

'Enough, Brother,' he said quietly, giving Priest a meaningful look that his Brother ignored, preferring to stand and mount his steed instead.

'Going to scout ahead,' he announced, casting one more scathing look at the female before he turned his horse and rode off down the road, leaving a cloud of dust in his wake.

'Don't mind him,' Drax said.

Eve merely shrugged as they mounted their horses and went slowly after Priest. She pretended she didn't care what Priest said, but Drax knew the truth. Priest's anger towards her and his cutting comments were beginning to take their toll on her. He could feel how anxious she got whenever she was the focus of his ire.

'Where are we going now?' she asked. 'Will there be another inn?'

Drax didn't need the bond to hear the hope in her voice. She may be uncomfortable in the lavish surroundings they took for granted, but she'd enjoyed the fine room they'd stayed at the night before … just as she'd enjoyed what he'd done to her though it was clear by her shock that she'd never been brought to her peak before. He looked forward to expanding her education, but it would have to wait.

'There are no more towns between here and the Ice Plains,' Drax told her. 'It'll get colder. The road will become more treacherous. Stay close to us. Keep your eyes and your ears open.'

She nodded, gazing around at the forest that surrounded them.

'You don't like it, do you?' Drax muttered, gesturing at the trees.

'There are a lot of things I don't like,' she said, her voice just as low as his.

THEY DIDN'T SEE Priest for the rest of the day. Their small party kept to the road and, as it began to get dark, Drax looked around for his Brother's tell-tale markings to show where he had left the track, for it was not safe to camp too close to the main thoroughfare. The woods were dangerous, it was true, but the road was doubly so.

He saw two sticks on the ground, pointing into the underbrush and he led his horse off the packed dirt and into the trees. He felt the female's fear spike, but she didn't say anything as they went deeper into the forest.

They hadn't gone far when Drax smelled the smoke from the fire. He dismounted, hearing Fie and Eve do the same behind. They walked the rest of the way on foot, coming to a small clearing with meat cooking and the bedrolls already laid out. Priest had made a circle of stones large enough for them and the horses as well.

Drax made sure not to disturb them as they passed over the threshold and into the clearing. They'd be necessary later out here.

'Hurry up,' Priest said. 'We're not alone. I left some rabbits as a decoy, but as soon as the sun is down, we need to make sure the circle is cast unless you want to spend the entire night fighting,' he stifled a yawn, 'which I do not.'

Drax made sure that the female and her horse were within the circle's boundaries. He nodded to Priest who took his amulet, runes carved into the surface, out of the pouch at his belt. His Brother muttered the words to ensure their safety for the night.

'You must not leave the circle,' he said to Eve.

She didn't question him, though Drax knew she was curious.

She wasn't much of a talker. In some ways, that was a good thing. It was irritating to travel with a companion who constantly needed to fill the silences with mindless chatter, but he did wish she would volunteer more information about herself.

He supposed that she didn't trust them. Of course, they didn't trust her either, he reminded himself, though he wasn't sure he believed that anymore. Since the claiming, it had been getting harder and harder to remember that her being a Fourth was a necessity, a temporary state. They hadn't chosen her. She had forced their hand. They'd neither wanted nor needed a Fourth. That hadn't changed, had it?

The subject of his thoughts sat on a log by the fire, staring at the rabbit and practically salivating. Priest scoffed at her, but said nothing, focusing on sharpening his knives.

Drax walked to the edge of the circle and looked out into the rapidly darkening forest.

'How many are out there?'

Priest didn't get up from what he was doing, nor did his actions falter.

'There are about twenty in that direction.' He pointed to the north. 'And something larger makes its way towards us from the south. Nothing we aren't prepared for,' he said. 'We know what dangers lurk out here. In truth, I was surprised that the human mercenaries we sent north returned.'

Drax nodded, remembering when the former unit of the Dark Army they'd sent had returned to Kitore weeks after they'd left with the news that they'd been unable to enter the Underhill because there was nothing left of the portals at all.

'I was as well,' he admitted.

He looked back at Eve and Fie. His Brother was trying to engage her in conversation, but she was having none of it, giving him absent, one-word answers whilst staring at the meat cooking on the fire with longing.

She sighed and looked at Priest, daring to speak to him. 'Are they not ready? They look ready.'

'As if you'd know,' Priest called over his shoulder. 'When was the last time you even had rabbit?'

She shook her head. 'Never, but it smells delicious.'

Priest looked shocked. 'Never?'

'Beef?' Fie asked.

She shook her head. 'I ... they never gave me meat,' she said.

Priest, Drax and Fie all looked at her with varying degrees of shock. Meat was a staple in every fae's diet. To not have any at all was tantamount to starvation.

'None?' Fie asked, sounding horrified.

She shook her head.

'What did you eat then?'

She shrugged. 'Whatever I was given. Bread, cheese, nuts, sometimes apples when they were in season.'

Priest stomped across their camp in a huff, but in this case, he was all bluster. He took one of their tin plates, threw one of the rabbits on it, and handed it to her.

'Gods, woman, fucking eat.'

She took it with obvious glee, shaking slightly as she tore at the flesh, stuffing it into her mouth even though it was steaming and clearly much too hot. She gave a moan of appreciation that had Drax's cock hardening.

He shook his head. He usually had no trouble separating mission from leisure, but it was becoming more and more difficult.

The others received their dinners and ate in silence. It was dark by the time they were finished and that was when they heard something rustling in the forest close by.

Eve stood up immediately, her plate dropping to the ground empty but for a pile of bones. She'd eaten every piece of flesh, even sucked the marrow out.

'What was that?' she asked, unable to keep the fear from her tone.

'Nothing to worry about,' Drax said vaguely. 'Just stay inside the circle of stones.'

Something else rustled to the other side of them and she turned. There was nothing there.

'What is it?' she asked.

Drax stood beside her. 'Dark Realm creatures. Wraiths probably. They're fucking everywhere these days.'

At her blank expression, Priest elaborated. 'They look like shadows until they feed. Then they turn solid-*ish* as they suck the very life essence from you.'

Eve's eyes widened.

'You *have* heard of the other realms, haven't you?' Priest asked impatiently. 'Gods, it's like trying to instruct a child. How are you my Fourth?'

Eve turned her hard gaze on him, her eyes narrowing. 'I am not simple,' she growled. 'I am not a child. I'm not a fool.' She practically bared her teeth at him. 'And I am not yours.'

Priest's face emulated hers, and he stood, stalking towards her. She held her ground though Drax could feel her fear rising.

'Open a portal,' Priest commanded.

She looked perplexed and glanced at Drax.

'That is what we need, female.' He poked her in the chest. 'That is the only thing you are good for.'

She raised her chin, looking him in the eye defiantly.

'Go on,' Priest mocked. 'Make a portal. Use your magick. Show us you're not completely worthless.'

She shook her head. 'I have no magick,' she said and Drax recoiled as he felt her sudden desolation at Priest's words. She believed everything he said, Drax realized, feeling an overwhelming sense of sadness that their Fourth thought so little of herself that Priest could cut her this deeply.

'Enough,' Drax said, rising to his feet, but Priest ignored him.

'Then you're no good to us.'

Priest grabbed Eve by the front of her tunic and began to stride forward, dragging her backwards with him towards the edge of the circle. As soon as she realized where he was taking her, she began to struggle violently, digging her heels into the earth, but it was no use. He was too strong, and she couldn't regain her balance.

'I said ENOUGH!' Drax commanded, taking Priest by the tunic and shaking him, angry that he'd let Priest go this far.

They were now precariously close to the edge. Something rustled in the undergrowth very close to Eve, and she screamed, clawing at Priest's hands, but he wouldn't release her.

'Let him do what he must,' Fie said to Drax, pulling him away from Priest.

Drax turned on him.

'She's our Fourth!' Drax yelled, pushing Fie hard enough for him to fall in the dirt by the fire and turning back to Priest.

'No!' Fie said vehemently. 'She's a means to an end and if she can't use her magick then we need to find another way to the Underhill. You're forgetting our mission, Brother. The bond with her is clouding your mind.'

With a growl, Drax sprang forward again to stop Priest, furious that his Brothers were doing this, but before he could get to Eve, she broke through her fear, made a fist, and hit Priest square in the face. Priest staggered back slightly with the force of the blow, looking incredulous as he pulled her back from the edge.

He bent down so that his face was level with hers.

'If you cannot do what we need you to do, female, you're dead weight, and there's no point dragging you along with us.'

He let her go with a growl and she fell on her arse. Realizing she was still close too to the edge of the circle, she scrambled away from it with a cry, leaping back to the middle of the clearing, breathing heavily.

Giving Priest a wide berth, Eve lay on one of the bedrolls by the fire, turning away from them and curling into a ball.

Drax trailed Priest across the clearing. 'I gave you a fucking order,' he snarled.

'You know what I say is true,' Priest said, shrugging. 'If the female cannot open a portal, she is useless to us. I must make her magick manifest,' he added in a whisper.

'Find another way,' he ordered.

Priest let out a huff. 'How do you propose I get us into the Underhill if I cannot make her create a bridge? Pray really hard?'

'I don't give a fuck, but you won't touch her like that again.'

Pushing past Priest, Drax chose the bedroll nearest to Eve and lay in it. The others followed suit and Drax closed his eyes, thinking of how she'd felt when Priest was tormenting her and vowing that he wouldn't let his Brother treat their Fourth like that again.

THE NEXT MORNING, he woke at the same time as his Brothers. The sun was just rising and the air was cold. Checking their Fourth still slumbered, he motioned for Priest and Fie to join him on the other side of the circle, far away from the female, so she couldn't hear them while they discussed her even if she did wake.

He was still angry at Priest and Fie for their mutinous actions last night, but he could understand. They thought him addled by the bond. Perhaps he was, but that was immaterial. This mission was important to him, but it was even more so to his Brothers. They had kin in the Underhill, and they didn't believe he was doing everything he could to get them there.

'Last night will have a comeuppance,' he said first in warning, 'but for now, we have more important matters to discuss. I think I know why her magick has never presented itself.'

His Brothers looked at him expectantly, waiting for him to go on.

'Since she's been traveling with us, she's been ravenous, and she admitted freely that she was given little food by her keepers.'

Priest shrugged. 'I don't understand what you're getting at, Brother.'

Drax's eyes found her, huddled in her bedroll across the clearing. 'When she hit you last night. How did it feel?'

'Hard.'

'Harder than when you fought her in the ring?'

Priest nodded slowly. 'Aye, harder than that.'

'Then she's getting stronger. How long did they have her? How many years was she made to fight in the rings?'

'You think they starved her for a long time?' Fie asked.

'If they did it from her being a child, that would be reason enough for her to be on the small side, even for human female,' Drax said.

'But why starve a fighter?' Fie asked quietly. 'They wanted her to win, didn't they?'

'There is only one reason why they would do such a thing,' Priest said grimly, 'They knew she was fae even though she didn't … doesn't. They kept her weak, probably even slipped iron shavings into the food they did give her because they knew that if she became too powerful, she would have been impossible to control.'

'You think she's that strong?' Fie asked.

'If she is her father's daughter, then she will be. If she reaches her full potential, she'll give any of us run for our money,' Drax said.

'What do you suggest we do then?' Fie asked. 'Put her in chains? Starve her as they did?'

'No,' Drax said. 'The opposite. We let her have all the food she wants and let her rest when she needs it. I don't think it will take long. By the time we reach the Underhill, she'll be strong enough to reach her magick, to do what we need her to do.'

'And if she's too strong for us to control by then?' Priest asked with a snort.

'Then we chain her in iron, make sure we can subdue her with our own power,' Fie replied before Drax could.

'Even if all that works,' Drax piped up, 'she's never conjured before. It takes fae with magickal affinity years to control their gifts. Can she learn to conjure that quickly?'

'Priest,' Fie said, turning to his Brother. 'You're the best with magick. Is it possible? Can you teach her how to use hers in theory so that when her power does appear, she can find it? Otherwise, we'll get to the Underhill, and be stuck while we wait for her to understand.'

Priest gave a long-suffering sigh. 'Very well, but I make no promises.'

Drax shook his head. His Brothers didn't understand and, after last night, Drax had seen how precarious his command was. He needed to tread carefully or risk losing his unit and his Fourth for if Priest took over, Drax had no doubt that he'd break the bond and slit Eve's throat as soon as she was of no more use to them.

He changed the subject, letting the matter of their Fourth lie for now.

'Now that the Dark Realm beasts have begun to make themselves known, do we have enough amulets for all of us?'

Priest nodded. 'I always keep a spare or two. We have enough for us and the female.'

'Good,' Drax said. 'Give it to her when she wakes and tell her not to take it off. We don't need her being caught and killed by something as innocuous as a wraith.'

∼

Eve

Morning had come too quickly for Eve. She felt as if she hadn't slept at all. It didn't help that throughout the night she'd been woken by dreams of being thrust outside the protective circle and devoured by whatever lurked in the bushes.

The men were already awake and moving about the camp when she woke. After last night, her first impulse was to run. But that was foolish. How far would she conceivably get before they found her again now that she was bound to their unit? It was ironic that she was now a Dark Brother when that was what she'd wished for. She should have been more specific.

She stood up and walked into the edge of the circle, needing a piss, and wondering if it was too dangerous to leave it in the day. It would be easy enough to simply squat by the edge here and do it, but Eve was beginning to think she should begin using what manners she did have.

And she did possess some. She was simply out of practice.

When she'd first joined the gang, Talik had taken her to an older woman who'd taught her some of the rudiments of etiquette. Eve had only realized later that he must have intended to make her a courtesan. But then he'd seen her strength, and his plans had changed.

Since then, she'd always been in the company of men. She could not appear weak, so she had emulated their mannerisms. She walked differently, stood up straighter because she was small. She spat and swore. She had no shame, as Priest called it, because none of the men she'd been around ever had any either.

Perhaps all of this was making things worse for her while she was with them. These men were not like the men in the town. Perhaps it was because they were fae, but their values were different. They didn't see vulgarity as strength.

She stood and watched from inside the camp, surveying the trees around them. She still wasn't used to being in the dense forest. She felt closed in, and she could swear that she heard whispers on the wind, but that made no sense. They were alone here except for whatever creatures were out there and, as far as she knew, they didn't speak.

'Where are you going?' Drax muttered from the fire.

She looked back at him. The first thing that came to mind was to tell him in no uncertain terms that she needed to piss, but she best start tempering her words.

'I need to ...' She trailed off, having no idea what the polite way of saying it was.

Drax got to his feet and tied his bedroll to his horse.

'Come,' he said to the others. 'The light is upon us. It's time to go anyway. Break the circle.'

Priest muttered something and then held a necklace out to her. 'Keep this around your neck,' he said.

She looked at it suspiciously. 'What is it?'

'Protection,' Drax said simply. 'So long as you have this, you need not worry.'

She took it from Priest gingerly and put it on. It was an oval of dark, charred wood carved with runes hung on a leather cord.

Drax looked around, listening. 'They're gone now,' he said, 'but don't go too far.'

She nodded and went behind some bushes, finding herself hurrying, though, not liking being out of her Brother's sights. She paused as she was walking back to the camp. *Her Brothers.* It felt right and yet it was so, so wrong. They were not her anything, she reminded herself. Everything was so confusing...

Drax might be being almost friendly, but she couldn't afford to forget what he was ... what they all were. But then there was the other night at the inn ... what Drax had made her feel ... she shook herself free of the thoughts.

Fie wasn't being particularly cruel to her, but he didn't like her. Of that she was certain. And then there was Priest.

He hated her with a vile passion that made her want to recoil whenever he looked directly at her. She shuddered as she remembered what he'd done last night, terrifying her with his threats.

No, these men may be feeding her and not treating her so badly as the others had, but it would all come at a price. Everything did.

When she got back into the camp, they were already ready to go. The fire had been doused in sand and the men had mounted their steeds.

She looked at her own horse with barely concealed suspicion. Her thighs and arse hurt from all the riding yesterday. In truth, she'd rather walk, but she knew that it was foolish to expend that much energy simply because she didn't like riding a beast of burden, so she gamely got on the mare's back, taking the reins as Fie had shown her.

They got back onto the main road. It was so quiet, but what did she know about the wilderness? Perhaps this was how the forest always sounded.

The men stayed in formation, Drax at the head, Fie at the back and Priest riding next to her.

'Keep your eyes open,' Drax said, and she copied him as he scanned the forest in front and beside them. She looked back and saw that Fie was doing the same and also constantly turning his head to look behind.

'Is someone following us?' she asked.

Priest barely glanced at her. 'Some*thing* probably,' he answered her. 'This forest is practically Dark Realm now since the wards of the portals failed.'

Eve knew that some of the portals had collapsed in recent years. Everyone did. The one that had been closest to her town was one of them, which was why so many people had left when the trade route was no longer viable.

'Why did they close?' she asked.

Priest shrugged. 'That doesn't matter now. What's done is done. But it means we need to be extra careful, extra vigilant.'

'What's out there?' she asked.

'Wraiths mostly at the moment, great fire breathing reptiles that look like snakes with massive claws, great big talons, and scales so black, you can't see them in the dark. Just their eyes. Yellow, glowing slits.' He leaned forward, as her eyes were widening. 'Members of the Horde,' he said, 'with great horns coming out of their heads. Some have scales on half their bodies. Some can turn into beasts so terrifying they'd make you sh—'

'Priest,' warned Drax.

He looked back innocently. 'She should know what we may face. She is one of us now, isn't she?' he scoffed.

Eve tilted her head to the side, trying to force the fear that he had elicited away. What would she do if she met any of those creatures? She had no idea. She could fight men. She didn't know how to fight Dark Realm things. Shadows. Monsters. She knew he was trying to make her afraid, but all those things were real, weren't they?

'Is there a particular reason why you don't like me?' she asked Priest quietly.

His eyes found hers and she could see the loathing in them. The force of it made her want to turn away.

He didn't answer her.

THEY DIDN'T STOP TRAVELING all day, but when her stomach started to growl, Priest passed her a bag of dried meat and told her to eat while they moved. She did because she was hungry, and she tried not to look a gift horse in the mouth though none of the others partook. Why were they feeding her more?

That night, a bit before the sun had begun its descent

behind the craggy mountains to the west, Eve belatedly realized that they had changed direction during the course of the day. Where they had been traveling north, they now headed towards the east.

They found a cave for the night, which she was glad of as the weather was much colder now. Drax entered first to ensure it was safe before they lit a fire at the entrance.

Priest plied her with more food and water, and she took it without a word. Once she was finished, he beckoned her to him.

'Sit there on one of those flat stones and close your eyes,' he said.

She looked at him with suspicion. 'Why?'

He let out an impatient breath. 'In order for you to hold up your end of the bargain, you need to do as I say,' he said vaguely. 'Give me your amulet.'

She frowned, but took off the rounded, dark pendant and handed it to him, sitting on the rock and staring up at him. Last night, he'd been ready to throw her from the protection of their circle to the creatures that lay in wait. What did he have planned this time? She practically shook with fear, and she heard Drax growl from the mouth of the cave.

'Would it kill you to put the female at ease?'

Priest let out a weary sigh.

'I'm not going to hurt you, female. This is merely a mind exercise. Close your eyes,' he said again, waiting until she did as he wanted before continuing in a smooth, slow voice that had her calm in moments. 'Imagine that you're walking through a dark tunnel. The walls are black and smooth as glass. With each step, your body begins to glow, brighter and brighter with energy from inside of you. You can feel it growing. In front of you is a closed door with the same light shining through the cracks. In your hand, there's a key golden and heavy. You can feel the weight of it as you walk.

You put the key in the lock, and you turn it. As you open the door, you see that the glowing is drawn towards you and it envelopes you in warmth. You can smell a tang in the air. Magick. The ability to conjure. The runes of power appear on your skin,' he said, 'bright at first and they fade as the power recedes into you. Deep inside.'

The tone of his voice lowered, and she shivered as she felt her pulse quicken.

She opened her eyes immediately, suddenly afraid. 'What are you doing to me?'

His countenance was hard and unforgiving. 'Nothing yet. Did you feel anything?'

'What am I meant to feel?' she asked.

He turned away. 'That's enough for now.'

Eve scowled at his back, sick of his condescending tones. He hadn't told her anything. She realized it was now dark and she stifled a yawn, falling onto the bedroll that had been laid out for her.

She could hear Priest setting stones at the mouth of the cave in order to cast his circle of protection around their camp and sighed. What did they actually want from her? Surely their notion of her being able to open a portal was a jest. She was just a girl on the small side. She had no magick to speak of and she was glad of it. Gods only knew what Talik would have made her do for him if she'd had those sorts of skills.

EVE WOKE, breathing heavily and she thought she must have had a bad dream, but she couldn't remember it. She sat up in the dark, the dying embers of the fire at the front of the cave casting little light.

She felt stifled and hot, needed to be out of this cavern that was little more than a tomb.

She went to the cave entrance and slipped out into the night, taking a long, deep breath in the cold air.

She felt something brush against her face and drew back. She couldn't see anything. It was too dark. She heard something rustling next to her and jumped, going back the way she'd come and trying to find the entrance to the cave, but it wasn't there!

Eve felt for her amulet but remembered Priest taking it from her last night. Panic rose in her as something pushed her hard, banging her into the boulders at her back. She cried out, trying to fight back, her mind replaying what Priest had said to her about the Dark Realm creatures that roamed the forests.

She was pushed to the ground and felt something holding her down. She couldn't move her arms or legs and she screamed as pain began to lance through her.

There was a scuffle to the side. The pain stopped and something shrieked. Then all was silent, and she was left shaking on the ground. She tried to stand up, but her legs wouldn't hold, and she fell back with a cry.

A torch appeared next to her, and she startled before recognizing that it was Fie standing over her.

'Are you all right?' he asked.

She nodded.

'Come.'

He grabbed her by the arm and roughly pulled her to her feet, practically dragging her back into the cave. Inside, Drax and Priest were awake as well, both looking furious beyond words. Eve abruptly felt just as afraid as she had outside and turned to flee, but Fie stood in the way, his arms crossed. His glamor was gone. He looked bigger, more ferocious. They all did.

She turned back to the others, her stance widening in case she needed to fight. Priest exploded first.

'What the fuck were you doing out there without this?'

He threw the amulet at her, and she fumbled for it, putting it around her neck immediately.

'I forgot to put it back on.'

'You can't forget something like that, you stupid female,' Priest growled.

He came forward, his hand was raised, and she flinched away, knowing that he was about to hit her and remembering how much stronger he was than she.

He looked surprised by her reaction, lowering his arm and she saw he was only gesturing in his anger.

'You don't know me well, female,' he snarled, standing in front of her and putting his face close to hers, 'but the only time I will ever strike you is when you know it's coming.'

She took an odd comfort in his words as he turned around and walked back to where Drax stood.

'What were you thinking?' Drax asked. 'You cannot leave the safety of the circle at night without us. You were almost killed just now.'

'She is useless,' Priest muttered, 'A fae *child* could have saved itself.' He spat on the ground. 'If we hadn't bound her, we could kill her now and be on our way. Instead, we are pumping our resources into this *half-blood* who can't even find her magick!'

Eve, tried not to cringe at his awful words, but couldn't quite manage it. She turned away from them both, so they wouldn't see the foolish tears in her eyes. She would not cry, she said to herself, but she remembered promising the same with the Bull so many times and he'd always had her sobbing.

'Shut your mouth,' Drax snapped at Priest.

Then he looked at her, his expression grim and apologetic. 'This cannot go unpunished, Fourth. You put the unit in danger, and you were warned what would happen.'

'Will you give her the lash?' Priest looked pleased. 'That might at least instill some discipline into her.'

Eve looked from one to the other. *Lash?*

Drax shook his head. 'She's lived her life in the rings. The lash will do nothing.'

Priest stepped closer. 'I know what might.'

The gleam in his eye made her swallow hard. What was he going to do? She steeled herself. Whatever it was, she would not plead nor beg them for mercy.

'You will not move,' he ordered her, 'or we'll simply force you not to. Your choice.'

Her body quaked, but there was nothing she could do. There was no escape from whatever penalty he'd decided on.

His eyes didn't move from hers as his hands unbuckled her belt just as Drax had done at the inn. It fell to the cave floor with an echoing clang and Priest's hand slipped into her breeches, settling between her legs. He meant to hurt her. Eve's bottom lip trembled, and she shut her eyes.

'Look at me,' he commanded.

His fingers found the place the Bull would twist and pinch to cause her pain and she tensed, but instead his fingers moved over it gently and her eyes widened as she couldn't help the moan that burst from her.

His fingers rubbed and played, all the while his eyes bore into her intently, watching her reactions to his touch. She hated it because she liked what he was doing and he knew it, which made the humiliation of it practically unbearable.

The other two were staring too, seeing what Priest could do to her. A high-pitched sound came from her, the likes of which she'd never made before. The heel of his hand pressed against her while two of his fingers entered her, easing inside, and making her wince as they stretched her. His fingers began moving expertly, making pleasure crest and ebb inside her, pleasure she hadn't known existed until she'd met these men.

She tried to scramble back, but he hooked them inside her, holding her in place while he punished her.

'Take it, female,' he growled low. 'Let the others watch you come on my fingers. Let them see how easy it was for me to bring you to your release. *Now.*'

She cried out as it happened, making her legs feel like jelly and her hips undulate against his hand, riding it as she whimpered in ecstasy.

When the sensations had run their course, he removed his fingers from her and smirked.

'Thank me,' he said softly, and she forced herself to meet his eyes.

'Thank you,' Eve whispered, her cheeks burning. She wished she could sink into the floor.

'Good girl,' he said softly, licking his fingers.

She gasped at the warmth that coiled within her at those words, so different from the horrible things he usually said to her. She knew the shock was etched in her face as he looked her up and down before turning away and going back to his bedroll, the others doing the same – as if all this were commonplace.

She went to her own bed and lay down, at war with herself. What was happening to her? What were these fae doing to her?

~

Fie

THE FEMALE WAS SUBDUED TODAY, plodding along on her horse in front of him. Her shoulders were slumped, and her gaze had an unfocused look to it. His brow furrowed. Was she becoming ill? Drax and Priest hadn't seemed to notice. They were still angry with her for what had happened last night, but as far as he was concerned, she'd taken her punishment and that was the end of it. That was the Brothers' way, after all. And what a punishment it had been to watch. The way she'd responded to Priest had left him so hard he'd had to take a walk this morning before they broke camp to see to his needs. Even thinking of it now had him shifting on his horse's back. She might be the daughter of their worst enemy, but Fie was starting not to care.

He conceded that perhaps his Brothers were angrier that they hadn't realized that she had left the cave, whereas Fie had.

Things hadn't used to be like this when they were first a unit. They had been content with each having the skills they were best at. Fie was best at infiltrating an enemy, getting people to talk to him ... by any means. Priest could conjure much better than both he and Drax. And Drax, though they were all skilled fighters, was superior in skill as well as the best strategist. But with the infighting, with both Priest and Drax vying for the position of leadership, the unit was suffering. It was making them weak, but neither of his Brothers seemed to be able to see it.

Fie brought his horse up next to the female and caught her eye.

'Your riding is improving,' he said conversationally.

Her cheeks reddened and she avoided his eyes, but he noticed that she brightened at his words, though she tried to hide it. He wondered if he could get her to smile for him.

The forest had given way to windswept plains and soon they would reach the edge where the land met the sea. This part of the realm was a barren wasteland that looked more Dark Realm than Light Realm in his opinion, but the advantage was that they'd be able to see any enemies approaching them for there was nothing at all to conceal them. They could all let their guards down for a few moments at least.

Fie decided to take this time to educate her further on riding. After all, in another life, *these* had been the skills he'd been known for.

He slid both his legs to one side of the horse, sitting on its back as he would a chair and saw that her attention was already riveted on him. He gave her a wink and grinned at her surprise. She had not seen this playful side of him, and he could see that she didn't know what to make of his antics.

Jumping onto the horse's back with his feet, he balanced, taking the reins, and urging his mount into a gallop. At speed, he flipped his body so that he was on his hands, landing gracefully on the road behind the horse. He whistled for the great beast to turn back, and he grabbed the reins again as the horse galloped by, throwing himself back onto his back, and slowing him.

Before he got to his Brothers and the female, he grinned at her again and found she was smiling wide, entertained. Even his Brothers were shaking their heads in amusement.

'Gods,' Priest said. 'Don't teach her any of that. The poor female will break her neck.'

Fie gave Priest a half-smile. He couldn't remember the last time Priest had had a light-hearted word to say, but it had been a long time ago, probably before they'd been stuck in Kitore.

Now, Priest commanded the female's attention, telling her to close her eyes, and murmuring to her about mind journeys. Priest was trying hard to help her find her power, but Fie wondered if the female was too small and weak to have any real fae magick within her. All they had to go on were Drax's vague visions, dreams that came to him in the deepest, darkest nights, feelings in his gut.

Fie hadn't seen one iota of magick in this female. In truth, if it wasn't for her scent, he'd have wondered if she was part fae at all for she displayed almost none of the characteristics. She was not tall, nor lithe. She was painfully thin, though, granted, she was already filling out. But her eyes were not violet either though she had no glamor upon her. Her ears were slightly pointed he supposed, but he'd seen other such traits in humans before. Her strength was the only tell-tale sign. That, he conceded, was fae.

They didn't stop during the day, but again they plied the female with meat. Fie noticed that she was making an effort not to tear at it like an animal, nibbling on it slowly. Had her appetite finally abated or had Priest's constant set-downs finally struck home?

He wondered again if Drax would have Priest break the bond they had with her as soon as she was able to get them into the Underhill, or if he'd wait. Fie knew that as soon as they didn't need her, Priest would kill her and probably send her head to a father who might not even know she existed.

But Drax … Fie wasn't sure. Drax was protective of the female, and he hadn't seen his Brother act in that way before except perhaps with Fie himself when he first joined their unit. He'd tried to protect her from Priest as well.

Fie had truly thought his Brothers would fight for leadership that night in the clearing and he didn't like that he'd taken Priest's side so blatantly against Drax. That wasn't right. Drax was in command. There were laws that must be kept to in the Dark Army. You didn't turn on your Brothers, you didn't rebel against your commander.

THEY TRAVELLED INTO THE AFTERNOON, the terrain around them becoming more and more marked by the portal that was out here. Fie was surprised that they hadn't seen more creatures that shouldn't be in this realm. He'd assumed the land would be overrun with them up here. But perhaps they'd moved on to greener pastures for they'd not seen any animals, nor another human in some days.

The female stayed closer to them now. She had noticed the change. The sun was just a little bit dimmer here, the colors muted. The trees were starting to die as well.

'It shouldn't look like this,' Drax muttered.

Priest nodded. 'Too much magick,' he said.

'A conjurer?' Fie asked, but Priest shook his head.

'Doubtful. More likely this realm is out of balance with the others now. The power from the destroyed portals has to have somewhere to go. I suspect the other bridges will start to open more frequently, be larger, throw out more magick, be more dangerous to cross.'

'Aye,' Drax murmured, keeping his eyes moving to ensure they weren't ambushed.

Priest didn't say anything more as they journeyed along the path, treacherous in places as they moved up the mountain.

When they were about halfway, they took a path that meandered into the rocks and they all drew their swords just in case anyone or *thing* was waiting, but nothing came for them as they made their way to the base of a sheer cliff.

The female looked around them as they stopped. 'What now?' she asked.

Priest sat back on his horse. 'We wait.' He looked around. 'I don't think it will take long.'

Priest was right. Fie barely had time to double check that his amulet was around his neck before the air began to feel charged. He heard the first crackles of lightning and they huddled together, closer to Eve, who was looking around like a trapped doe.

'Nothing to worry about,' he said with a grin. 'This is the fastest way to the Ice Plains. If not for this portal, we'd have the wait until the thaw to take a ship. It would cost us weeks. Just follow us, and you'll be all right.'

The female didn't look soothed by Fie's words, but there was no more time as the hole opened in front of them with a thunderous sound, their amulets saving them from the stray bursts of energy that fizzled out into the air around them.

Drax look back at them. 'Come on,' he shouted, struggling to be heard over the roaring.

The female's horse began to dance around, and Priest took its reins tightly, ensuring that it would follow them and not bolt with Eve on its back.

Where only moments ago had been solid rock, there was now a tunnel stretching in front of them, dark in places, yet blindingly, beautifully light in others. The female was breathing hard, rapidly glancing around, and clutching at her horse's mane.

They moved forward as a group into the portal, the ground disappearing as they entered the breach.

Fie didn't know what happened, but the female was suddenly off her horse's back, and, inside of the portal next to them, there was another bridge opening.

Priest yelled at her to come back, throwing himself from his own horse and colliding with her. Fie reached out, grasping for Priest but both he and Eve were already gone. The second portal disappeared.

'We have to go back!' Fie yelled.

Drax shook his head. 'We can't stop in the middle of the tunnel. Keep going.'

He and Drax emerged on the other side to a bright, white snowscape and the bridge closed behind them.

Drax swung around, noting the bare backs of the horses. 'What happened?'

Fie stared in disbelief at where the portal had been.

'There was another breach inside the tunnel. They were both sucked through. They're gone.'

Drax swore, pulling up the hood of his fur cloak, and drawing it closely around them as the wind whipped, blowing snow into their faces.

'What are we going to do?' Fie asked.

Drax rubbed his face. 'Keep their horses fed and watered, pray to the gods that Priest didn't get separated from the female, and that he can get them to the Underhill by the time we get there.'

'But where—?'

'There's no way of knowing,' Drax interrupted. 'They could be in any realm, but if anyone can get them back, it's Priest. Come. Let's keep moving before we start to freeze.'

CHAPTER 7

PRIEST

*P*riest threw himself towards the female, realizing what the foolish girl had done a split second too late to stop her and wondering if they were going to survive to tell the tale of this catastrophe.

He felt the portal she had opened inside the other pull him in as his arms wrapped around her and they fell out of the air just far enough off the ground for Priest to groan as he hit the hard surface of the rock, cushioning the female's fall. At least he knew, firstly, that she was now strong enough to access her magick and, secondly, how it was triggered.

Sheer terror.

She got up, scrambling away from him, her head darting this way and that like a cornered mouse. Priest looked around, getting his bearings, and ensuring he had his weapons. He did, thank the gods, but little else besides the amulet around his neck. He could see that she had hers as well. Well, that was something at least.

'You foolish bitch,' he ground out.

Her eyes narrowed in anger.

'Me?' she exploded. 'You didn't even tell me what we were doing until it was happening.'

'You didn't need to know,' he said.

'Clearly I did,' she blustered.

He stepped towards her, and she did the same, standing in front of him and tilting her head up to glare into his face.

'You are the most bothersome female,' he muttered.

'Where are we?' she asked, ignoring him.

'In a dark realm,' he said. 'Look around you.'

He followed his own advice again, taking in the barren ground, the black rocks littering the landscape, the twin suns that were setting slowly in the sky, and the scraggly bushes that gave them next to no cover should they be attacked.

'Which one remains to be seen,' he muttered, but he had a feeling he'd been here before.

'Do you know all the Dark Realms,' she asked, a timidness in her voice making him remember that she'd never been outside her own realm and that making her afraid at the moment might have unpredictable consequences.

'There are too many to know them all,' he said. 'Come on. I think I know where we are and if I'm right, we're very, very lucky.'

He grabbed her by the arm, keeping her close and moving her with him as he walked briskly down the slight slope towards the valley in the distance.

He glanced at her. 'Well, at least we know Drax was correct. You have magick.'

'But–but,' she stuttered. 'How do you—'

'*You* opened that portal inside the other one.' He made a sound of disgust. 'Even the barest novice knows not to try something like that.'

'I didn't do it on purpose! Perhaps if you had told me what was happening,' she stated again, and he snorted.

'As if it would have made any difference in your tiny, human mind,' he taunted.

She made a sound deep in her throat at his latest insult and Priest felt her slam into him from behind. She tackled him to the ground, and he realized that she had indeed become much stronger since they'd been taking care of her. But she was still no match for him. Her fighting style, if it could even be called that, was rough where his movements were calculated, elegant, and sophisticated.

In a swift move, he used her strength against her, throwing her off him and onto the ground some paces away. She lay on her back, winded as he stood over her. He grasped her by the throat and was gratified to see her eyes widen just a fraction. He couldn't feel her as Drax could, but she was afraid. He had to ensure she didn't get *too* scared though, or else there'd be another portal to gods only knew where.

He tutted. 'Silly female. If you begin a fight,' he hauled her to her feet, 'you must be sure that you can win.'

He pushed her backwards hard enough that she fell on her arse, and he stood over her again. She looked at him with ill-concealed hatred and he grinned at her humiliation.

He squatted down in front of her and smiled darkly. 'You will never win against me, female. I'll admit your strength is, perhaps, now equal to mine and the others, but you do not have the skill.'

He watched her expression tighten and then she surprised him by looking away. Was she yielding to him, he wondered, lowering his guard? He stood, his mind still thinking on that. What would it be like for this female to submit to him as a full-blooded fae female? He couldn't help but think of the previous night when she'd writhed on his fingers for his Brothers to see.

His mind agreeably engaged with those imaginings, he

didn't see it coming as she jumped to her feet and flew at him again.

He found himself on *his* back and looking up at the pinkening sky. His eyes widened as he saw something coming towards them, its wings spanning three men.

He turned them both, rolling them out of the way as talons as thick as saplings struck the dark earth, sending shards of rock through the air around them.

He pulled Eve to her feet.

'Run!' he ordered, pulling her with him towards the boulders a short distance away. If they made it, they could lose the beast amongst the stones with help from their amulets.

The female was slowing him down so, he turned back, picking her up and throwing her over his shoulder. He sprinted as fast as he could, hearing its wings in the air behind them getting closer and closer. He'd never outrun it.

Priest stopped in his tracks, crouching down so that it overshot them, grabbing into the earth just in front of them. He stood, running again, and having successfully secured them precious moments as the creature had to fly up into the sky again to regain its momentum.

He reached the first boulders and put the female down. Holding both their amulets in his hands, he said a word in the old tongue. Then he took her shoulders and kept her in front of him, sitting on the ground.

'Don't move,' he breathed. 'Don't speak.'

She nodded, shaking, and Priest was overcome with an urge to tuck her beneath his arm and keep her safe.

But he ignored it, stretching the muscles of his back instead. It felt as if the skin had been gouged and was already knitting back together. The great beast must have caught him, but he'd heal so quickly it wouldn't be a problem. The female, though, had an injury on her arm somewhere. Blood was dripping down her fingers.

He put his hand on her arm, saying the words of an incantation, so that the beast could not smell her and, again, he lamented the fact that this female was half human. So vulnerable. But then, if magick truly was coming to her, he could teach her, he thought.

Why was he continually thinking about her in these future terms? She was temporary, he reminded himself, and, once they were finished with her, he was going to kill her. Wasn't he?

She huddled by the rock, quivering underneath the outcropping where the creature could not see them. She looked as if she might retch. Her gaze was unfocused, and he whispered to get her attention.

'Keep your mind from wandering,' he said. 'Do not let this realm play tricks on you.' He tapped the side of her head and she nodded.

They could still hear the creature above them, its wings flapping in the air, searching, but he had made them invisible. Now, they simply had to wait for it to give up, which he hoped wouldn't take too long.

'Did I really bring us here?' she whispered, and he wasn't sure if she was talking to him, but he answered anyway.

'Yes,' he said just as low. 'At the beginning, the magick will manifest at odd times. For you, it's clearly when you are afraid. You must work to keep your emotions in check. Does your arm hurt?'

She shook her head.

He couldn't see the blood now because of the conjure he had wrought, but he knew the wound beneath her clothing continued to flow.

'Take off your tunic,' he told her, 'but stay under the rocks.'

She did as he said, unbuttoning her clothes and hissing as

she took off her leather jerkin. As he'd suspected, the wound on her arm was deep and bloody, but it was not life threatening. He pulled a long, thornlike shard of rock from it and tossed it away.

'Use a piece of your chemise,' he said, remembering how stupidly long it was.

She pulled it from her breeches and ripped a large piece from it without hesitation. He tore it in two and used one to wipe the wound, tying the other strip tightly around it to stem the blood.

'We'll tend it properly later,' he said, 'when we have some supplies.'

She nodded. 'Thank you,' she said quietly.

'We can't chance building a fire,' he muttered, noticing her teeth chattering.

'I'm not cold.'

He frowned. She was much more frightened than she was letting on. He put a hand lightly on her shoulder, telling himself he wanted to calm her, so they didn't go missing in a dark realm if she lost control of herself again.

'There's nothing to fear while I'm with you. I've been to the Dark Realms a thousand times. We are safe now and we aren't stuck here. Our amulets are tied to the portal magick. They will lead us to the closest bridge, and we will yet arrive at the Underhill without much delay.'

'What else can your amulets do?' she asked.

'Protect us from some Dark Realm creatures. They got us past the wards and into the capital too,' he said. 'Couldn't get us back out when we got stuck though.'

'Why?'

'Gods only know. Kitore's magicks are ancient and jumbled. Even I don't have the skills to unpick that mess.'

'I'm sorry I put us in danger. *Again*,' she whispered, changing the subject.

He was surprised at her words. 'It wasn't your fault,' he said and could see *he* had surprised *her* as well.

He peeked out from the rocks where they hid instead of speaking further on the subject, not sure what to say.

'I think it's gone,' he breathed. 'Come on. We need to get through these rocks and, hopefully, the portal won't be too far away.'

~

Eve

EVE FOLLOWED PRIEST. Her arm wasn't hurting, but that hardly meant anything. Her mind was adrift. Could she really have opened a portal? Did she really have magick?

She glanced up at his retreating form in front of her.

'Am I fae?' she whispered, giving voice to the question that had been brewing in her mind since the day she met these men. She said it so quietly that he couldn't possibly hear ... and yet he did.

He looked back, his eyes assessing. 'Half.'

She gaped at his cavalier reply, tears coming unbidden to her eyes. 'I don't understand.'

How could this be possible? She was an orphan, a street child. She ran to catch up with him.

'If the nuances of how children are made escapes you, female, I'm afraid I cannot be the one to enlighten.'

Her tears dried as she gave him a look. 'Stop playing games. You know what I mean.'

Priest grunted his ascent. 'The fae aren't meant to take humans as slaves,' he began, 'but, like everywhere, those with power and wealth can do what they like without any real repercussions. In truth, your mother was probably a slave taken from your realm, sold to one of the lords.'

He glanced at her as if ensuring she was still listening to him. 'Halflings used to be rare. The human females taken weren't allowed to become pregnant, but that has changed in recent years.' He shrugged. 'In truth, I've no idea how you ended up in that town. There was once a portal nearby. Perhaps you were brought through it and left to die.'

He was silent then and Eve didn't ask him anything more.

Her mind was reeling. She'd always assumed that her mother had simply not wanted her. Perhaps if things had been different ... she would have had a family, people who'd loved her. Her eyes prickled again, and she turned her face into the wind. That hadn't happened and it was useless to dwell on it now.

'Who are you looking for in the Underhill?'

She hadn't really spoken much to Priest in general, so she didn't really expect him to answer. She was surprised when he did.

'I had kin there, h*ave* kin there,' he said, his jaw tightening.

'Your mother or father?' she asked.

'No. My mother and father are ... they live their own privileged lives in the fae courts. We rarely speak since I joined the Dark Army. They didn't approve.' He was quiet for a moment. 'My younger sister is there. She'll be old enough to leave the Underhill by the summer.'

Eve nodded and they lapsed again into silence as they trudged down the slope into the valley before them. Small shrubs and leggy plants were growing in patches, more of them as they descended.

'You spent all your life in that town?' Priest asked.

She nodded, surprised that he was keeping the conversation going.

'I grew up on the streets with the other orphaned children. I was stronger than them, but I tried to keep it hidden. I aligned myself with the strongest gang when I was old enough.'

'You have to join, or you die,' she explained at his questioning look. 'But, in truth, their leader had always looked out for me, so it was an easy decision. They decided I was pretty enough to make money for them on my back, but then there was an accident, a foolish thing and I ended up saving someone's life. Talik saw my strength and decided I'd earn my keep another way. I was grateful he didn't kill me for being Dark Realm.'

'How old were you when you began to fight for them?' he asked, not looking at her.

'I was taken to the rings when I was about twelve or thirteen.'

Priest's tone was neutral. 'Did you always win for them?'

She snorted. 'I could have, but I won when I was told to win, and I lost when I was told to lose.'

'Ah,' he said with a nod. 'No doubt you made your gang much coin in the rigged fights.'

She nodded her assent. 'Probably.'

They were getting dangerously close to things she didn't want to discuss as they made their way across the landscape, and she hoped his line of questioning was at an end. She decided to change the subject to ensure that it was.

'Why doesn't it get dark here?' she asked, looking up at the two suns that were low in the sky. They hadn't moved since they'd been here.

'The days and the nights can vary in different realms,' he stated. 'The day here might last several of the ones you're used to in the light realm. The nights as well.'

'How many Dark Realms have you been to?' she asked him.

He shrugged. 'Many. The fae aren't so afraid of them as the humans are and we can navigate them better. We have magick for it. The fae can still die, but it's more likely that we'll survive a Dark Realm than a human will.' He chuckled. 'Less likely we will shit ourselves when we see a Dark Realm beast.'

'Come,' he said. 'My amulet is warm to the touch. That means we're close.'

'Would it not be faster if I tried ...' she trailed off.

'To open another portal yourself?'

She nodded; a bit embarrassed that she hadn't thought of doing so before. They could be back in the Light Realm by now.

'No,' he said simply. 'You're a novice. Gods only know where we'd end up. If we are where I think we are, the nearest bridge will take us to a main trade route anyway. That's typically how these things work.'

He turned towards her seriously. 'You must do as you are told, female. Humans are coveted in this place. If I tell you to put your hood up, you put your fucking hood up. Understand?'

She nodded.

'Do you understand? Say it aloud.'

'Yes.'

'Good girl,' he said, and though she wanted to bristle at his condescension, she found that those words did something else to her entirely just as they had last night when he'd touched her.

Surely, she could not want this patronizing fae male as well. It had to be this realm playing tricks on her mind as Priest had warned her it might.

The object of her thoughts stopped in front of her, making her bang into him.

'There,' he said, pointing at the air a few paces away.

'I see nothing.'

'Hold your amulet,' he said.

Eve put it in her hand and gasped as it appeared in her vision; a hole with a bright circle around it like the sun looked during an eclipse in the Light Realm.

'Is it open?' she breathed.

'Aye, this one's always open. That's why it's not hurling lightning at us like the other one did. Its power is a trickling constant.' He looked back at her, grasping her arm. 'Keep hold of me, female, and do not fear. It's no different than walking down a path.'

She went with Priest, gripping onto him as they walked to the tunnel before them. She was still afraid of him, but she feared all these unknowns more. She clenched her eyes shut when they stepped through, but she felt nothing but a slight charge in the air, a rush of warmth like a breeze rustling in the trees.

She finally worked up the courage to open her eyes and found herself in the middle of a bustling town. A market. There were no humans at all as far as she could see. There were groups of men, but they weren't Light Realm *men*. Some had horns tipped in shining metal. Others were covered in black scales. There were females too, many tall and strong. Some were dressed in battle armor with weapons hanging from their sides or slung over their shoulders, but most had on long gowns that looked similar to what the women wore where she was from.

There was a great beast tethered by what appeared to be a tavern; it was a working animal of burden like a horse or a pony, except that it was five times the size, with great big teeth and eyes that followed everything that moved around it.

She was hustled forward by Priest.

'Stay calm,' he warned, and she nodded, practically grasping at his cloak, so afraid was she that she might get lost in this place.

'Don't speak to anyone, even if they speak to you,' he advised quietly, and Eve nodded again.

She knew when to keep her mouth shut.

'Stay behind me,' he said. 'Close by, but still within arm's reach.'

Falling behind, she trailed after him as they walked around the market full of trinkets she'd never seen before, food she'd never eaten, cloth that shimmered in the light, artifacts that glowed with magick ... and a slavers block where humans sat in cages. Some looked bored, some afraid.

'Hood up.'

She did as Priest commanded immediately so that the only her face showed.

'If only you weren't so short,' he muttered as they walked by the raised platform, and Eve's eyes were drawn to a woman. She was visibly shaking.

'Probably snatched from the Light Realm only a day or so ago,' Priest said as he saw the direction of her gaze. 'There's nothing I can do even if I wanted to, which I don't. Stop looking at her.'

He gestured to the crowd that was gathering. 'Any and all these folk would strike us both down before we'd got five steps. This is the grim reality of all the realms. Humans are chattel to be bought and sold ... even within your own world. Though since the wards were destroyed, they're being brought here by the dozens to be sold.'

'Does no one notice the disappearances in the Light Realm?' she asked.

'Even if they did, what would they do about it?' Priest shrugged. 'Most aren't noticed anyway. They go missing in the towns or from peasant houses. No one gives a fuck about them.'

What he said was true, she thought. How many people had she seen killed in the streets while soldiers looked on?

How many more had simply gone missing, and no one cared enough to even try to find them?

Priest gestured to a female and a man who were locked together by chains on their ankles. 'Those ones are sold as a breeding pair.'

Eve's eyes widened. She looked at him and he nodded. 'But what if they don't want to …'

The look on Priest's face was enough to stay her words, then he actually chuckled. 'The male will be willing enough; they won't have let him rut for weeks.'

Eve saw that Priest was right. The man was staring at the woman by his side, hands twitching, clearly just waiting for the order to get her with child. Her lips turned up in disgust. She hadn't thought the Light and Dark Realms would be so similar.

'And them?' she asked, looking at another cage full of men and women who did not look afraid at all.

'Those ones have been here a while,' he said. 'Note the scars of the lash, the rags they wear, their hardened expressions. It's not their first times here on one of the blocks.' He pointed at the last cage full of massive men, all of whom looked angry. 'They are for the Horde.'

'The Horde?'

'The Dark Realm army. They move even now, fighting wars on multiple fronts. They always need fodder for the frontlines. Once those fine specimens are sold, their minds will be altered so they'll do as they're instructed. They'll fight until the death and then others will take their places.'

'Is it only humans who are sold?'

Priest shook his head. 'Here, yes, but anyone can be bought for a price. Stay close to me and don't let anyone see what you are. I don't need any trouble when I don't have anyone else to call upon for help.'

They kept walking until they reached a large square with an empty ring standing on its side in the middle.

'Is that the portal?' Eve asked him.

'Aye.' He swore. 'But it's just closed. Might not be active again for days.'

'Days?' Eve regarded it dubiously. 'How do we know it will take us to where we want to go when it does open again?'

He gave a long sigh. 'Some of them have an intuitive way about them. Come. No more questions now. Let's get out of the street. Trouble is inevitably going to find us as the night draws in.'

She did as he said, keeping her head down and following him around the town that was actually quite similar to her own, except for the odd creatures.

Priest found a small, disreputable-looking establishment down a small alleyway. She was surprised. From what she knew of him, he preferred inns that were much nicer than this.

He opened the door, hustling her over the threshold and she was met with a grand entrance hall that looked larger than the entire building had from the street. She gaped and Priest gave her a knowing grin.

'As if I'd stay in a hovel,' he said.

He put some coins on the table by the door, took a key from a hook, and started up a shining stone staircase with carpeted steps.

He beckoned her. 'Don't dawdle, female.'

She trailed after him like a lost pup and, at the top of the stairs, there was just one door.

He opened it with the key and went inside.

She was met with plain, stone walls, a floor covered in thick rugs and a warm fire. There was food already on the table, and a steaming bath waiting.

Priest immediately began to take off his clothes and she turned away, cheeks heating. She heard him step into the water and give an audible groan as he lay back.

Eve took off her cloak and tunic, sitting down in one of the chairs heavily. Her arm was throbbing, and her stomach was hurting low down. She felt tired as well and hoped she wasn't getting some Dark Realm malady.

She ate some bread and meat from the table because she was still feeling hungry despite her pains and fatigue, but as soon as she was finished, she longed to climb into the bed and sleep.

She realized Priest was watching her and she hoped their odd truce wasn't already at an end. She couldn't endure any more of his barbed comments today.

She tried to ignore his eyes on her, untying the cloth that was over her arm to have a look. Her arm was covered in dried blood and beneath the bandage, the gash was only just beginning to knit together. She'd noticed the holes in Priest's cloak that was draped over the chair, but he'd clearly already healed from whatever damage the beast's talons had inflicted. It must be good to be fae she thought. Then she frowned. *Full-fae*, she corrected.

Could it really be true? Was she really half fae?

'Do you know who my father might be?' she asked, wondering if she had kin somewhere.

He watched her impassively. 'No,' he said finally. 'There are many fae lords.'

She nodded, pretending not to care, but inwardly she was disappointed.

Priest began to wash himself with the soap and her gaze was fixed on him. She knew she shouldn't watch, but she couldn't seem to help herself. She swallowed hard. His glamor was gone and had been since they'd arrived in this realm. His muscles rippled with his movements, defined and alluring. His eyes met hers in amusement.

'Do you like what you see, female?'

She turned away quickly before he could see her blush, dying of mortification that he'd caught her ogling him.

She lay on the bed, turning away from him and closing her eyes.

A DROP of water fell on her, and she turned to find Priest standing over her, a drying cloth wrapped around his waist.

'You should clean that wound on your arm before it closes on the outside,' he said, turning away and gathering his clothes.

Eve sprang from the bed in her nervousness and, taking advantage of Priest's turned back, she practically ripped her clothes from her. She darted to the bath, clamoring into it, and sitting down hard, making the water slosh onto the floor.

It was miraculously still hot, and completely clean though Priest had already washed himself in it. This place was full of magick.

After scrubbing the dirt from herself, she leant back, resting her head on the side, and dozing.

'Don't fall asleep in the water, female. Don't want you drowning,' came Priest's sardonic voice, cutting through her relaxation and she rolled her eyes at him though she noticed he was dressed in only his breeches now and quickly looked away from the sight of his toned, muscled torso.

'If I was foolish enough to drown in my own bath,' she said, 'I deserve to die.'

But she did get out, waiting until he was turned away again. The water ran down her body as she wrung out her hair. She looked over her shoulder and caught sight of Priest staring. Though she wanted to cover herself, she resisted and instead smirked at him.

'Like what you see, male?' She echoed his earlier question to her and almost laughed when his cheeks tinged pink.

She grabbed a larger drying sheet that was folded on a small table by the bath and wrapped herself in it, finding that she couldn't look at him again, her bravado having vanished. She wanted to sleep, but it was not to be.

'Sit down,' Priest ordered her.

She winced as he probed the wound.

'Infection's setting it,' he murmured. 'Must have been the talons.'

'But you're all right,' she pointed out.

'I'm a full-blood. Clearly this realm is no place for a halfling.'

She closed her eyes and ignored his words, not giving into his baiting. She heard him cross the room and open a cupboard. Inside were clean bandages and black vials. He brought one to her and held it out.

'Drink this,' he said, and she eyed it dubiously.

'It will allow you to heal faster.'

She sighed and downed the brackish liquid in one, making a face. He then rubbed something that stung into her wound and wrapped it.

She tried to stand, but he pushed her back down. She frowned.

'I'm tired,' she said.

'And you can sleep, female, when we're finished.'

The tone of his voice made her pause, looking up as he stood over her.

'Tell me,' he said, leaning closer. 'Did you pleasure yourself the other night at the inn while Drax lay in the other bed asleep?'

She gawked at him. 'No!'

'It's nothing to be ashamed of, female,' he said, looking quite entertained by her reaction.

'B–but I didn't! Drax ...'

She went quiet and his eyes danced as they surveyed her.

'Drax what? What did he do, Eve?' Priest murmured, his large hands settling on her shoulders, kneading them gently and making her close her eyes with how wonderful his touch felt on her sore body.

'I smelled you in the air,' he went on. 'As soon as I entered, I knew you'd come in that room not long before. So, what did Drax do to elicit such pleasure from our Fourth?' His fingers trailed lower, pulling on the blanket she wore so it fell to her waist.

She instinctively tried to cover herself, but he tutted, drawing her to her feet and pulling the blanket away completely.

'No, don't hide from me, female. I want to see you and I always get what I want. Now, answer my question. Did he do what I did to you? Use his fingers on you?'

She shook her head, unable to say the words aloud.

'Something else?'

'Um ...'

He chuckled low. 'Something else then. What? A candlestick?'

Her eyes flew open in scandalized shock. 'A candlestick!?'

Priest guffawed. 'Not a candlestick then.' Then he smiled salaciously and licked his bottom lip slowly. 'Did he fuck you with his tongue, Fourth?'

Her expression gave him his answer and he shook his head. 'Not very imaginative, but I'll wager you taste sweet.'

Her eyes widened as she looked up at him in bafflement. But Priest hated her ... didn't he?

He seemed oblivious to that fact now as he stood in front

of her, and his eyes flicked down over her figure that was nowhere near as gaunt as it had been only days ago.

She looked up at him. 'But—'

He silenced her with his lips on hers, gentle but demanding. He drew back for a moment, his eyes questioning, but he said nothing aloud, descending on her again and groaning when her lips parted, and he finally gained access to her mouth. His tongue touched hers and she drew back, startled, but he chased her lips, kissing her again and not letting her get away.

She felt his hands on her, her skin tingling pleasurably wherever he touched her. He caressed up her arms to her shoulders and down her back, suddenly clutching the bare globes of her arse and pulling her to him as he sat back in the chair behind him. She gasped as he had her straddle one of his legs, the pressure on her core making her clench her thighs as much as she could around his. She ground her hips against him; couldn't help it.

He chuckled, murmured something about her making his breeches wet.

She felt odd, her mind not able to focus. Before she knew quite what had happened, they were lying on the bed together, his legs intertwined with hers.

His breeches were gone, and they were both completely bare. He held her in his strong arms, kissing her shoulder and then her breast. He sucked on one of her nipples, his sharp teeth scraping her skin and she moaned.

He moved over her in a swift motion as if he'd gotten bored, wrapping her legs around him as he thrust into her. Eve gave a high-pitched cry at his sudden invasion.

'Drax was right, you are tight,' he grunted.

She whimpered as he set a punishing pace, rutting her hard, holding her legs around him so she couldn't get away, not that she'd want to. She loved the feel of him inside her, his hands touching her. He brought her to release quickly, but not himself, continuing to plunge into her over and over again until she couldn't take anymore and screamed his name at the top of her lungs as her body tightened around him. Only then did he give a final, hard thrust, spilling deep inside her with a low growl through gritted teeth.

He lay next to her panting. 'Well, that was easier than expected,' he muttered.

She looked over at him and her stomach turned leaden as she saw his cruel expression.

His friendliness had disappeared and what they'd just done was like a haze in her memory. It had been a ruse.

'What did you do?' she asked.

His expression turned rueful. 'You're too trusting,' he said.

Her eyes flew to the cupboard. 'The potion you gave me,' she said faintly. 'But why?'

'I need to know a few things and Fie wasn't getting anywhere with you.' He shrugged. 'I'm not the leader of the unit at the moment so, unlike Drax, I couldn't compel you until we were bonded properly. It was this or torture. Surely bedding me was preferable.' He let out a small sigh as if this were an inconvenience for him. 'Would that you were fully human. It would have worked on you without the power of the bond and none of this would have been necessary.'

She covered her nakedness as best she could.

'I hate you,' she said, looking away.

'It's for the best, my sweet.'

His voice took on that same eerie quality that she'd heard Drax use the first time in the Camp. 'Tell me what you fear, female. What are the horrors that keep you up at night? The memories that make you quiver?'

She didn't want to tell him, but she couldn't help it. How could she have been so foolish as to trust him even for a moment?

'The Bull,' she said, a fat tear rolling down her cheek.

He watched it fall and his face softened for a moment. She saw remorse, but it was gone as soon as she knew it.

'Who is the Bull?' he asked, his voice cold.

'Another fighter. Talik's enforcer.'

'Why do you fear him so? Did you lose your little fights to him?'

'When I was told to.'

'Ah, of course. Did he humiliate you badly in the ring? Make it look good for the crowd?'

'Yes,' she said, closing her mouth to try and stop the words.

He chuckled. 'If you try to fight it, you'll just hurt yourself. What did he do? What's made you so scared of him?'

'He would strip me, touch me in front of the crowd. Tell them what he was going to do to me later.' The words burst out of her, and she hung her head, trying to stop the tears. 'I had to take it, or Jays wouldn't bring me food … for days.'

'What else?' Priest's voice was sharp.

'Whenever I lost to him, he would come for his payment the same night.'

'And the payment?'

'Me.'

'Go on.'

'I would be shackled. Jays would let him in and leave him with me. He'd laugh at me, grab the chain, and pull me to him. Sometimes he did it quickly, other nights he would take his time. He liked to hurt me. He knew I'd heal before my next fight anyway so Talik wouldn't care what he did so long as I wasn't dead.'

Priest's voice was tight with the next question. 'What did he do, Eve?'

'Everything. Broke my bones, crushed them sometimes.

Burned me, cut me. He liked to make me cry, liked to see how long it would take before I begged him to stop.'

'And did he take your body as well?'

'Always.'

Priest didn't ask her anything for a long time. She closed her eyes next to him.

'One more thing and then I promise you I'll let you sleep.'

She nodded, not bothering to open her eyes.

'Tell me about the first time you were bedded.'

Eve didn't even try to fight the compulsion to tell him. He already knew the things she'd been too ashamed of anyone knowing.

'I'd just lost my first fight to the Bull as Talik had told me to. He came to my room. I didn't know why he was there until he wound my tether around my neck. He choked me while he did it.'

'When I woke, it was the next morning. I was bloodied and hurt and … he told me all the things he did to me while I'd been unconscious the next time he had me.'

He was silent again and she thought perhaps she should open her eyes but didn't want to face him.

'Sleep, Eve,' he said very softly, 'You won't remember any of this when you wake. I promise.'

EVE HAD BEEN asleep for several Light Realm days while she healed, Priest told her after he shook her awake gently and thrust a plate of food in her hands. The portal was open once more. It was time to leave the Dark Realm.

Something niggled at her as she ate the food he'd given her. There was something she felt as if she should remember, but every time she got close to it, it would move further away from her.

They left the inn with what little they'd brought with

them, and Eve found it was full-dark when they emerged out onto the street.

'How long does the night here last?' she asked

'Many days go by in the Light Realm while all who call this realm their home live in darkness,' he answered absently, keeping an eye on those around them.

They went through the market again, finding it bustling with the same sorts of odd creatures. But whereas during the day there had been a calmness to the place, in the night it was much different. Females stood outside doorways, dressed in silks and gauzes, transparent clothes showed their bodies to passers-by. Some looked human. Most were not.

Eve looked away. Though she had seen such females before, she'd never been so close. She stayed next to Priest, keeping her hood well up.

But as they walked down the street, a scuffle broke out next to her between two of the horned warriors who seemed to frequent the town and someone jostled her, knocking her to the ground. She went sprawling with a cry, her hood coming down to show him and his friend what she was.

'A human girl.'

The horned beast stood over her, dressed in black mail and leather. Various weapons hung from his belt, but the way he looked her up and down made her blood run cold.

Priest was suddenly in between them.

'Mine,' he growled.

The warrior sneered at Priest. 'She's only yours if you can keep her, elf.'

It appeared that 'elf' was a grievous insult because Priest's countenance turned more menacing than even she'd ever seen it. He moved with such speed that Eve wasn't sure exactly what he'd done, but the warrior was suddenly on the ground, clutching his abdomen.

Priest laughed, grabbing her by the wrist and pulling her

with him. They ran down the streets towards the main square.

As Priest had said, the portal was open, and no one even looked their way as they went across the bridge – though Eve once again screwed her eyes shut and gripped onto Priest.

A moment later they were standing on a sunny hillside. It was late morning and Eve was sure she'd never been so happy to be anywhere in her life before.

Unless...

'We *are* back in the Light Realm, aren't we?' she asked Priest, looking around her. Everything *appeared* as it ought, but what if there were Dark Realms that looked like the Light Realm? How would they know...

'Aye, calm yourself,' Priest said, 'but we're not in the Ice Plains yet. Come. We have a journey ahead of us.'

Eve went with him, and they traveled the rest of the day on foot. By the time the sun was setting and they stopped to make camp, they were exhausted.

'Start a fire,' Priest ordered.

He was gone before she could tell him she had no idea how to do such a thing without a hot coal to start with. She couldn't make fire out of nothing.

She sat in the middle of the clearing he'd chosen for a time, wondering if she should get some rocks together to make a circle as he had done before. She gathered what she could find, making a smaller boundary around where they would sleep tonight.

Priest returned not long after, a rabbit hanging from a snare.

'Got lucky,' he said. Then he scowled. 'Why haven't you built a fire, woman?'

She looked away and he came to stand over her, clearly fuming.

'Are you a fool? Is your mind addled?'

She shook her head, embarrassed to tell him that she had no idea how to do such a simple thing.

He took a step back suddenly, shaking his head and did it himself, starting a blaze in no time at all, giving her odd looks as he did so.

'Can you skin the rabbit?' he asked.

Again, she shook her head.

He sighed.

Eve stood up, finally deciding she'd had enough.

'I am not foolish,' she snarled. 'I am not addled either. Am I not meant to be your Fourth? Do I not deserve some small amount of respect?'

He stood up with her, throwing down what he was doing as he stomped towards her.

'Enough!' He drew a hand through his dark hair, considering something.

'Might as well try it,' he said seemingly to himself, then he turned on her.

'You think your *my* Fourth?' he snarled. 'You might be Drax's, but you aren't mine. You never will be. What was done at the Camp was done because we had to do it, because you left us with no other choice, because you are a stupid, useless female.'

He advanced on her, making her step back.

'If you hadn't run to the Dark Army with your pathetic notions, we would have arrived at the Ice Plains already. We'd have gone through into the Underhill, and we would know what happened to our kin. But, because of you, we are constantly delayed!'

He picked her up by the scruff of the neck and shook her. She pushed him back, her body readying for the fight. It wouldn't be in a ring, but she didn't care. She needed the violence of it. Now.

But instead of hitting her, he kicked her legs out from

under her, sending her to the forest floor on her back and, before she could do anything to counter, he had somehow immobilized her hands over her head. They were stuck to the hard earth, and she couldn't move them. He leaned over her with a sneer.

'Is this how he did it?'

Eve's heart began to thud in her chest, her lungs becoming tighter with each quick breath she took.

'W-Who?' she whispered.

'The Bull.'

All at once, she recalled him making her tell him about her past in their room in that Dark Realm, about all the things the Bull did, about how he had hurt her, tortured her, raped her countless times while she'd been bound and weak and at his mercy. Priest had made her forget what he'd forced her to tell him, but she remembered now what he'd done ... after he'd tricked her into his bed.

She stifled a sob, but traitorous tears came to her eyes and spilled down her temples as she lay on the cold ground. He must truly hate her. How else could he have done these things to her?

He knelt down, straddling her body, and ripped her tunic apart roughly, untying her chemise as well. He stared at her chest that she could feel was exposed, though she couldn't raise her head to see, and he loosened her breeches. Then, he hesitated for a breath, his eyes impossible to read, before one hand took hold of her throat and the other grazed the sensitive part between her legs where she'd confessed to him that the Bull had always hurt her first.

Memories of being crushed beneath the Bull's great, hulking form beset her and Eve shut her eyes and screamed as she fell head-long into them.

She vaguely heard him yell, 'the Ice Plains'.

And then they were dropping out of the sky into deep

snow. She blinked. Priest was on top of her, but his hand wasn't *on* her anymore. Everything as far as the eye could see was white. It was snowing and the wind was bitter.

He deftly retied her chemise and pulled her tunic together while she shook beneath him with cold ... and with fear, but he no longer seemed interested in doing what he'd been about to do. He touched his forehead to hers and sighed, stilling over her for a moment.

Then, he stood, pulling her up by her tunic when she didn't take his outstretched hand.

'Well,' he looked around. 'It *looks* like the Ice Plains.'

He pulled his hood up and then hers as well, almost a protective gesture which confused her considering what he'd done.

She didn't speak, her mind whirling, her body shaking so badly she could scarcely walk.

'Come,' he said, trudging ahead through the snow.

Not knowing what else to do, Eve tried to keep up. The snow was too deep though, coming up to her thighs in places whereas for him it was only up to his knees.

When he saw her struggling, he picked her up, putting one arm across her back and the other underneath her knees, carrying her like a babe.

She didn't look at him, didn't say anything, but she vowed to kill him. He'd tricked her, used the unit's bond to make her tell him the worst things that had happened to her, the things that scared her most ... and then he had used them to make her conjure.

∼

Drax

'WHERE THE FUCK ARE THEY?' Fie asked for probably the millionth time.

Drax looked over at him and sighed. 'They'll be here.'

Fie bared his teeth. 'You've been saying that for days. I'm fucking frozen,' he growled.

Drax rolled his eyes. 'It will take time if they were transported to a far-reaching realm. It may take more than one portal to get to the main trade routes.'

Fie growled something under his breath, going back to his rock, the only thing that wasn't covered in snow because he kept brushing it off.

Drax looked out into the distance. Well, as much as he could see of it anyway. The snow was coming down thick and heavy and had been for hours. Such were the Ice Plains.

He saw something. Black. Moving. He squinted, trying to pick out what it was.

'There,' he said, pointing. 'Can you make it out?'

Fie stared. 'It's Priest,' he said at last.

'Where's Eve?'

'I think he carries her,' his Brother replied.

As they got closer, Drax could feel her. She was upset and miserable. But then, her only companion had been Priest for days, so that was a given.

They waited until they were closer, and Priest finally made it to the rocks where they stood. Drax gave him a nod and Priest returned it, setting the female down into the snow that almost came up to her waist.

Still, Eve tried to edge away from Priest and his Brother's expression turned grim. She shivered with cold, her teeth chattering. Her tunic gaped, and the buttons were missing. Drax's eyes narrowed at Priest, but his Brother didn't look his way.

'Come,' Drax said gruffly, not quite willing to admit to himself that he had missed her. That couldn't be what he was feeling. He looked her up and down. Misery and fear came off her in waves the likes of which he'd not felt before, not even close. He frowned, looking at Priest who avoided his gaze. What was wrong with their Fourth?

Was it whatever realm they'd been thrust into that had scared her, or was it simply being in Priest's company for an extended period of time? His gaze turned back to Priest, who gave nothing away, of course, but Drax could guess how the last days with him had been for her.

He'd speak to her later about it but, first, they needed to do what they'd come here for. He only hoped that Priest had readied her during the time they'd been together.

He led them down the gully that he and Fie had been clearing of snow everyday to where one of the Underhill's portals had once been. There were rocks strewn about, owing to whatever cataclysm had occurred to make the bridges collapse so abruptly.

Priest, Fie, and Drax looked at her expectantly and she stared back.

'Well?' Drax asked.

She glanced at Priest and then looked down.

'I can't,' she said miserably.

Drax threw up his hands at his Brother. 'What have you been doing all these days you've been gone? I thought you would have taught her how to manifest—'

Priest stepped forward, his eyes cutting into her.

'Do it.' His tone was almost pleading.

She shook her head, wrapping her arms around herself and cringing before him in a display that was very unlike their strong, proud Fourth.

'I can't,' she said again.

Without a word, Priest took her by the throat, his other hand grabbing between her legs. She gave a broken cry, grasping at his hand and trying to claw him off her, but he was too strong.

He whispered something in her ear and Drax felt her terror increase ten-fold, palpable in the air around them. He staggered back a step, feeling sick. What was Priest doing?

Eve flailed and there was an ungodly sound of the stones around them cracking. Lightning flashed and the portal opened. The roar of it was deafening, and Drax screamed at them to get through the doorway before it buckled. They lunged as it sputtered and Drax was sure they'd be killed as rocks began to fall around them from the cliffs surrounding the gully.

They found themselves by a gurgling stream in the warm sun and Drax thanked the gods that there had been enough power for the portal to bring them here. He looked around him, taking in the vibrant colors of the foliage and flowers around them. It was always high summer here. There were birds tweeting, fish swimming lazily in the river. It was a beautiful realm where everything grew and thrived.

'The Underhill,' Fie breathed.

Drax looked back for the others. They'd all made it through; the horses as well. The portal was gone and though the others wouldn't like that as there was now no quick escape, Drax found himself relieved, for it meant that they still needed Eve's magick to leave this place. Priest couldn't yet break their bond with her.

'Is she all right?' he asked.

Priest was staring down at their unconscious female who he now carried once more, looking at her in a way that Drax had never seen his Brother look at anyone. Could it be that Priest was forming an attachment with her since they'd been traveling in each other's companies?

'I believe bringing us here drained her. Her magick is new and it was only earlier today that she brought us to the Ice

Plains. It may be some time before she'll be able to reopen a portal to the outside.'

Drax frowned. 'Are you going to tell us what happened in the Dark Realms?' he asked his Brother.

Priest's face was shuttered, his tone emotionless. 'It doesn't matter. I got us to the Underhill.'

Drax's jaw clenched, remembering the fear Eve had been feeling. What had Priest done to her while Drax hadn't been there to stop him?

Realization dawned. 'Fear is her magick's trigger,' he guessed aloud, but Priest didn't answer, beginning to walk in the direction of the realm's only town with Eve in his arms.

Drax caught up with him, taking him by his shoulder and turning him.

'What did you do?'

For a brief moment, Drax saw his Brother's emotions flit over his face, and he held Eve tighter. Drax knew without a shadow of a doubt that Priest had done something unforgivable, but then his face again became a hard mask and Priest thrust Eve's sleeping form at Drax.

'You take the bothersome female,' he said. 'I've had my fill of her over the past days. Let's find the children, the proof we need to implicate Gerling for the destruction of the portals, and get this fucking mission done.'

He stalked off down into the valley, Fie oddly silent and following on his heels, both of them leaving Drax standing in the road holding the female.

He looked down at her. Physically she seemed fine, but when she woke, he would find out what Priest had done.

Drax began to follow his Brothers down the hill, leaving their mounts to wander. There was nowhere for them to run off to after all.

He closed his eyes and smelled the air as he walked,

memories assailing him from when he had spent his time here as a boy, as all the fae did in their youths.

He hoped to the gods they'd find the children. They had to be here.

As they entered the town, they took off their cloaks and their tunics, for the weather was completely the opposite to where they'd just been.

All was silent. For the first time in millennia, there were no children playing here, no laughter. The tinkling of the stream that ran through the village was all they could hear as they explored slowly. The whole place looked abandoned. There was no one and nothing. A goat ran in front of them, bleated and then ambled away again.

Drax put Eve down in the moss under the shade of a tree and walked into a house. It was deserted. Food had molded and withered to nothing on the table. It was as if everything had been left in one moment.

'There's no one here,' Fie called, 'but whatever happened, it happened quickly.'

Drax nodded. Everything pointed to that assessment.

'The horses starved to death in the stables,' Priest muttered.

'Here,' Fie called.

Drax found him in an alley across the way standing over the skeletons of two fae males.

'There are more. All male warriors.'

'So, the few male protectors died here, and the females were captured and murdered by the First Scholar in Kitore when they went to seek aid. But what of the children?'

'They definitely aren't here,' Priest said, his voice devoid of emotion.

He turned on his heel and left them both in the alley.

'Where the fuck are they?' Fie yelled, kicking one of the

dead fae in the head and sending the sun-bleached skull hurtling into the outer wall of the adjacent house.

'We'll find them,' Drax promised his Brother. 'We'll find your brother and Priest's sister. We'll find the evidence that Gerling orchestrated all of this.'

'Well not here we won't,' Fie said. 'This place is nothing more than a beautiful tomb.'

'Perhaps it's time we went back to Kitore,' Drax said.

'I'm not setting my foot inside that fucking city again,' Fie said, shoulders slumping.

'You'll do it if you want to find out what happened here,' Drax snarled. 'This isn't just about you. These are all that are left of the fae children. We must keep our heads and find them.'

He left Fie to calm down, finding Priest standing in the street, staring at nothing.

'I was sure they'd be here,' Priest whispered. 'Scared, perhaps, wondering what had happened but here. Safe.'

'We will find them, Brother.'

Priest bared his teeth in anger, and then he abruptly deflated, running his hands through his hair and looking more exhausted than Drax had seen him before – even when he'd been their unit's commander, even when they'd tried every day for weeks to escape Kitore to no avail.

'You don't understand.' He turned to Drax. 'Getting to the Underhill is all I've thought about since Kitore. I was sure that if we were able to discover a way in, we'd find them …' he broke off, looking *ashamed*. 'I've done something …'

CHAPTER 8

EVE

The Underhill was not what she'd expected, Eve thought as she wandered around. It was summertime here. Everything was in bloom. Everything was so beautiful; the opposite of the Dark Realms she'd seen, though she supposed there were thousands of realms and she shouldn't use just those two for comparison. For all she knew, there were many lovely Dark Realms as well.

The men were talking amongst themselves in the middle of the street, leaving her out of their conversation, and she was glad of it. She'd woken up here not long ago, Priest's actions fresh in her mind. She'd never felt so defiled. Not even by the Bull. She'd never felt anything with the Bull but hatred, she realized. He'd simply been a bad thing that happened sometimes. But this ... Eve didn't know why she felt so betrayed. She wasn't sure she had the right. She and Priest were nothing to each other, after all. He'd made that clear by what he'd done. Simple hatred had been easier.

She stopped by a door, leaning on it for support as she tried to get herself under control. She was angry and scared and sad.

She supposed that some part of her had thought they might perhaps keep her as their Fourth when all this was over, that they might want her to stay with them. She hadn't even realized that was what she wanted until Priest had done ... what he'd done, and she'd understood that she truly was simply a means to an end to them. She had harbored a hope, though she hadn't known it; a hope that was now dashed. Gods, she was pathetic. Was it because she had no one else? What were these men becoming to her?

She let out a breath. It didn't matter now. They were here, and Priest would terrify her again so that they could leave and then they'd do whatever it was that they had planned all along. Would they free her, she wondered? Maybe death would be preferable than trying to navigate a world she knew so little about.

Eve walked through a door in the village, and a small bell chimed. It looked like an apothecary shop. She studied the various vials and potions, one of them looking very much like the one Priest had tricked her with. She turned away, trying to put it from her mind though her body was already responding to thoughts of him. In truth, she had enjoyed their time in that bed and that made his deception worse.

She shook her head to clear it, focusing on what was in front of her.

Everything in the town had just been left where it had fallen.

On the table in front of her were various bowls filled with colorful powders. There were bundles of dried herbs she didn't recognize, and, in the dead center, there was a tiny black disk. On it sat a little puffball, pink and pretty. It was so beautiful, and Eve ached to touch it as she stared, not able to take her eyes off it.

Her hand hesitantly moved towards it, something telling her she shouldn't and yet she couldn't help herself. She grazed it with her fingertip, and it exploded into a white mist that settled over her despite her waving her hands to dispel it.

Eve sneezed, rearing back, and leaving the shop with itchy eyes, hoping the men wouldn't find out about this. They'd call her all kinds of foolish, she muttered to herself as she went down to the stream to wash her face in the cool, clear waters, choking slightly as the dust caught in her throat.

She looked slowly down at the stones of the riverbed, smoothed by the running water. It was so hot here, she thought, pulling her boots off, and letting her breeches fall into the water. A tiny voice in her head was telling her not to, that this wasn't right, but she silenced it, pulling her chemise over her head. The clothes had been itchy and confining. Now she felt free. She wandered in the sun, naked as a nymph, through the trees into the forest, following the river until she came to a waterfall and a pool. She waded in, sighing as the water touched her over-heated flesh.

She knelt in it, throwing the water over her arms and her breasts. She bit her lip and did something she'd never done before. She touched her nipples, her mouth opening on a gasp as her core throbbed. She needed ...

She caught sight of Fie walking towards her. He was saying something, but she couldn't make out the words.

It was him. She needed him.

She stood, going to meet him, saw his eyes move over her body. She looked up at him, not breaking eye contact as she began to unlace his shirt. He let her, helped her pull it off him, showing his broad shoulders, toned chest and defined torso.

'I knew you wanted me, female,' he said gruffly, kicking off his boots and pushing his breeches down to show her his large cock, already standing to attention.

'Get on your knees,' he ordered, and she did as he told her, a part of her surprised when he put his hard staff in her mouth.

She knew how to do this. The Bull had made her do it many times. But he had not been so big. She struggled, choking as he grabbed her hair and moved her head to fuck her mouth at his own leisure.

She kept staring into his eyes, and he into hers, all the while moving her for his pleasure. And then he finally threw back his head and growled his release, and she felt his seed spurting down her throat.

Only then did he let her go and she sank to the earth, looking up at him.

There was something wrong with her, she thought dimly as he lay her out on her back, spreading her legs. Her body was languid as he moved her thighs wide and looked down at her. Without further preamble, he lay on top of her, licking her nipples, playing with them, moving up and kissing her mouth. Soon, her hips were undulating, needing more.

Fie didn't speak as he lined himself up and eased himself inside of her tight channel and she moaned, wrapping her legs around him as he began to move in slow, easy strokes that made her eyes roll into the back of her head.

She whimpered for more and he ordered her to touch herself, showing her how when she looked at him in confusion.

She arched her back, seeing stars as pleasure erupted through her, making her disjointed body feel relaxed but also alive – just like this place was, she thought dreamily as he found his release again and finally removed his softening rod from her.

He pulled up his breeches and put his shirt back on. Only then did he look down at her with something akin to concern.

'Eve?' he asked.

His voice sounded so far away.

'Eve?' he asked again. 'Female, are you well?'

She smiled at him, and his expression changed to one of shock.

'Fuck,' he muttered. 'I'm sorry. I didn't know. I didn't realize.'

He picked her up and cuddled her to him and she smiled again, touching his face, down his soft cheek, his angular features so beautiful. She gave a small sigh, relaxing in his arms.

HER EYES SNAPPED OPEN. She remembered Fie fucking her mouth and then her ... it had been a dream, hadn't it? She was in a room, sun streaming through the casement.

She looked down to find she was on a bed, her arms and legs tied down. She gave a screech and tried to struggle, but it was if the ribbons were made of iron. She could hardly move. What if the Bull was here, her sluggish mind thought? She screamed again, and the door burst open.

'Let me go!' she cried at Drax, but he shook his head.

'I'm sorry, female. We can't do that until you're yourself again.'

'Keep her calm! Let her go if you must or you'll find a breach opening in the fucking corridor!' shouted Priest from another room.

'I am myself,' she cried at Drax.

Drax hushed her, ignoring Priest's words. 'You are safe, Eve, but you are not yourself,' he said. 'You touched something you shouldn't have and now you're under an enthrallment. Fie will be punished for taking advantage.'

Fie was lurking in the doorway, looking concerned. 'I'm

sorry, Eve,' he said quietly. 'I didn't know. I thought you wanted...'

She looked at him in consternation. 'It wasn't a dream?' she asked.

He shook his head, opened his mouth to say more, and then shut it again, turning on his heel and leaving the room.

Eve belatedly realized that she had no clothes on and tried to turn away.

Her breathing stuttered as she tried to quell tears, but they begin to stream down into her hair anyway, and she cursed herself for bawling in front of them.

Priest entered, looking at her on the bed with a clinical eye. 'She's still under the thrall?' he asked. 'You shouldn't have touched anything,' he said, and her lip quivered under his anger.

'Leave her alone,' Drax ordered. 'You've done enough. You both have.'

Priest ran a hand through his hair.

'Fuck,' he muttered, turning around, and leaving.

Drax stood over her, hushing her again. 'I can feel your upset. I won't hurt you.'

But that was what the Bull said too. It was all part of the game. She had to do what he wanted and then he wouldn't hurt her, but then he always did anyway.

'Don't lie,' she whispered, 'I know what men like you do.'

She'd given too much away. She didn't want to see the pity in his eyes.

'I will set you free,' he relented, 'but you must touch nothing else while you're here and if you feel odd, you must tell one of us immediately. What you've done is very dangerous. I only hope your fae side is strong enough to expel the magick.'

He untied her and she sat up, covering her nakedness,

crawling up on the bed in a sitting position and drawing her knees to her chest.

'Here,' he said throwing an ivory, homespun dress to her. 'You threw your clothes in the river.'

She put it on, finding that it was the right length for her and feeling much better now that she was covered.

'What happened to me?' she asked in a small voice.

'An enchantment,' Drax replied 'A game that most fae would have been able to see right through, but you were caught in the enthrallment. It made you want—'

'Fie?' she asked.

His face was bleak. 'Fie didn't realize that you weren't yourself or he'd never have …'

∼

Fie

FIE SAT ALONE in a dusty corner of a storeroom, hoping that no one would find him, his head in his hands. He was a fool. He'd never forced a woman, and although Eve had been more than willing at the time … why hadn't he noticed that look in her eyes? He'd seen it often enough in the fae courts with the human women who were under the control of the lords. An enthrallment was nothing to be glib about. It may be little more than a child's toy to the fae, but in the human realms such things could wreak havoc.

She hadn't really wanted him, and he didn't know why that cut so deeply. He threw a shard of wood at the wall, sighing.

He could feel her now their bond was complete. He'd been ready and willing to cut her loose yesterday, but now he felt a powerful, albeit faint connection to the female. He could feel her emotions, her confusion and fear. That surprised him. He hadn't realized she was so afraid and that was his fault, as well as his Brothers.

He stood up, going back upstairs in the house they had commandeered for their use while they were stuck here. There were worse places to be sure, but this was just another gilded prison.

He ascended the steps slowly. He knew that Drax had left Eve alone, and Priest was scouting the rest of the Underhill to make sure they hadn't missed anything. He'd be back later on today as this realm was tiny compared with all the others.

Walking into her chamber, Fie found her lying in the bed, staring at the wall. Her fear was palpable when she heard him enter, but relief was on its heels when she saw it was him. That gave him hope that perhaps he could salvage whatever this was between them even after what he'd done.

He sat in a chair in her view.

'Can I get you anything?'

She shook her head and Fie's gaze fell onto the table where a plate of uneaten food sat, growing cold. She wasn't eating and he found that there was little that would have worried him more. She was always hungry, after all.

'I'm sorry, female,' he said, staring at the ground, unable to look her in the eye.

She said nothing for so long that he looked up.

'It wasn't your fault. I'm sorry that I ...'

He frowned. What could she be sorry for?

'I'm sorry that I forced you to do something that you didn't want to do. I know that you do not find me ...' This time she looked down. 'I know that I'm not like a fae female.'

Fie wanted to throw back his head and laugh. She thought *he* hadn't wanted *her*?

He stood up, taking two steps closer, wanting to ensure she heard every word and could not mistake him.

'You didn't force me to do anything I didn't want to do. That's why I'm sorry. I thought you wanted me.'

She sat up in the bed. 'There's nothing for you to be sorry for,' she said quietly.

He looked incredulous and spoke slowly. 'You weren't willing. Not really,' he said. 'I've seen enthrallment on a human enough times to know what it looks like. I should have realized. Please, forgive me.'

Eve regarded him. She wasn't afraid at the moment, he didn't think, but understanding the link between them was going to take time.

'It may have been fae magick,' Eve continued, 'but in my own mind, I was not struggling. Believe me when I say that I know what it is to be truly forced,' she said, meeting his eyes and daring him to pity her. 'It wasn't the same.'

Fie felt rage wash over him at the thought, though it didn't escape him that both Drax and he had not had her consent either. The time with Drax had been unavoidable. There simply hadn't been any other way. The pleasure tents would have killed her. But he'd made everything worse with his stupidity. How could he have thought she wanted him? She'd been forced into this. She was practically their prisoner, and he hadn't been kind.

She drew back and he frowned. Had he scared her anew?

'You're ... angry,' she said. 'Why?'

'You can feel that from me?' he asked in surprise. Drax hadn't told him that she'd be able to feel him as well.

She nodded slowly. 'But it's different; like a muffled sound that I can only just hear. Can you feel my emotions too?'

'Yes, when we're close to each other.'

'And Drax?'

'And Drax,' he confirmed.

Eve got out of the bed and stood in front of him.

'What am I feeling now?' she asked, looking up at him.

Surprised, Fie stepped back as he felt her arousal spiking. That couldn't be right, could it?

Very slowly, needing to make sure, he stepped closer to her and the emotion intensified.

'Tell me you are not still under the thrall,' he murmured in her ear.

'My head is as clear as the river outside,' she whispered. 'but ...' she hesitated and Fie could feel her warring with herself.

'Speak,' he said.

'I want ... When I lost in the rings, it was always because I was ordered to; so that money could be made.'

Fie's eyes narrowed. 'What happened if you refused to fight?'

She shrugged, giving him a vague smile as if what she recalled was just an amusing memory.

'I was starved until I relented, but that doesn't matter now. I want you to understand. When I was made to lose, it was to one man – always the same one. For his payment, he never wanted coin.'

'He wanted you,' Fie guessed, his hands forming fists at his sides.

She nodded. 'I was his reward for putting on a good show,' she murmured. 'I may not have been in my right mind when you found me by the waterfall, but ... with you was nothing like it was with him.'

The darkness in her eyes made him wish he could take this pain, banish it from her. Whatever this man she spoke of had done, it had left its mark on her as keenly as a blade on her flesh.

'What would you like me to do?' he asked, taking her chin in his fingers so that she would look at him.

She bit her lip and he almost groaned aloud.

'Take off your shirt,' she said, sounding excited and thrilled. She wasn't enthralled, just intrigued.

He did as she told him, pulling it off in one swift movement and basking in the attention she paid to his body with her eyes.

Her breath quickened at the sight of him. He kept his face carefully blank, not wanting to scare her. This was for her.

'Your breeches?' It was a question, not a command, but he did as she asked, taking off his boots as well, and standing in front of her so that she could see him in full.

'Would you like me to turn?' he asked quietly, giving her a quick grin when she looked shy.

She nodded tentatively, and he turned for her in a slow circle so that she could see all of him.

She stepped closer, and then froze.

'You can touch,' he said, taking her hand and laying it on his chest. Eve's fingers felt the contours of his muscles, the warmth of his skin and her other hand joined it, caressing his shoulders and down his corded forearms.

Her fingers interlaced with his for a moment and he felt their connection, the bonds between them flare to life. She felt it too. She closed her eyes on a small sigh.

'It's different with you,' she murmured, her hands leaving his to trail up his arms again to his chest and then down his abdomen. He sucked in a breath, and she looked down to find his staff already hard. The tip glistened with a bead of moisture. Her hand moved toward it, and he gritted his teeth as she touched him, her thumb swirling over him.

'Lie on the bed,' she said quietly, and he did.

Eve took off the dress that she'd been given and knelt between his legs, her hands moving up his calves to slide over his hips.

She stretched herself over him, connecting their bodies.

She lay her head next to his and looked at him, uncertainty in her countenance.

'Is this all right?' she asked.

Fie nodded, his arms coming around to hold her to him. He wanted her, but at this moment he didn't mind if they stayed like this. He'd not felt so close to anyone for a long, long time. He hadn't realized how lonely he'd been with his Brothers always at odds with each other.

'Would you tell me about yourself?' she asked, eyes closing.

'I was born here in the Underhill. I stayed here until my magick came.'

'You have magick as well?'

'Yes, but I'm not very good at conjuring.' He shifted in the bed to get more comfortable. 'When I was old enough to take care of myself, I left for the fae courts. I come from a family of well-known performers. Faire folk. I grew up tumbling, making people laugh, doing tricks for the other children, riding horses.' He grinned. 'Amazing others with my clever, entertaining skills.'

'And your family?' she asked.

'Both my parents were killed in a Dark Realm. They were performing at a faire, and it was attacked by the Horde. I have a brother. Rogue. He was in the Underhill.' Fie sighed. 'My mother should have been here, but she left to meet up with my father at the faire.' Fie smiled at the memory. 'They loved to perform together when they could, but she was slain with him in the attack.' He looked at her, her eyes still closed, but she wasn't asleep. 'Rogue was meant to be safe here,' he whispered.

'Where is everyone else?' Eve asked.

'You mean the adults? The only males here at the time were a small band of warriors. The mothers and other females who lived here to care for the children went to seek refuge in the capital as per the ancient agreements in place between Kitore and the Underhill when the portals began to fail, but they were betrayed and killed there.'

'The children weren't taken with them?'

'No one can remember.'

He looked down to find her staring at him.

'I don't understand. How can no one remember?' she asked.

'Kitore is an old city with its own defenses to contend with. Its wards can manipulate the minds of its citizens. Originally, in order to keep them safe, but, in the wrong hands, a powerful weapon. We were able to find out that the females who went to Kitore were murdered for their magick by Nixus, the First Scholar on the orders of a fae lord, and we don't believe the children were with them. There's no record of them at all.'

He lay his head back, staring at the ceiling. 'We all hoped they'd be here, that the portals had been destroyed to keep them safe until help could come.'

'Where will you search next?'

'Kitore.'

'And what about me?' she asked.

Fie pretended nonchalance, but inside he tensed. She was finished what she'd been brought to do. Priest at the very least wanted her gone and, at most, dead. Would Priest insist the bond be broken? *No!* He wouldn't let his Brothers have their way in this. She was his, theirs.'

She suddenly moved over him, and he groaned, clutching her to him, and pulling her against his hard length.

'Tell me you want this as well,' he said. When she nodded, he let out the breath he'd been holding. 'Then my body is yours, female,' he said, letting her go. 'Be gentle with me.'

She stilled over him for a moment. 'I don't really know what to do,' she confessed. 'I was always tied down before.'

She said it so matter-of-factly, as if such a thing were normal to do to a female during the act and Fie seethed. Whoever had hurt her, he vowed he would find them and seek revenge for their Fourth.

He turned them both, so they were facing each other.

'Tell me what you like,' he said low in her ear.

'I don't ... well, what Priest did before in the cave ...'

He groaned. 'I knew you enjoyed that. You came on Priest's fingers so hard. The way you ground against his hand ... What else?'

'I ... Drax used his mouth at an inn. I liked that too.'

Fie's hands moved over her, pinching one of her nipples hard enough for her to cry out.

'That?' he asked.

She looked away, embarrassed. 'Yes.'

His fingers traced her breast and down her stomach, cupping her, pressing into her slit with the heel of his hand and rubbing in slow circles.

'That?'

She nodded mutely, her eyes not leaving his.

He pinched the bead between her legs and she jerked, moaning loudly.

'Please,' she whispered, 'I need—'

'I know what you need, female,' Fie said, caressing her face as he pushed a finger into her channel.

'You're so wet,' he murmured. 'Do you need my cock, Eve?'

She nodded, her body shuddering.

'Enough to beg for me to fill that tight, needy cunt?'

Again, she nodded, opening her mouth to do just that, but he silenced her with a finger to her lips.

'As much as I'd love to hear you pleading for me to fuck you, I have another idea,' he said.

Fie picked Eve up, moving her over him before taking her

by her hips and easing her down on his length. Then he let go, allowing her to move how she liked.

She rolled her hips inexpertly, impaling herself fully on him with a low moan. She moved up again, and then down, gasping, and then she took his hands and moved them to her breasts, looking bashful as she showed him what she wanted.

His hips rocked involuntarily, and her mouth opened on a whimper. 'Do that again,' she begged. He grinned, repeating the motion, and making her cry out.

'Do you like that, female?' he asked, and she nodded.

In the background, he saw that Drax was standing in the corner, watching them.

'I need more,' she whimpered, and, in one swift movement, Fie turned them so that she was on her back beneath him.

He pushed into her gently, wanting this to be something different than it had been in her past. He knew that Drax still watched them. His Brother liked to do that, and Fie hoped they were giving his Brother a good enough show that he would think twice about casting their Fourth aside.

He dragged Eve down the bed. Her hands were on his shoulders, holding on to him as he pumped into her with slow, easy strokes. With his thumb, he rubbed the small bud at the apex of her thighs, enjoying how she writhed beneath him as he rode her.

He could feel how excited she was, how close she was to her peak. It was an odd sensation to feel hers as well as his looming on the horizon. He took her a little faster, the friction between their bodies making them both moan.

His body clenched as his seed erupted from him at the same time as she arched her back and cried out her own release. His fingers turned bruising as he claimed his female properly, pushing every inch of him into her, an age-old need being fulfilled, yet one he'd never wanted to satisfy before. It scared him and as soon as his pleasure had ebbed, he pulled himself from her, sitting back on the bed.

She was panting, glistening with sweat and, not wanting her to know the direction of his thoughts, he brushed the hair from her brow, and kissed her forehead gently before covering her with a blanket.

When he looked behind him, Drax was gone.

∼

Priest

'Try again.'

Priest's tone was harsh as he tried to get Eve to open a portal. But the female could still not reach her magick on her own. She needed the terror only he could provide. He gritted his teeth, not wanting to have to instill it in her anymore.

She sat on the ground, back straight and eyes closed, trying to open a portal. She was failing miserably.

Shame welled up in him as he watched her try again and again, accomplishing nothing and becoming more and more panicked. If she couldn't do it on her own, she knew what he would do and how well he could do it thanks to his deceit.

He thought back to that night with self-loathing. How could he have known that that fucking potion that was meant to relax her would work so well that she'd been too dazed to tell him no?

Securing the bond with her and learning her fears had been the plan from the moment he knew she had magick and they'd been sucked into the Dark Realms, he reminded himself. But it had not gone the way he'd thought. Listening to her answer his questions about her past, her treatment and men who had hurt her so many times had been harder than he'd expected. In truth he'd not thought it would shock him, but it had. He'd taken her memory of the interrogation he'd subjected her to away, hoping to spare her that ... and selfishly so she wouldn't think even worse of him. But, somehow, she'd remembered all of it.

The anguish he'd seen in her eyes, that he'd felt in his very being now that they were bound together properly had almost made his legs buckle.

He looked away from her for a moment, disgusted to the core with himself. He was no better than Talik ... the Bull. It was right that she should hate him and feeling the agony that he was causing her ... there was a justice in that.

But if she couldn't find her magick, he was going to have to hurt her again and the thought of it made him want to retch.

Having not found their kin here in the Underhill, they'd be obliged to return to the fae court soon to relay their findings, as no one else had been able to breach the portal. But first they would go to the capital where all of this had begun.

He looked over at Drax and Fie, who were staring at the female, their horses' reins in their hands as they waited patiently. All three of them had claimed her now ... as if she were truly theirs, as if any of this was right.

His Brothers would not want to break the bond as they'd originally planned.

Priest shook his head. Their minds were clouded, and he was fighting to keep sight of what he needed to do. Eve should never have been their Fourth. If Drax and Fie were no longer present in their minds enough to see it, then Priest would have to be the one to break the bond ... for all their sakes, even hers.

Luckily, he had the skill and didn't need the Dark Army Commander to perform the rites to destroy it.

'Try it again,' he said.

Her eyes opened, flashing at him. 'There's no magick there. Do what you must.'

'You can find it,' he insisted, not believing that she was resigned to him tormenting her. Why wouldn't she keep trying?

She stood up, not backing down. 'Just do it!'

He growled at her and was amused when she growled back, even though he was not looking forward to what he was going to have to do. *Again.* The other two looked away from the intimate moment, and he smirked at her. If she knew what that sound meant from a female, if she understood that, for the fae, it was the beginning of a courtship ritual, he knew she'd be horrified.

But he didn't tell her. Instead, he gritted his teeth, and prepared himself for the pain he'd have to put them both through now otherwise they'd be here for gods only knew how long before she found her magick on her own.

He grabbed her, ignoring her cry of surprise even though she'd known something was coming as he turned her around and pushed her into the thick trunk of a nearby tree, face first. He leaned in close to her as he pulled up the dress she wore with one hand, knowing there was nothing underneath.

'Remember how the Bull would punish you, female?' he whispered in her ear, trying not to react to her stiffening body. 'Did he beat you as I'm going to do before he fucked you?'

This was the fastest way. They didn't have time to get stuck in this purgatory.

Drax and Fie were coming towards them, looking murderous. They didn't understand, but she needed to feel that terror, that base need to flee and it would be less painful to do it quickly in the long run.

She squealed when his hand came down hard on her

backside and a bridge opened next to them almost immediately. He picked her up with one arm, and thrust them both through the window she'd made, not waiting for the others.

They walked out into a forest and the portal disappeared. He let the female go and she fell to her knees, breathing heavily, pulling away from the others with a cry as they went to her.

Priest stopped himself from doing the same. He couldn't comfort her when he was the cause of her suffering.

'I didn't really hurt—' he began, but Drax lunged at him, knocking them both to the ground and striking him across the face.

'You will never do that to her again,' he warned, his voice low; dangerous. 'Never or, by the gods, I swear I will kill you, Brother.'

'And I will do whatever is necessary for us to complete our mission. As always.' He let out an exasperated sound, throwing Drax off him with ease. 'Do you think I want to do this to her?' he ground out.

'Yes,' Drax said without hesitation. 'You've made no secret of how much you loath her.'

Priest got to his feet with a snarl. 'This is why you never should have been given command. You cannot do what needs to be done. Emotions cloud your judgement.'

'Fuck you, Priest,' Drax spat.

'While you argue, we stand in the open like Dark Realm bait,' Fie interrupted, sounding angry with them both. 'Where are we?'

Priest took a step back, trying to curb his anger as he looked around them, noting the flora and fauna.

'It looks like she's brought us south. Come. Let's find a road and get our bearings. If we're in luck, we won't be too far from Kitore.'

Their argument finished for the moment, they mounted

their horses and began to make their way through the dense forest, on their guard in case anything should appear that wished them ill. They broke through the brush onto a small road and began to travel west.

If they were where Priest suspected, they were heading towards the capital, but they wouldn't know for certain until they reached a main thoroughfare.

Fortunately for them, it wasn't long before they found a signposted fork and the north road that would lead them directly to Kitore. By then it was getting dark, however, so they left the main path and found a secluded clearing by a trickling stream to make camp for the night.

Priest conjured the circle as usual, making sure Eve still had her amulet as well, just in case she went wandering.

They'd brought some fae foods from the Underhill with them; fruits and fine, aged cheeses and the like, but Priest wasn't hungry. His thoughts over the course of the day had kept his stomach pitching and rolling as had the fact the Eve wouldn't even look at him. He could feel her misery through the bond they now shared, and he fucking hated it. If it was even possible for him to make her feel better, he had no idea how to go about it.

Drax and Fie made sure she ate something and, though she seemed to like the fayre, she only picked at what was on her plate until Priest snapped at her to eat lest she slow them down the next day. In truth, he'd become so used to her eating copious amounts that seeing her imbibe so little concerned him.

The tear-filled eyes that she tried to hide at his comments made him hate himself even more. He feared he had broken her; something even her enemy the Bull had never done.

His Brothers both gave him looks of animosity and, swearing to himself, he strode to the edge of the circle, looking out into the dark forest.

He'd never cared before whether a female liked him or not, thought him charming or not, but he did with this one and, fuck the gods, he had to keep her at arm's length.

As he was trying to calm his mind, think of the next step, he heard a sound from behind him that he remembered her making when he was toying with her body that night in the Dark Realm. He twisted around, unable to help himself.

His gaze was riveted on her, lying with Fie, that silly, tight dress bunched around her waist ... gods, he could see everything. He swallowed hard as he watched Fie's fingers fuck her, twisting in her and making her whimper and sob with frustration as he whispered lovers' words into her ear that Priest could just make out. How wet she was for him, how much she loved being fucked, what else Fie was going to do to her before the night was out. One finger. Two. Plunging in and out of her, the squelching sounds a testament to how aroused she was.

Gods, he could hear it, smell it, and, on a slight delay, *feel it.*

Priest pulled at the collar of his tunic, suddenly hot and glanced at Drax who was staring as well, his mouth very slightly open as if he couldn't believe that Fie – out of all of them – had gotten the female to submit to him willingly out here in front of them all.

And submit she had.

The sounds she was uttering made Priest want to stride over, steal her from Fie and pull her onto his hard, throbbing staff. But he couldn't. After what he'd done, she wouldn't welcome his hands on her ever again. He stifled a growl as his female mewled for release and wished he hadn't claimed her, hadn't solidified the bond between them.

He was about to turn away and try to block what was happening out when Drax got to his feet and stalked towards

Fie. Priest thought his Brother was going to pull Fie off the female, but he didn't.

'Use another finger,' Drax ordered. 'Stretch her but be gentle. Make her beg you for it.'

'You want to come, don't you?' Drax asked her, staring at her body, and using his boot to nudge her legs further apart. 'You're aching for Fie's thick length to fill that hungry void between your legs. Answer.'

'Yes,' the female moaned, practically holding her legs open for Fie.

'Then do it. Beg for your release. If you do it prettily enough, Fie might just give you what you need.'

'Please,' she begged. 'Please, Fie.'

Drax chuckled. 'You'll need to do better than that, Eve.'

She opened her eyes and stared at them, her eyes landing on Priest and not straying from him for a moment.

'Please, Fie,' she said again, transferring her gaze to the fae male in front of her who was still moving his fingers in and out of her, slowing down when she got to close to her pleasure, keeping her on the precipice of release.

'Not good enough,' Drax said, sounding amused. 'Do you want me to help?'

She nodded vigorously and he chuckled. 'Repeat my words then. Fie, please put your thick cock in me.'

Eve shuddered, her eyes pleading, and Priest snorted. She wasn't going to say it.

'Fie, please put your cock in me,' she mewled, and Priest's mouth dropped open.

'You didn't say 'thick'. For that ... Please fuck me hard and fast. Stretch my tight little cunt in front of my unit.' Drax said, leaning over her.

She squirmed, her cheeks reddening with her embarrassment. 'Fie, please,' she stopped and moaned instead and Fie's fingers left her body.

'Say it,' Fir ordered her, 'or I'll leave you like this.'

'Please, Fie, fuck me hard. Fast. Stretch my tight little …' she looked away, 'cunt in front of my unit.'

'Make me submit and scream your name.'

'Make me submit and scream your name,' she echoed, saying the words in a rush.

'Well?' Drax said to Fie. 'What are you waiting for? Pleasure our female.'

Fie needed no more prompting, surging forward and burying himself in her in one, swift movement.

She screamed so loudly it echoed off the trees around them. She clawed at Fie's tunic as he pistoned in and out of her. Her legs shook, the sounds coming from her almost made Priest spend in his breeches like a green youth. Eve writhed and moaned, whimpered and gasped as Fie continued to take her, grunting and panting. He leaned down and took her mouth with his, groaning into it as that sent him over the edge.

'You're everything to me,' Fie said in her ear and Priest felt her surprise.

He turned away and quietly seethed. The link between him and her was torture for him and it was clearly influencing his Brothers.

THEY REACHED the city late morning the next day and, as they approached from the east looking at its white towers, Priest had a feeling of foreboding.

'What if we get stuck again?' Fie asked quietly, giving voice to their concerns.

He glanced at Drax who too looked grim. 'Then we kill that witch from the Library and steal the ward key. It was made by the fae anyway.'

'But she's a Fourth; the new First Scholar's Fourth.'

Priest snorted. 'Fuck Drake, his unit, and fuck his Fourth too.'

His eyes moved over Eve, but she didn't look his way. She hadn't since they'd got back to the Light Realm. She looked tired and, as he looked to his Brothers, he knew they were all feeling her misery despite trying to cheer her up with their pleasurable interlude yestereve. They didn't seem to realize it was too late to salvage this – whatever it was – with their Fourth.

They went down to the eastern gate and got in the queue to enter the city. At least Nixus, the former First Scholar and the bane of their existence, was dead. That was the only reason they'd been able to escape the cursed city's wards last time. Priest hoped they wouldn't get caught by them again. If they did, he meant what he'd said. He'd kill that bitch, Fourth or no, and deal with her unit afterwards.

They walked through the massive archway under the gate house. They crossed the threshold and looked at each other. Nothing happened. No one came. No one rushed out to attack. There were no alarm bells. They didn't even feel anything. If the wards were still there, then they were now allowed into the city.

Fie shrugged. 'Let's go home.'

'This isn't my home,' Priest growled.

The female stayed behind them and Priest tried not to pay her any mind, but he couldn't help it. She was clearly fascinated by the big city. She'd never been anywhere before. She'd told him that while he'd been asking his questions of her and compelling her to answer him.

'Stay close,' Drax said to her.

They went down to the river where their house was. It was understated from the outside, but the interior held the finest luxuries that could be bought in Kitore, of which there were many, for it was a port city with countless trade routes, both of this realm and others.

They went in, leaving their horses at the stable nearby. Priest noted that Drax kept the female close by his side as her gaze went this way and that, gawking like a provincial slave girl. It marked her as a visitor here and Priest kept his eyes on everyone who noticed her, warning them off with his menacing gaze.

They went into their richly furnished house and her eyes widened further as she looked around.

'Try not to steal anything,' Priest muttered, stomping up the stairs and entering his chamber.

He slammed the door behind him, knowing all of this would be easier while she hated him, but wishing for her to take pleasure in his arms as she clearly did in Fie and Drax's.

CHAPTER 9

EVE

The Brothers' house in Kitore was … Eve looked around Priest's room slowly … lavish was an understatement and every room was like this, but she wasn't surprised that they enjoyed their comforts. The chairs were plush and newly stuffed. There were expensive trinkets everywhere that held no purpose other than to be beautiful. The walls were covered in murals and tapestries that rivalled even the ones she'd seen at the inn they'd stayed at on their way to the Ice Plains. She wondered if all the fae lived this way though she'd noticed in the Underhill that everything had been quite simple and understated in comparison to this.

Drax, Priest and Fie's house was anything but simple. It was a statement of wealth and power, which was odd because she thought they'd been prisoners in the city. She wondered what they had done to make so much coin. Perhaps she didn't want to know.

Eve drifted around slowly, exploring, but not touching anything; having learned her lesson in the Underhill. At present, all of the men were gone, leaving her alone in their grand house in the middle of the city. She could see the wide river from the window. The road in front was mostly silent though they were close to the center where the markets and shops seemed to be.

They'd been in the city for three days and she had been sequestered in the Brothers' home for all of that time. She thought they might release her here. Gods knew the fighting rings of this city were so legendary even she had heard of them. But they hadn't even spoken of letting her go.

In fact, Drax and Fie seemed to always be close to her, and gods help her, she had begun to enjoy their company. She felt something when she was with them that she'd never had before. Safety.

Her innards clenched at the memory of what Fie had done in the forest, the things Drax had made her say to him ... of Priest watching. She'd never taken pleasure in the act before. After the Bull, she'd not thought she could, but these men ... even Priest's skills in bed were practically inconceivable to her.

Priest was a different story. He kept his distance, and she was glad of it she told herself. She didn't fault him for his loyalty to his kind, but he was single-minded in their mission. He would destroy her if he needed to and not even think twice.

The front door banged, and she heard Priest and Fie arguing quietly while they climbed the stairs. She hurried out of Priest's room, not wanting him to think that she was curious about him, which of course she wasn't.

Laughably, this morning Priest had left her in their library with a pile of books and told her to read up on fae magick. He clearly hadn't even thought to ask Eve if she could read, and she'd been too embarrassed to tell him that she could not.

She'd spent some time looking at the symbols after they'd

gone, trying to make heads or tails of them, but failed miserably and soon gave up, feeling stupid.

Priest went to his chamber, slamming the door, and Fie left the house a moment later. Only then did she venture out of her semi-hiding place, going down to the kitchens. Some bread sat out on the counter, but whereas before her odd hunger would have had her gulping it down as quickly as she could, it had abated over the past few days. She felt stronger than she had when she'd fought in the rings, and her body was no longer skin and bone. Her hips and breasts were rounder, and her stomach had a bit of paunch to it when only days ago it had been concave.

She meandered back to her room, bored and wishing she had something to do. She was full of nervous energy, and she didn't like feeling stuck in this grand house where she didn't feel like she belonged.

An idea came to her. Drax had advised her not to fight in the rings close to her town, but surely it didn't matter now. They were in a massive city and there was more than one fighting ring.

She donned her cloak and tall boots that matched a new tunic of supple black leather the Brothers had brought her when they'd returned to Kitore and noticed that her clothes were becoming too tight for her. After that, things had begun appearing in her room frequently; trinkets like brushes and shining baubles, scented oils for bathing, and a myriad of clothes for her to choose from. Eve was starting to find that she enjoyed these things as well, developing a taste for some of the frills they gave her.

Slipping out the front door, she went towards the river, knowing that if she followed it, she'd get to the docks. There was always a fighting ring near the docks.

She walked slowly, enjoying the city after being inside for

so long, her eyes taking in the patterned cobblestones of the streets and the stone buildings that lined them.

She heard the ring before she saw it, the sound of the fights a balm to her senses. She knew this. She understood this. Her skin began to prickle in anticipation, her blood pumping faster through her veins as her body readied itself for battle. She cracked her knuckles and stretched her neck as she walked, warming up her body to move.

It was only midafternoon, so when she found the rings there weren't many people there. She was glad as she stood at the edge, nervousness making her stomach roll. She'd only fought in one ring before, after all. What if it was different here?

The fight in front of her ended with one man begging for mercy and receiving it much to the disappointment of the men watching who wanted to see some blood. She stepped in to take the place of the loser who was dragged out unceremoniously and left by the edge.

The small crowd jeered, which she'd expected for there were no other women fighting that day and, of course, she was so small that no one ever thought she was a threat. The fight began immediately and her opponent, while not a large man, had the movements of a seasoned fighter. He had a short, graying beard and scars intermingled with small tattoos that gave his skin a mottled look. He watched her closely, looking for her weaknesses. He knew his way around a ring that was for sure, and he was not underestimating her, which she was glad of. It made for a better fight.

He came at her, testing her, and she drove him back. She could tell he was surprised, though it barely registered on his face, but he was more careful after that. They danced around each other, well matched in movement at least. He blocked her strikes, and she blocked his. Then he got a lucky punch into her face, splitting her lip. She grinned and he looked uncertain, but this was what she loved, what she needed.

She lunged forward to retaliate, but, at that very moment, a sharp pain radiated out from her chest like hot coals being poured into her. She cried out, falling to her knees, and doubling over, clutching her heart.

Her opponent didn't hesitate, kicking her hard in the stomach. She fell to her side in the dirt, unable to get up, the pain still debilitating her.

She looked up at him through the tears of agony she couldn't help. He was going to kill her.

She tried to get up and failed as her muscles cramped. It felt as if something was being ripped from her. What was happening to her? She'd never felt such torture in her life.

Her opponent leaned over her and grabbed her by the throat, lifting her. She pleaded with her eyes, her hand grasping over his as she struggled to breathe. She saw mercy in his countenance and sagged in relief as he dropped her to the ground and said something about the victory not being true because she was clearly in the midst of some malaise.

The crowd, again denied the violence they craved, booed and hissed as she was dragged from the ring and left at the edge. Perhaps they'd call for a healer, but like as not they'd simply leave her there to live or die as the gods willed.

As she lay on the ground and her vision swam, she noticed a face in the crowd that she recognized, and her stomach dropped. It couldn't be. She fought to stay awake, but the pain was too much and, unbidden, her eyes closed.

∼

Priest

PRIEST DOUBLED OVER IN PAIN, steeling himself, forcing himself to stand upright, to finish the ritual. He would break this bond if it was the last thing he fucking did and, once they were free of its influence, his Brothers would thank him. He might even get his command back once they realized what he'd done; when their minds were not clouded by a bond that meant nothing.

He snuffed the candle, letting the strings that represented their bonds burn down to nothing in a silver dish and, only then did the pain in his chest finally subside. He stared at the ashes. Had the pain been so severe for them all?

The door to his room burst open and both Drax and Fie stood on the other side, their expressions thunderous.

'What have you done?' Drax shouted, still clutching his chest.

'What had to be done. We have no more use for the female. Cut her loose or slit her throat. You both decide. I don't give a fuck, but she is not our Fourth. This was a business transaction and nothing more. You two fools forgot that. Hopefully, you will soon remember now that your judgement isn't impaired.'

'It was not your decision to make,' Fie hissed and Priest was taken aback.

He hadn't thought Fie would care once the emotions the bond made him feel were gone.

'Where is she?' Drax said looking around.

Priest shrugged. 'In the house somewhere abouts as usual.'

'Come on,' Drax ordered, staggering from the room. 'We have to find her, ensure she's safe.'

Priest rolled his eyes. 'She's no fainting wench. She's as strong as you and I. She'll be sitting in her room, lying asleep in her bed, or, more likely, eating through our stores in the kitchen.'

Fie looked back, giving Priest a venomous look. 'You don't even know her.'

Priest barked a laugh. 'As if you do. Look at you, falling in love with the first female who doesn't want you back? He ground out another laugh. 'And you,' he said to Drax. 'I lost leadership of this unit because my magick got us trapped here in the first place. As far as I'm concerned, I just saved us all. I want my command back!'

'It takes two of us to make that decision!' Drax roared, 'What say you, Fie?'

Fie didn't even look at Priest as he left the room. 'Your power games have torn us apart,' he ground out. 'Fuck you both.'

Priest threw the plate of ashes to the floor with a curse.

'She's not here,' Fie said from down the hall.

He heard his Brothers stomping down the stairs and followed at a distance, not wanting to admit he was worried. Where was Eve?

They went down to the kitchens, finding them deserted, and Priest frowned. He'd have bet good coin that she'd be here stuffing her pretty face.

'She's not in the house,' Drax said, coming in from the parlor. 'Where could she have gone?'

They turned on Priest who threw up his hands. 'I don't know.'

He didn't see Drax's fist before it hit him. He slammed into the wall. Putting a deep dent in the painted plaster. He righted himself and lunged at Drax but was pulled back by Fie. Both his Brothers were attacking him.

No, he realized, they were *punishing* him the Brothers' way.

'I did what was best,' he ground out as his head was pulled back and his arms locked behind him by Fie. He struggled, but his Brother was strong and imbued by a righteous anger the likes of which Priest had never seen before; not in Fie at any rate.

Drax stood in front of him, striking him in the abdomen and again across the face. He didn't stop hitting him and Priest didn't say a word. He didn't beg for release or for Drax to stop. He took the beating and, finally, when Drax was finished, Fie let him go and he dropped to the floor, coughing up blood. Fie kicked him hard in the face and he fell back into the stone floor on his back, groaning.

~

Drax

DRAX DIDN'T SPARE Priest another look and they left him prone on the flagstones, bleeding.

How could their Brother have done such a thing to them? Drax knew Priest didn't like the female, but he never thought he'd do that. Breaking a bond was not something done lightly, and it definitely wasn't something one did without anyone's knowledge. Drax didn't know if he'd ever forgive Priest for this. How far was his Brother willing to go to get his command back? Perhaps their unit was already too fractured to ever be whole again. He leaned against the wall as his head began to ache. A vision. He hadn't had one since before they'd found Eve. Fie stood next to him.

'What do you see?' he asked.

'I see nothing,' Drax murmured. 'It's a feeling only. Eve is in danger.'

'Where would she have gone?'

'The fights,' they both said in unison.

'Where's the closest one?'

'Down by the docks.'

They donned their cloaks and left the house, practically

running down to the river. The day was grey and soon it would snow. Drax knew this realm well enough to deduce that much. The wind had started to howl through the streets and the day had gotten darker though it was still early.

They reached the rings, a fight already in progress, but Eve was nowhere to be seen.

'Where else could she have gone?' Fie muttered.

'Come. Perhaps I'll get another vision,' Drax said quietly as they moved around the ring, listening to the fighters and the spectators alike.

Drax noticed a man looking at them, a fighter; thin and sinewy – weathered if the scars were anything to go by. The man had the sight. Drax could usually tell such things, so he was not surprised when the fighter approached them.

'You search for a female,' he said. 'She fought me earlier. She lost.'

His heart in his throat as he thought about her death at the hands of this man, Drax took the fighter by his shirt, dragging him close.

'Did you kill her?'

He put his hands up. 'No. In the middle of the fight, she suffered a fit of some kind. She was dragged to the side of the pit, and another took her away. He was a large man I've not seen here before though he was clearly no stranger to the rings by the looks of him. He wasn't from Kitore.' The fighter hesitated before he spoke again. 'He looked pleased to see her. I thought perhaps they were friends.'

'And what was she doing during all this?' Fie asked.

'She was insensible,' he said. 'She seemed to suffer a great pain that left her unable to even stand.'

Drax and Fie shared a grim look. The anguish of the bond being broken would have been worse for her as she had been tied to all three of them. If Priest had cost them their Fourth, Drax would find a way to get around the wards of the Dark Army, and he would kill his Brother himself.

'Where did they take her?' Drax asked, letting the man go.

'They went in that direction.' He nodded with his head.

Fie and Drax left the rings, walking the way the fighter had indicated. A child stood by a corner, and Drax approached him.

'We're looking for a female.'

The boy gave a bored yawn. 'Two streets over.'

'A *specific* female,' Drax said, producing a gold coin.

His young eyes took on a feral gleam. 'I'm sure I can find her for you.'

Drax held out a coin. 'One now. One when you can show us where she is. She's small, was being carried by a much larger man from the rings.'

'Wait here,' he said, disappearing down the alley nearest to them.

He came back a moment later.

'You're in luck. Come with me,' he said, leading them into the narrow street and down another to a spot not far from the river's edge.

'In there,' he said, pointing to a ramshackle building that looked like it might collapse under a persistent breeze.

Drax gave the child the second coin. 'If we find her, I'll give you five more.'

He nodded, his fingers curling around the money and secreting it away in his rags. 'She's in there.'

They slunk towards the building, drawing their knives when they heard someone approaching. Drax turned to find Priest. His Brother had already healed from the beating he and Fie had given him. Drax sneered at him. They should have used iron to hurt him.

'What the fuck are you doing here?' Fie snarled and Priest subtly flinched at his tone.

'Where's the female?' Priest asked, ignoring Fie's question and looking around as if she might appear.

'What do you care?' Drax ground out, his voice sounding like a prelude to further violence.

'Silence,' Fie snarled at them both.

Drax looked at his Brother in surprise.

'She's in there,' Fie said to Priest. 'She's been taken.'

Priest stared at the house. 'By whom?'

'We're going to find out.'

Drawing their weapons, they opened the door a crack and slunk into the house if it could even be called that for it was practically a ruin. The floorboards were rotten underfoot, and they had to be careful not to fall through them as they walked across the interior. The stairs down into the cellar were holey and rotten, but the ones that led up to the next floor were completely impassable.

The decision of where to begin made for him, Drax descended into the cellar slowly, keeping an eye out the front, knowing that Priest was at least doing his duty and watching behind them.

As soon as he reached the bottom, Drax grunted, falling to his knees with a thud as his strength was ripped away in an instant. He heard Fie and Priest fall as well, and a light enveloped them.

'What have we caught here?' a male voice said from the shadows. 'Three fae poking their noses where they don't belong.'

Drax saw that they were in the middle of a crude circle of stones. They'd been caught in some kind of conjuring net.

'Who the fuck are you?' he snarled.

'Talik. Did little Eve not tell you about me? I'm hurt.' He grinned. 'I'm your slave's true master.'

CHAPTER 10

EVE

Eve's eyes snapped open as she woke on a gasp. It couldn't be true. It couldn't be true. She looked around frantically. She was on a filthy pallet on the floor in a corner. Her wrists were chained with iron.

She struggled into a sitting position, looking around for the Bull. He was here, she'd seen him in the crowd. And where the Bull was, Talik was. Why were they in Kitore? Surely, they hadn't made the journey in search of her. She wasn't worth that much to Talik.

Eve rubbed her chest. Besides the weakness from the iron, her heart pained her. She felt hollow, as if something important had been ripped away. She recognized what little was left. This was how she'd felt for all those years in the rings when the fights were her only companion. The warmth she had felt was gone and there was only a cold void in its place.

The bond had been broken. She had fulfilled her purpose and they'd released her and themselves just as they'd said. That had been the agreement.

Eve didn't know why that made her want to rail and sob,

but it did. She didn't have the strength to do either though, so she lay her head down on the dirty, stinking pallet and let her tears fall now while she was alone.

She wondered if they'd drag her back to the town or simply kill her after the Bull was finished with her, for no doubt Talik would reward his pet for finding her.

The door was unlocked and the boss himself strolled in, looking as immaculate as he always did.

'Eve,' he drawled, and she looked up at him, thrusting out her chin. 'You've caused me no end of annoyance.'

She noticed the hulking figure of the Bull come into the room behind him, staying in the shadows and leaving the door ajar. Talik ignored him, but she could not and, though she tried to hide her body's shaking, the beast noticed her instinctive cowering and looked pleased at her blatant terror of him.

'But now we've found you again,' Talik continued, stepping forward, and bending down to touch her face.

Eve lunged at him and tried to bite him, but he pushed her back down to the floor easily, the chains doing their work well.

'Still that same fire,' he chuckled, taking hold of her wrists, 'and even stronger than before despite the improved grade of iron. You're going to make me a lot of money in this city, but,' he looked back at Bull, 'it's time to be reminded of your place.'

He let her hands fall and gave her cheek a light slap, turning towards the Bull still waiting behind him. 'Torment her however you like. You've earned it.'

The Bull's expression made dread coil in her belly as Talik left the room, closing the door behind him with a final, awful bang. The Bull approached her, and, to her shame, she shrank away.

He lifted her by the bonds around her wrists until her feet

came off the floor and she hung in front of him like a rat by its tail.

'Such fine clothes you have now,' he said softly, wrenching her tunic open and watching her face to see how much he scared her, but she showed nothing, raising her head in defiance.

He brought her closer to him, his foul breath landing on her as he kissed her hard on the lips and then he bit her brutally enough for her to squeal. She felt blood dripping down her chin and let out a stuttering breath.

'There's that fear,' he breathed, 'and I'll see so much more of it before this day is done. You know I always keep my promises, Eve, and I vow you are going to be weeping at my feet by the time I'm finished with you … in front of those friends of yours.'

Eve's stomach dropped at the Bull's words. Friends? The Brothers were *here*? Had they been in league with Talik all along? Had they delivered her back to him now that they no longer needed her? Despite her promise to herself, tears came to her eyes at the thought.

'What friends?' she croaked, feigning ignorance.

'The three downstairs,' he laughed, not believing her for a moment.

'Not my friends,' she snorted, looking away.

'They're going to watch everything I do to you,' he promised darkly. 'Perhaps I'll let them join in the fun with you before I sell them to the Horde.'

Eve struggled in his grip as his meaty hand grasped her breast and kneaded it hard through what was left of her clothes. She looked away, clenching her jaw, and not giving him the satisfaction of her pained whimpers. She would give him nothing.

After a few moments, when she did not react, he snorted.

'Trying to ruin my fun, Eve?' He tutted. 'I can make you play my games.'

He picked her up and slung her over his shoulder, carrying her from the room and down the creaking stairs, into the cellars lit by only one, lone candle.

The three Brothers sat looking bored and frustrated as if they'd been waiting awhile and her lip curled in disgust and disbelief, her worst suspicions realized. They'd been working for Talik. That was why they'd come to the city, so that they could return her to him. Why else would they be here?

When they noticed her, they all stood – even Priest – their eyes moving over her, lingering on her ruined clothes.

She sent them a venomous look as the Bull dropped her to the ground in front of him, but what she saw in their faces confused her. Their countenances ranged from anger to horror to fear.

'Leave her be,' said Fie and the Bull laughed.

'I must thank whichever one of you destroyed her iron bonds,' he said to them. 'Talik has provided me with much better ones. In these,' he kicked at them, making them clank, 'she can hardly move.' He looked down at her. 'This will be much easier without you fighting the inevitable.'

Eve hung her head.

'On your knees.'

She pulled herself up from the dirt floor, kneeling and expecting the blow that would come next. The Bull was nothing if not predictable.

The strike sent her sprawling to the floor again.

'Get up,' he ordered, and she returned to her position in front of him, her body swaying.

She looked past the Bull to the Brothers who were all standing across the room, the pain of their betrayal cutting deep. She'd been foolish enough to think that at least some of their kindnesses had been real, but they'd been using her just like everyone always had.

She blinked back tears, but one tracked its way down her cheek and the Bull laughed at her.

'Crying already?' he taunted. 'Time outside the rings has made you weak, woman.'

He unbuttoned his breeches and she stared down at the floor, knowing what he was going to make her do in front of the Brothers. Maybe they would jeer at her and join in, she thought. Perhaps they'd all take their turn with her.

But then the cellar door creaked opened and Talik called down to the Bull. 'He is coming. I need you upstairs,' he said, sounding panicked. 'NOW!'

The Bull cursed, picked Eve up, and flung her across the room like a child playing roughly with a ragdoll.

She thudded into the crumbling stones of the wall and fell to the floor with a groan, her back and head throbbing.

'If I come back down here and find you've moved, I'll break your arms and legs before you pleasure me,' he grunted, stomping up the stairs and leaving her and the Brothers alone.

She struggled to sit up.

'Eve,' Drax said, trying to come closer, but flinching away from the edge of the stones they stood behind. 'Are you all right?'

She looked at him and the others dispassionately. 'As if you care,' she said dully, looking away.

She was broken and defeated. She watched them from the corner of her eye as they began to fight amongst themselves.

'Look what you've done,' Drax said to Priest. 'Is this what you wanted? Look at her! What do you think he's going to do to her when he comes back?'

He pushed Priest and Priest swore as his back touched the edge of the circle, leaping forwards as if it burned him.

'How did they know how to catch us?' Fie asked.

Because they have experience with fae,' Drax muttered, his eyes back on Eve.

She looked up at him, listening to them but didn't speak. Perhaps she'd been wrong about them. She hoped she was.

'You think they knew what she is all along?'

Drax nodded. 'I think they knew *who she is.*'

'He probably had her brought here,' Priest said. 'Her mother didn't escape to this realm at all.'

'But even a half fae child is precious to our dwindling numbers,' Fie said, frowning. 'Why would he do such a thing? Why would he risk the Council finding out?'

'You know how little he values humans,' Drax answered.

Eve looked at them in question. 'Who are you talking about?' she asked aloud.

All three of them looked at her as if they'd forgotten she was even there.

'Your father,' Drax said.

'But you said it could be any number of fae,' she said to Priest.

He didn't meet her eyes.

'Eve, we've known who your father is since the day we met you, since we first smelled your blood,' Drax said.

'Tell her all of it,' growled Fie.

Eve took a breath. How much more was there? How much had they not told her?

'We knew you'd be able to open portals before you yourself did because your father's family line is known for that particular skill.'

'And you believe he left me here to be raised as human?' she asked.

Drax looked at the others and then at her. 'Eve,' he said gently, 'You father likely gave you to Talik in return for something. Payment for a debt.'

She breathed out slowly, struggling to sit up, wondering how she was going to get out of these bonds before the Bull came back. She was not going to simply sit here and wait for him to return to wreak havoc upon her. She would not be defiled by him anymore. She would no longer be a pawn for a father she'd never met, for Talik, for the Bull, and not for these three men. She meant nothing to them.

Although it hurt, she began to pull at the chain, hoping it wouldn't take much to destroy it. She could feel the iron in the metal now that her fae side was so much stronger, and though it was of a higher grade than her previous bonds, it was nowhere near as pure as Talik seemed to think it was. They underestimated her. She was stronger than she'd ever been before. The metal began to burn her flesh where the links bit into her skin, but she ignored the pain. Worse was in store for her at the hands of the Bull.

The bonds snapped with a clang and her hands came free. Immediately, she began to feel better, at least in body. She stood on shaky legs and hobbled across the cellar.

She was tempted to leave them. She should, but she might need them to escape. And, though she knew she was a fool, she couldn't let them be sold to the Horde.

'How do I free you?' she asked on a sigh.

Priest was one who answered. 'Break the circle,' he said. 'Don't touch it with your hands or you'll be caught as well but move one of the stones and we'll no longer be trapped.'

She nodded, limping to the back of the cellar, searching for something she could use. Upstairs, the door opened, and she heard the Bull's heavy footsteps as he began to come back down.

Frantically, she looked around. There was nothing save some old bricks in a pile. She grabbed one and she threw it as hard as she could at the stones of the circle, pushing one of them just enough for Drax to step through.

He went to her immediately and grabbed her, thrusting her at Fie. 'Keep her safe,' he ordered.

He and Priest hid in the shadows as the Bull descended. She pulled herself from Fie's arms and was glad when he let her go easily. She was not going to let them do this for her and perhaps he understood that she needed to avenge herself. Her strength had already returned enough that she knew she could kill him.

And she would.

As soon as she saw him, she leapt at him, dragging her nails down his face. He bellowed and tried to thrust her away from him, but she locked her legs around him and wouldn't let go. She grabbed his shoulders and butted him in the face with her head. Blood sprayed from his nose, and he screamed for Talik.

She sneered at him. Talik was even more of a coward than he was. He wouldn't come without guards now that there was danger.

She bit the Bull's neck where it met his shoulder. He grabbed her hair, trying to pull her head away, but she held on, ripping his flesh, blood coating her. She spat out a piece of him, grinning at him, and was gratified by his terrified eyes, loving every moment of her revenge.

But she wanted Talik too. Suddenly in a hurry, she took the sides of his head in her hands and squeezed as hard as she could, his body bucking under her, until she heard his skull crack and he fell to the floor, twitching for a moment.

Eve stood over him until he went still, and she was sure he was truly dead.

She spat on his corpse.

'Fuck you,' she whispered and then she looked up to see the three Brother watching with a mixture of approval and pride.

Without a word, she turned and tiptoed up the stairs, going after Talik, but he was already gone.

Huffing, she walked out onto the street, ignoring the looks from passers-by, realizing belatedly that she was covered in the Bull's blood.

The Brothers, who she was half-surprised to discover were following her, covered her with a cloak. They took the lead, guiding her away from the broken-down hovel. Eve wasn't sure what else to do, feeling a numbness settling over her now, so she went with them willingly as they followed the river back up to their fine house.

They went inside and one of them picked her up, taking her to her room and putting her on the bed. She heard them clattering about downstairs.

A bit later, they returned. As she stared listlessly at the ceiling, what was left of her clothes were taken off. She didn't fight as she was gently lowered into a tub of steaming water, hissing at the pain of it on the raw skin of her wrists.

Fie bathed the blood from her while Drax and Priest looked on, their faces blank, their eyes moving over her bruises as more and more were uncovered. It looked like the Bull had beaten her while she'd been unconscious after the fight as well.

When Fie was finished, he lifted her out of the bath and into a waiting blanket in Drax's arms. She was carried back to bed where she stared at the ceiling again, listening to them muttering to each other in soft tones, as if she couldn't hear them.

'What's wrong with her?' Fie asked. 'What does she need?'

It was Priest who answered him. 'Time.'

The men left her alone, closing the door with a soft click.

The numbness was being replaced, she realized, with an overwhelming sadness that she didn't quite understand. She had no one to turn to, nowhere to go, which meant she had to stay here until their guilts were assuaged and they discarded her again. She meant nothing, not to anyone.

~

Fie

FIE CLOSED THE DOOR QUIETLY. Drax thought it best, but he didn't want to leave Eve alone. Though their bond had only been solidified in the past few days, Fie felt bereft without it. Empty. From the look on Drax's face, he felt the same.

His eyes cut to Priest, anger rising up all over again even though his Brother had already been punished and that should be the end of it. That was the Brothers' way. But Fie couldn't forget, nor forgive.

'How could you have done this?' he asked quietly. 'We were meant to be Brothers. But you ... and you as well,' he said, looking at Drax. He shook his head. 'You've both been vying for power in this unit for too long and now it has cost us our strength, severed our bond with our Fourth, and broken our female.'

Fie drew his knife and stabbed it into the polished table in front of him angrily, forever marring its perfect surface.

'Learn how to be Brothers once more and mend our unit,' he said them. 'I am going to do what we should have done and try to comfort our mate. And when you have decided which of you is to be our leader, we are going to bind ourselves to her again. She is ours.'

With that, he stood and left the room, going back to Eve. He opened the door and let himself in. She was laying just as he'd left her on the bed, staring at nothing.

'Eve,' he said, but she didn't even react to his presence, or his words. 'Fourth.' That got an expression of disdain. 'It was not I, nor Drax, who broke the bond,' he said. 'Priest did it in some misguided notion—'

'Because he despises me,' she finished quietly. 'As you all do. You hate my father. I could see it when you spoke of him.' She didn't look at Fie. 'Was all of this somehow to take revenge on him for something?'

He sat on the bed next to her.

'I can't speak for the others, but not for me. Not now.'

He drew her into his arms and frowned when she stayed rigid, trying to keep away from him.

'Enough, female,' he said. 'You are our Fourth. You will be again.'

'What if I don't wish it?' she asked. 'Will you force it upon me like in the Camp?'

Fie flinched, feeling as if an arrow had pierced his chest. 'You are our female,' he said, 'even without the bond, even if you are not our Fourth. You know it in your heart as well as I, as well as Drax, and even that fool Priest.'

She sighed heavily and, to his shock, Eve began to cry broken, heavy sobs. She clung to him, her nails digging into him, and he held her as she let all her sadness and her fear pour from her.

He let everything come forth, knowing that she'd feel better for it though he hated the sound of her sorrow more than anything. Eventually, she fell into an exhausted sleep in his arms.

While he lay with her, Priest and Drax entered, both of them looking chastened.

'Have you decided?' Fie whispered.

'Aye,' said Drax. 'Priest and I should never have been put in a unit together. That was Greygor's fault. We all know he did what he wanted while he was the Dark Army Commander. He didn't listen to the gods. We were never meant to be together, but what's done is done. We can either fracture our unit or we can do what we should have in the beginning.'

Priest stepped forward. 'We give the leadership to you, Brother. Drax and I will ever be at odds if one of us is higher than the other, so you will take command. We will follow your orders.'

Fie's mouth dropped open. He had not foreseen this. He wasn't a leader. 'B–but,' he stuttered. 'But I'm the youngest.'

'It is no matter,' Drax said, 'so long as you're able to take counsel. We will follow you, Brother, in a way we cannot follow each other. This is how it must be if our unit is to survive.'

'And what of Eve?' Fie asked.

Priest sighed, the weariness in his eyes showing them that he felt the emptiness as keenly as Fie and Drax. 'I truly thought the bond had clouded your minds. I sought to keep our unit strong. You must believe I never meant for this.' He looked yearningly at Eve. 'But I see now that it wasn't simply the bond that made us care for her. I can remake it without need for the blood ritual.'

Fie nodded. 'We can't let her escape us now.' He looked at Priest. 'If I'm truly in command, then I order you to do it before she wakes.'

Priest nodded once. Turning, he left the room without another word and Drax approached.

'Are you sure about putting me in command, Brother?' Fie asked.

'If you're sure about having Priest remake the bond. If I know anything about our female, she's going to be very angry when she wakes and it's already been done.'

Fie's lips turned up into the ghost of a smile. 'She'll be in a fury all right, but something about Eve calls to you and I.'

'And to Priest,' Drax muttered.

Fie made a noise of derision. 'Priest can hardly stand to be near her.'

Drax shook his head. 'You're wrong. She's under his skin and he doesn't like it. This female has taken over his thoughts. Have you not seen how he is with her?'

'Aye. Rude, boorish, callous.' Fie listed them on his fingers.

Drax let out a small laugh. 'He has been trying to teach her magick. He has been more patient with her than I've ever seen him be with anyone. He may have terrified her into conjuring, but he hated every moment of her pain.'

Fie shrugged. 'That remains to be seen, but he will treat our Fourth with respect from now on and if he ever does anything like this again, we fracture the unit and kill him.'

'Agreed.' Drax put a hand on Fie's shoulder. 'But all will be well, Brother.'

Fie snorted. 'Have we heard back from the First Scholar?'

'A message was on the table. We go to the Library tomorrow. They believe they have found something.'

Fie leaned back, not wanting to leave Eve alone. She sighed, guileless in her sleep.

'Then let us hope to the gods that whatever it is leads us to our quarry,' he said.

He heard Drax leave the room, and cuddled Eve closer, hoping she wouldn't hate him in the morning when she found out what he'd ordered Priest to do even knowing she didn't want it. She'd be furious, but anything was better than her tears.

He felt a rush of pride when he thought of what she'd done to the Bull. She was a fae warrior through and through.

CHAPTER 11

EVE

Something was different. She could feel it as soon as she opened her eyes. The sun was streaming through the casement. By all accounts it was a fine day and Eve felt ... better than she should. Her body still hurt from the Bull's beatings; her wrists still chafed from the iron.

But her lips turned up into a grim smile as she recalled how she'd killed him. That wasn't the reason for her elation though, which confused her. She thought finally having her revenge would have felt more *momentous*. Talik was still out there, it was true, and her business with him was unfinished. She knew he would turn up again. His pride wouldn't allow him to be bettered by her for long. Perhaps once he was dead as well it would feel like more of an occasion.

Eve sat up, wincing as her back reminded her that the many injuries from yesterday would take more time to heal properly. She was alone in her room, the fire in the grate making the room cozy and warm.

She remembered them coming back here and, vaguely, Fie bathing her. She should be embarrassed but it had felt nice. She couldn't remember the last time someone had taken care of her. Not really.

She saw some clothes folded neatly on a chair and padded across the room towards them, donning a short chemise under a black shirt, fitted breeches and a black fitted tunic. She stared at herself in the looking glass as she plaited her hair and her brow furrowed. Brothers' blacks. Her hand flew to her mouth on a gasp as she understood why she felt the way she did.

She could feel the bond that had been ripped away yesterday strong in her chest, warm and whole. Anger flowing through her veins with an intensity that would see these Brothers dead, Eve wrenched her door open, screaming all of their names as she stomped down to the parlor. All three of them sat there as if there was nothing wrong, Priest drinking one of his expensive wines regally in one of their comfortable chairs. Drax stoking the fire and Fie reading, relaxing in their home as if they hadn't done what they'd done.

Eve practically leapt across the room to Fie and, without hesitation, she slapped him hard across his face.

'I told you I didn't want it,' she barked. 'I told you.'

She felt like crying and cursed herself. If she cried now, they'd see her as weak. They wouldn't understand that these tears were of fury, not sadness. But tears were tears to men like them, so she blinked them back and levelled her livid gaze at him.

Fie was rubbing his jaw. Luckily for him, he was taking her seriously for if she saw one of his smirks …

He stood up, towering over her, but didn't make a move towards her. He was calm and collected. There was something different about him. He exuded an air of confidence that he hadn't had yesterday.

'I ordered Priest to do it,' he said. 'I know you don't want it but it's time you got it into your head. You are ours, female.'

His hand came out to brush against her cheek, and she flinched away.

'I am not yours,' she spat.

He shrugged. 'Well, we are yours.'

Eve took a step back, her eyes widening in surprise at his words. She glanced at the others, expecting to see her own disbelief mirrored in their faces, but it wasn't. Even Priest was nodding.

'Mine?' she asked faintly.

Fie nodded, sitting down again. He surveyed the other two. 'We all agree it.'

She scowled. 'And if I do not?'

'Time will tell,' was all he said, going back to his book and leaving her standing there, her anger having burnt itself out too soon.

Feeling foolish, she grabbed a spiced bun from the table with a huff, not sure what to make of any of this. She thought yesterday that they'd simply jumped at the chance to be rid of her, that they had been in league with Talik. But nothing outside the rings was simple.

'It's time,' Drax said from behind her, donning his thick cloak.

'Where are you going?' she asked.

'*We* go to the Library, Fourth. They've found something they want us to see.'

'They know where the children are?' Eve asked.

'We hope,' Fie said, standing once more.

They left the house and made their way up the wide streets of Kitore's center, Eve in the middle of the Brothers' formation like some cherished possession.

Fie was at the front of their little party, which was new. It had always been Drax before, but he wasn't acting as the leader now. Neither had she heard Drax and Priest arguing the entire morning, vying as they always did for control. Something else had happened since yesterday. Fie had clearly been given the unit.

Eve stifled a snort. She'd have wagered good coin that both Drax and Priest would have fought each other to the death before giving the leadership up to anyone else but it looked as if they had both stepped back.

'I don't understand,' she said quietly.

Next to her, Drax turned his head towards her. 'What is there to understand?'

'None of you even like me,' she muttered. 'Why remake the bond after destroying it? What do you get out of it? Is there something else you need me to do for you?'

Drax didn't answer her, his expression remaining blank.

They arrived in front of an imposing building with wide, shallow steps leading up into a great edifice of white stone columns and intricate carvings.

They ascended, walking past guards who let them into the building without question.

The door banged closed with an echo that reverberated through the entire structure, announcing their presence before any servant could.

Eve's mouth dropped open at the sight before her. Books; mountains of them, stacks and stacks, columns and rows. In the middle of the enormous hall was a great island rising up from the floor, an elaborate stone mezzanine where she could see four figures dressed in black.

Fie didn't hesitate, walking forward through the books as if he knew exactly where he was going. He took them directly to a small set of steps and led them up.

Eve followed, her eyes wide.

At the top of the mezzanine, a woman and three large men sat around a large, round table, all focused on the table in front of them that was covered in documents and books. One of the men stood as they entered.

'You received my message.'

The woman looked up as well. Her gaze wandered over them, assessing them. Eve wondered what she was thinking and was surprised when the woman gave her a genuine smile. She stood then, coming forward.

'You must be Eve,' she said.

Taken aback, Eve gave a nod. 'How do you know me?'

'I had a bird from the Camp; from the Commander's Fourth, Lily. I believe you know her.'

Eve nodded, remembering the kind woman from the Camp when she'd been so afraid.

'I'm Vie,' she said. 'I spent some time in the Camp myself.' Shadows appeared in her eyes. 'Though it was not a pleasant experience.'

The imposing man who'd risen from the desk was immediately by her side, his arm around her waist as he whispered into her ear. He drew back as she relaxed, their eyes locking together for a moment and Eve could practically feel the connection between them. A part of her yearned for the same with her Brothers, but she shook off the feeling.

'Why are we here?' Priest asked from behind them, sounding bored. 'Do you have news, or not?'

Vie nodded. 'I was going through Nixus's papers, and I came across a payment.'

'How does that help us?' Fie asked.

'Because it has nothing to do with Kitore or the Library. It was to a temple high in the mountains. Nixus rarely gave Library funds to god houses unless he was paying for something, and it was a sizeable amount.'

'He could have put the children there for safe keeping,' Fie said and she nodded.

'We know that he killed all the adult females,' she flinched as she said it, 'but there is no record of the children at all, and no one can remember anything. He must have had them taken somewhere and this could well be the place. It's deep in the mountains and high up; practically a defensible keep.'

'It will be a dangerous journey so far into that part of the realm with the portal wards gone,' one of the other men murmured.

'For us, but not so much for our fae Brothers,' another chuckled and Eve shot him a look of surprise.

She hadn't realized this unit knew they were fae.

Vie grinned at her. 'In case you haven't realized, you have full reign of the city now. The wards won't stop you from going anywhere you will, and you can come and go as you please through any of the gates and the port. You will never again be trapped here.'

'Our thanks, witch.'

Yet again Eve's eyes widened as they fell on Vie. Vie was a witch? She'd thought they were only myths and Vie certainly didn't look the way the stories said either. Her long dark hair was beautiful, thick, and shiny with not a hint of grey or white and she couldn't be much older than Eve was. She found that Vie was watching her, a very tiny line between her brows as if she was trying to make out something.

Vie stepped towards her. 'Forgive me. I know we don't know each other, but are you,' she came closer still. 'Are you fae?'

Eve glanced at her Brothers, not sure what to say, but they were all in deep conversations with the First Scholar and the other Brothers and didn't notice her, so she nodded slowly.

'Half,' she muttered.

Vie grinned. 'That explains it.' At Eve's questioning expression, she elaborated. 'There's something different about you. Most wouldn't notice it but ...'

'But you're a witch.' Eve finished for her. 'What else can you tell?'

Vie shrugged. 'Your magick is strong or at least it will be when you learn how to wield it.'

Eve canted her head. 'Can you show me how?'

'I have fae magick, but it comes to me differently than it does to fae conjurers,' she said giving Eve a rueful smile. 'In truth, I don't know the first thing about fae magicks, but that one,' she nodded at Priest, 'he's relatively powerful. Can he not help you?'

Eve flinched, thinking about what Priest did to make her use her power.

'No,' she said, 'he can't.'

She turned away, walking to the edge of the mezzanine, and staring over the Library. 'I had no idea there were so many books here. I suppose you've read them all.'

Vie laughed. 'I haven't even put a dent in them!'

'Forgive me if I was rude,' Eve said, casting a look back at her unit.

Vie gave her a sympathetic look. 'Lily told me you were forced into the unit,' she said low.

Eve nodded jerkily.

'And now?' Vie lowered her voice further. 'I could petition the Commander to break the bond …'

'No,' Eve said. 'I don't … I don't know what I want, but they've made it clear I'm theirs.'

'I find that sometimes Brothers are a bit too used to getting everything their way,' she said, giving Eve a look and Eve snorted.

'Aye, that's true enough.'

She turned to glance at the Brothers, finding that they were saying their goodbyes.

Vie gave her a wink as she walked back to her unit, one of

them casually throwing an arm around her and pulling her to him to cuddle her close.

The Brothers filed out with purpose in their strides, and she followed after them.

'I hope to see you again, Eve,' Vie called as she descended the stairs back to the main Library floor.

They left the way they'd come, briskly walking the short distance back to the house that, despite her better judgement, Eve kept thinking of as a home. Her home. It was an odd feeling for she'd never had one before. She was also beginning to feel more at ease in the casual opulence of her surroundings, more often than not finding peace in the beauty of it.

She caught Priest staring with an indiscernible look on his face and stared back, still angry with him for what he'd done, both the breaking and the remaking of the bond. She made a face at him. It was childish, but it made her feel better.

She got back up to her room and lay on the bed, feeling fatigued.

Someone knocked on her door and she told him to go away.

'Gather your things. We leave before midday,' came Drax's muffled voice from the hall.

Spirits plummeting, Eve got up and packed a spare set of clothes for herself as well as a few trinkets that had appeared in her chamber, including a carved, wooden hairbrush that she loved. She didn't know which of the Brothers had given it to her though. She supposed she should throw it in the fire, not take anything from them except the barest necessities, but then she'd not have a hairbrush and she'd found it invaluable for her long tresses.

A voice in her head said she should give it back anyway along with a firm rebuke to ensure they knew that she had no need of their frivolities, but she couldn't bring herself to. She liked it. It made it easier to plait her hair back, and she enjoyed the feel of it.

She made her way down to the front hall, finding all three ready and awaiting her and, again, she wondered why they'd bound her to them anew. What did they want from her; more portals made?

She looked at Priest, not giving anything away, but her heart began to beat faster as she thought about how he might terrorize her into making her magick manifest for them in future.

She swallowed hard, moving her eyes away from him quickly when he looked at her, her pride not wanting him to know how she dreaded him.

In truth she didn't want to leave now. She wasn't feeling quite right. She felt tired and her back was hurting, she supposed from the Bull's throw. Low down in her tummy throbbed as well. She hoped she healed fully soon.

∼

Priest

HE WISHED he didn't know what she was thinking, that they weren't connected by the bond again, but as Priest glanced at the female from the corner of his eye, he could feel it all. She was angry and afraid of him. Confused. After what he'd done, she should keep her distance from him. He told himself he hoped she would, ruthlessly silencing the tiny voice in the back of his mind that said the opposite. He'd thought that breaking the bond would allow his Brothers' minds to be unclouded. But none of it had gone to plan. Instead, having to rebind her had ensnared him more than ever.

He shook his head. How could one tiny female cause such

havoc? Before they'd met her, they'd had no thoughts of a Fourth, no need for a female in their lives. And now both Drax and Fie were besotted and he wasn't far behind. She consumed his thoughts. Even when he tried to think of something else, he drifted back. He had to stop this.

THEY LEFT the city in haste as soon as they had ensured they had all the supplies needed for their journey now that they had their first real lead as to the whereabouts of the children from the Underhill. After so many months, they were all impatient to find out if what the witch had found in that bastard Nixus's papers would bear fruit. He hoped the gods it did, or he doubted he would ever see his sister again.

They took the road south that would lead to the flat plains and the grasslands. Though this time of year, the lowlands wouldn't be much more than frozen mires with some dead spindles of grass poking out next to pools of ice.

The wind whipped as they rode and even Priest found his teeth chattering.

They got as far as they could, finding an inn before the sun went down and the temperature plummeted further though it hardly mattered in Priest's opinion. They were already well and truly frozen to the bone.

The inn, it turned out, was full so they bedded down in the stables for the night.

Priest found himself too tired to care that there were no creature comforts, that he was laying his head in straw instead of a downy pillow.

Fie had he and Drax see to the horses and sort a meal for them and, although he hid it well, Priest could see that his Brother was subtly enjoying his newfound control. Not too much, but he was clearly remembering all the times those had been his duties under both his and Drax's commands.

But now as Priest saw to the horses and looked into the stall where they'd be bedding for the night, he saw Fie sitting very close to the female, talking to her in soft tones, putting a hand on her shoulder. The woman looked almost shy as she spoke back and even he, with his sharp fae ears, could not hear what they said to each other.

He was curious, having never seen Fie speak very much to any female besides Eve. In the past, his Brother tended to pay for their time, and it wasn't to talk.

Drax came back a few moments later with some bread and meat. They ate heartily and, all of them fatigued from their travels that day, soon bedded down for the night amongst the intermittent noises of their four-legged companions in the other stalls.

The next morning brought with it even colder conditions and Priest was reminded of the ice plains though, granted, he had not spent as much time there as Drax and Fie had. He'd been with Eve in the Dark Realms after all.

Their female sat on her horse, huddled under her ermine cloak; the finest one he could find for her in Kitore before they left. He had ensured that she was well provided for during this journey with sheepskin-lined boots and thick woolen clothes to keep her warm.

He hadn't examined too closely what made him want to take care of a woman who hated the very ground he walked on. Guilt for what had happened, perhaps. How it had been his fault that she'd been caught by the Bull. He gritted his teeth, remembering how the great beast of a man had pushed their tiny female to her knees, beaten her. Priest had never felt so powerless as when he was stuck in that conjuring circle, waiting for their Fourth to be defiled before their eyes and unable to do anything but watch. He was proud of how she had killed her enemy.

He grinned at that memory. He and his Brothers would

gladly have avenged their Fourth for even that one blow he'd dealt her, but, like the true fighter she was, she hadn't needed them to. She'd done it herself. Priest knew he'd remember the sound of the bastard's skull cracking until his dying day. Even the thought of it filled him with satisfaction.

He gazed at Eve, watching her ride. He could see that she was keeping her seat better now, not looking constantly uneasy on her horse's back. He'd also noticed that her cravings for food had calmed down considerably. They'd all been worried at first, but her body was still filling out despite her no longer eating all and sundry. She looked healthier; her skin having taken on the glow typical of a fertile fae female.

Priest averted his eyes, for some reason embarrassed by the realization that their female was now well enough to get with child.

That night they found a cave; one of many now that they were past the wind-swept planes and heading into the mountains. Fie and Drax went together to hunt as Fie had ordered that no one was to go anywhere alone, leaving him and Eve to keep each other company in the small cave.

She regarded him warily as he approached her. He tossed a book on her bedroll.

'Read this,' he said, making an effort not to sound gruff. 'It will at least give you some idea of what your power can do if you learn to control it properly.'

She gazed at the book but made no attempt to pick it up. He frowned at her.

'Is fighting all you want to know? All you want from your life, Fourth?'

She gave him a look, rolling her eyes at him as she picked up the book and opened it.

He turned away, satisfied that she was at least trying to learn. He stoked the fire and busied himself with the normal camp tasks that needed to be done while the others were hopefully securing their dinners. He made a circle of stones around the perimeter of the cave, ensuring it was ready to be cast as soon as the sun was going down. Now that they were back in the mountains, it would become more dangerous again. But when he turned around to observe Eve's progress, he found the woman still on the same page, staring down with a vague expression as if she was daydreaming.

He went over to her again, tapping her lightly on her boot with his own. 'Do you not want to learn how to control your gifts?' he asked, deliberately keeping his tone calm and devoid of anger.

She still flinched and he turned away with a curse. She'd kill her tormentor, a monster she feared and hated, and yet she recoiled from him even when he was trying to help her.

'You're not even trying,' he said, suddenly angry at himself and snatching the book from her. 'Do you think you'll simply be able to conjure without putting the effort in to learn?'

He looked at the open book in his hand and frowned. She'd been trying to read the pages upside down. His eyes narrowed as he looked at her and realization dawned. He was the worst kind of fool.

'Female,' he said gently, he squatted down in front of her.

She didn't meet his eye.

'You can't read, can you?' he asked her.

Knowing that only weeks ago, he'd have made a jest at her expense made it worse. Of course, she'd have tried to keep this from him for as long as possible.

Her cheeks colored, and she deflated, not answering him.

'I could teach you,' he blurted before he could think better of it and she looked suspicious, as if she thought he was tricking her in some way.

She was playing with her fingernails, something he had noticed she did when she was nervous.

He stood up and turned away from her, rubbing his eyes

and wondering what it was about this female that made him act like a charmless boar.

'Perhaps you could read it to me,' she murmured.

He didn't show his surprise, but it was an olive branch if there ever was one.

'Very well,' he said. 'But I'll teach you to read for yourself as well.'

He could tell there was something else on her mind, but she didn't say anything as he sat next to her and began to read from the book slowly, answering her questions when she finally relaxed enough to ask them.

When Fie and Drax returned, it was before the sun had set. They both looked surprised to find Priest and Eve sitting side by side, but neither of them commented as they began to prepare supper.

Eve got to her feet, announcing that she needed to go outside. As per Fie's command, Priest went with her to ensure her safety. She went behind a tree and he stayed a discreet distance away, waiting for her to finish.

A moment later he heard a low cry and raced towards the sound, finding her still sitting on her heels.

She looked up in alarm.

'Don't come any closer.' she cried, her lip trembling. 'Go away!'

His nostrils flared as he scented her blood.

'I said, go away!'

Eve straightened, her tunic covering her down to her thighs. She gave him an angry stare, clutching her belly low, and Priest suddenly understood.

He canted his head, confused by her behavior. This wasn't simply embarrassment; she was genuinely afraid.

'It's just your courses,' he muttered, turning away, intending to go back behind the tree and let her sort herself out, but her low voice behind him made him pause.

'My what?'

He turned back around to see her looking confused.

'Your courses.'

At her blank look, he elaborated. 'Your monthly bleeding.'

Her mouth opened and closed, but she said nothing.

'Wait here,' he said more tersely than he'd meant to, running quickly back into the cave, and cutting up one of their spare blankets with his knife. The other two looked at him curiously as he strode from the cave, a bundle of rags in his hand, to where she still stood.

'Here.' He handed them to her.

She looked at them and then back at him.

'Put them in your small clothes,' he said, 'to catch the … it'll stop you from making a mess.'

Lips still trembling, she did as he said, her cheeks crimson as she pulled up her breeches and fastened her belt.

'Am I dying?' she asked in a quiet voice.

He chuckled at her innocence. 'How is it that you don't know this? You must be, what, twenty winters?'

She shrugged. 'Never happened before.'

He remembered how she'd been starved. 'They kept you too thin and weak,' he said. 'I've heard of such things. They never came, but now that you are hail and strong …'

'This happens to everyone?' she asked.

'Only females,' he informed her. 'Humans and fae alike.'

She took a breath. 'My stomach hurts and my back. I thought it was from … my injuries. Will it go away?'

He approached her and put a hand on her shoulder. 'It will last but a few days at most. Come. Let's get back to camp. The sun is about to set, and we need to be within the confines of the circle before it does.'

She nodded and followed him back into the cave, head down.

Priest said the words and the invisible dome enveloped the cave to keep them safe for the night.

Eve sat back on her bedroll stiffly and lay in a fetal position. He frowned, knowing what would probably help but wondering if she would accept it. He emptied a waterskin into a cooking pot and let it simmer on the fire until it was hot. He then decanted it back, and closed it up securely. It warmed in his hands, the heat of the water seeping through. He held it out to her.

'Here.'

She took it and looked at him in question.

'Put it where it hurts,' he said. 'It'll make you feel better.'

Still looking mortified, she took it from him and lay it on her abdomen, closing her eyes with a sigh of relief.

'How did you know to do that?' she asked.

'I have two older sisters as well as the younger one.'

She opened her eyes and looked up at him.

'Thank you,' she murmured, wrapping herself around the heat of the vessel and falling asleep.

He looked to the fire to find both his Brothers regarding him in something akin to shock. He shrugged.

'Not as if one of you would have had the first notion of what would help,' he muttered before sitting before the flames, not ready to go to sleep just yet.

He looked back at the female, sleeping soundly on her bedroll. He'd misjudged her since the beginning. In truth, he had no idea what her life had been like before them except for what he'd made her tell him about the Bull ... and what he'd seen with his own eyes, of course.

Human females being mistreated was not uncommon in this realm and in the others. It was simply their lot and never had he felt any particular sympathy towards them. But when she had told him of how she had suffered, he had been angry that their Fourth had been treated thus. He'd wished that they had met her sooner so that they could have saved her from the torments that she had endured.

It was clear that her father had orchestrated all of this, though Priest wasn't sure what his game was. Surely there must be one, however, for Gerling was not known to do things in half measures, nor did he typically make rash decisions without having an airtight plan.

He had given his halfling daughter to humans in the Light Realm to be used as they saw fit. That was not normal behavior for a fae, even a ruthless lord like him. The halflings were treasured in the fae lands now. Though many full-bloods might look down on the half-breeds, the Council's law was clear where the children were concerned. Many inherited the magicks of their fae parent's bloodline. They were as important as the scarce, fully fae children and all of them were coddled in the Underhill until they were old enough for full fae mates to be found for them. That Gerling had not given her to the Underhill was a punishable crime and it wasn't the only one he'd committed if only they could find proof that it had been him who had been behind the Underhill's downfall.

He gazed at the flames for a long time, sometimes staring at the female while she slept. She looked pale and fatigued from her courses. One of his sisters had suffered in such a way as well, so Priest could guess at how she was feeling.

He lay down in his bedroll after ensuring that their circle was still strong and he fell asleep, wondering how he was going to teach the female to control her magick before they found the children of the Underhill and she needed to create a bridge to take them to the fae court.

~

Eve

They were riding again, and Eve's back was starting to feel a little bit easier thanks to another hot waterskin that was currently sitting on her tummy under her cloak that Priest had made for her this morning. She didn't know what to make of his kindness. He was nothing like the man who had coerced her into telling him about the Bull only weeks ago ... or was it days?

Time was mashing together, days and nights slipping by, and she no longer knew how long she'd been with the Brothers. The Army Camp seemed so long ago now, a distant memory from another life. It surely could only be a few days since they'd been there but so much had happened since then.

She glanced at Priest again. No. She didn't know what to make of him at all. Perhaps it was a trick. Perhaps he was trying to get her to lower her guard for some nefarious reason, but she didn't care. She decided if that was the price she had to pay for having a hot waterskin to ease the pain of these 'monthly courses', then so be it. He had given her more rags as well and she was grateful he hadn't made any of his typical cutting comments to her about any of it, not even about her not being able to read.

He'd even sat with her more than once since that night and read to her from his book, showing her what the words meant, how to say them, having her repeat them back to him. And although she had no idea still what any of the symbols meant, she was at least starting to recognize them. They weren't as jumbled as they had been before. She was starting to believe that being able to read wasn't an impossible dream, maybe she could do more than fight ... maybe she wasn't too stupid to learn as she had always thought.

She kept her eyes sharp, watching for movement. They were well into the mountains now and she wasn't sure how long it would take to get to the temple where they hoped to find their missing kin, but by the way the Brothers had been talking, it was a treacherous journey at the best of times and fortune wasn't on their side. Besides the Dark Realm creatures roaming the roads, it was the wrong time of year to be heading for the high passes. Even Eve knew that. The Brothers had also mentioned something about secret doors being the only ways in and out of the temple itself, or so the First Scholar had told them.

But if they found the children, any danger they faced would be worth it. The Brothers believed that, and Eve had realized that she did as well. The fae children, and even the halflings, were seen as precious treasures. Eve liked that. It was so far removed from her own youth where lives were cheap and young bodies in the gutter was a daily sight. More than one night before her strength had appeared, she'd thought she'd be among them come morning.

She shook herself from unpleasant thoughts.

There were no inns this far up in the ranges and they camped out under the stars at night where they could, Eve usually sandwiched between Fie and Drax for warmth when it had become apparent that her body became much colder, much more quickly than theirs' did.

They'd been travelling endlessly, the bitter cold seeping into Eve's very being. She wasn't dying from it – at least, she didn't think she was – but it was so, so cold all the time that she was afraid she'd never feel warm again.

That afternoon, they found a spot under the trees where there wasn't as much snow on the ground and set about moving what snow there was, banking it around them and forming a circle, a kind of pit that was slightly sheltered from the whipping winds. This was their routine. Then one of them would make a fire in the middle. Today it was Drax while she and Fie unloaded their supplies and Priest went to hunt alone. He and Fie had had words about this as Fie was adamant that no one should go anywhere by themselves, but, in the end, Priest had murmured something to Fie that had had his eyes flitting to her and, finally, he assented, and Priest had left them.

Priest liked to go off by himself she'd noticed and, since Kitore, though he interacted with her and his Brothers, he and Drax were no longer at each other's throats all the time. They were cold with each other as if there was no love lost between them, but no more altercations. There was a stillness around them when they were together, much like there was in these mountains, and Eve wondered if they would mend whatever rift still lay between them.

As soon as Priest was gone, Fie and Drax practically pounced on her, sandwiching her between them and making her sit with them by the fire. They said it was important to stay very close in this colder weather and she found herself grinning at their ploy. She knew they simply wanted to be close to her. They'd both become more tactile; innocuous touches, helping her with her clothes when her fingers were numb, or rubbing her extremities if she complained she was cold. She secretly liked their hands on her. Something inside of her was telling her that she wanted, nay needed, to be as close to them as possible, and when she was, she felt warm and whole for the first time in her life. Was this what happiness felt like?

Eve wasn't quite sure she understood any of it. Perhaps it was a trick of the bond.

Fie's arm draped around her shoulders carelessly while Drax's fingers made lazy circles on her thigh. Neither of them seemed to realize what they were doing and neither of them touched her any further.

'Are you feeling all right, Eve?' Drax asked.

She nodded, giving a small sigh between them.

He frowned slightly, his nostrils flaring.

'Are you still bleeding?' he asked.

She wrinkled her nose at him, bothered that they could smell such a thing.

'Does it still pain you?' Fie asked and she shook her head.

The blood had mostly stopped so the rags still had some rust-colored stains, but that was all. Priest had told her that it wouldn't last more than a few days, so she hoped it would be finished by the morrow.

'Priest said you'd never had one before,' Fie fished and she frowned.

They talked about her with each other? Why were they so interested?

'No,' she murmured, cheeks coloring. 'Priest said it was because my body was too thin.'

Fie nodded. 'I've heard of this regarding slaves in the Dark Realms,' he said. 'That's one of the reasons the breeding slaves are always fed well.'

Fie glanced at her expression and coughed. 'Apologies. I forgot you're ...' He trailed off.

'A half-breed?' she asked, looking away towards the fire.

An awkward silence descended, and Eve glanced at them both.

'Are human and fae pairings frequent in the Dark Realms?' she asked, wondering if there were many like her.

'More so now because of the fae's dwindling numbers,' Drax said, 'but—'

Fie nudged him and he quieted.

Eve frowned at Fie. 'Don't keep things from me. I'm not an infant who needs coddling.' Turning back to Drax, she nudged him. 'What were you going to say?' she insisted.

Drax grimaced. 'The most attractive human slaves are usually bought by the wealthiest fae for the purposes of breeding regardless of the laws. The auctions are simply held in non-fae dark realms.'

'You mean women are made to …'

'And men,' Fie interjected. 'Remember, the fae are able to enthrall humans to do what they will. The slaves aren't *made* to do anything. At least, not in the way you're picturing they are.'

She couldn't help her shudder. Fie was too perceptive by half. She *had* been thinking about her own experiences with the Bull, but his words made her think of the time with him in the Underhill when she had been enchanted by the pink dust. He was right. It wasn't the *same*, but to be taken from your home and family to a fae realm, enthralled and *bred* …

'There must be another way,' she muttered.

Fie and Drax both looked sympathetic.

'If there is, I hope we find it,' Drax said, 'But until then, with many full-blooded fae unable to have children of their own, humans will continue to be taken for the purpose.'

'Do you have slaves?' Eve asked, wondering if the Brothers owned enthralled humans and hoping to the gods they didn't.

'No,' Fie said. 'Most fae who own slaves are wealthy, same as it is in the Light Realm. My family were humble faire folk as I told you before.'

She looked at Drax who grimaced.

'No,' he said. 'My father may have, but he died when I was very small. I lived in the Underhill until I was fifteen. I joined the Brothers as soon as I left.'

Eve canted her head, sensing a sadness in him. 'Where is your mother?'

A look she couldn't discern passed between them and Fie quietly busied himself with the feeding the fire. 'When I was a small child, she was stolen by a wealthy fae lord.'

'What?' Eve asked in shock, drawing closer to him.

'At the time, the birthing rates were starting to decrease,

and no one knew why. A fae female who'd already successfully birthed a babe was coveted to beget more.'

Drax looked into the fire. 'My mother loved my father and, when he died, she refused to marry again. The fae male wouldn't take no for an answer. He took her and kept her.'

Eve put her hand on his arm, feeling his sadness. 'What happened to her?'

'He treated her badly, punished her when he couldn't breed her. She finally got with child, but she didn't survive the birth and both she and the babe died.'

'I'm sorry,' she breathed.

'It was a long time ago,' he said, clearing his throat. 'I didn't find out until much later, after I'd left the Underhill.'

Eve reached up and put an arm around him as Priest returned, carrying a small deer with short legs and little tusks protruding upwards from its jaw.

He set it down on the ground with a thump and his gaze lingered on where his Brother touched her, but he didn't say anything as he began to prepare the meat. He cut it with a skill that spoke of many nights traveling out on the roads, and it wasn't long before her mouth was watering at the mere smell of it as it cooked.

It was late when supper was finally ready, and Eve moaned as she bit into it while the Brothers looked amused.

'I like meat,' she said defensively and Drax chuckled.

'Aye,' he said. 'All fae love meat. It sustains us better than anything else. It's a staple of our daily lives. Without it we would be—'

'Weak?' she asked.

All three Brothers frowned, looking uncomfortable; obviously not wanting to draw attention to her years of starvation.

'It's all right. We can speak of it,' she said. 'The Bull is dead. That time is finished.'

She couldn't help her grin as she said it, still feeling as much satisfaction now as she had in the moment she had killed him.

'What happens after we find the children?' she asked. 'What happens then?'

The three of them looked at each other.

'Then nothing,' Fie said. 'We have fulfilled our mission. We get our money.'

'I meant ...' Eve halted, frowned, and sat up straighter as she took in Fie's reply. 'You're trying to find the children *for coin?*'

They all chuckled.

'We're still Dark Brothers,' Drax said. 'We have stake in finding them of course, but the three of us are also in the best position to do so as we have more ties in this realm than most others.'

'Who is paying you?' she asked

'The fae Council.'

Eve's brow furrowed. 'What if they hadn't been able to pay you?' she wondered aloud.

'We still would have done it,' Fie said, looking as if he couldn't help his smile. 'We aren't cruel. They're still our kin, but the fae Council would never not pay for something. It's not the way of our kind. Everything has its price. To do something for free would be remarked upon, thought less of.'

She nodded slowly, not really understanding him. 'Why did you—' she stopped, wondering if they would answer, wondering if she wanted them to.

'Go on,' Drax said.

All of them were looking at her and she bit her lip as she stared at them.

'You want to know why we brought you with us from Kitore when you'd already fulfilled your purpose. You want to know why we reneged on our bargain.'

She nodded slowly. 'When you broke the bond …'

Eve didn't look at Priest when she spoke, flinching as she remembered the pain of it being ripped away.

'Why did you bother to remake it?' she asked.

Fie and Drax opened their mouths, but it was Priest who spoke.

'You are our Fourth … more than our Fourth,' he said. 'I shouldn't have broken the bond and I'm sorry for it.' He looked uncomfortable. 'I'm sorry for everything you suffered because of what I've done.'

Eve knew he wasn't just talking about Kitore. He must feel her surprise. She'd never thought he'd be one to apologize for anything.

Drax moved closer to her. 'It isn't just the bond that we feel. Fae aren't the same as humans. We have those we are destined to be with. Fated mates, Eve. When we find the other part of ourselves, we know it.'

Eve's eyes widened. 'Fated mates? You don't think I'm …'

'Yes,' Drax replied, putting his hand back on her thigh. 'Fie and I knew it as soon as the bond was remade. You are ours and we are yours. There's no escaping it.'

She wasn't sure what to say. She'd never considered being with one man, let alone two fae males.

'And you?' she asked Priest.

Priest snorted. 'I don't believe in fated mates,' he muttered, towering over their trio, and then snorting derisively as he went to his bedroll and lay upon it.

She rolled her eyes at him. There was the Priest she knew. Cold, mocking, caring for no one but himself. She sighed as she leaned into Fie, wanting to believe what they were saying was true; was possible. She didn't say out loud that she had her doubts. Perhaps they wanted it to be so, but she was simply a half-blood stray whose father hadn't wanted her. She wasn't special.

That night, she slept between Fie and Drax as usual. They continued to say it was simply to keep her warm. But regardless of their reasons, she had never slept so peacefully as she did when they were lying next to her with their arms draped over her.

In the morning, Eve felt more herself. The bloods had stopped, and she was not so fatigued. The day brought with it a storm, however. Snow blew into their faces as they tried to navigate the high paths and, more than once, they ventured too close to the cliff edges because they couldn't see much more than a hair's breadth in front of them. Only part of the day had gone by before they decided it was too dangerous to continue on already treacherous paths until the blizzard had abated.

They found a rocky outcropping nearby that afforded them at least some shelter, staking a tent into the rocks to improvise a better refuge from the cold and wind when they noticed that Eve's lips were turning blue.

Drax and Fie made a fire under the awning, cooking meat from the deer that Priest had slain.

Priest sat with her, reading to her from the book and showing her some more of the symbols. She still had a long way to go before she could actually read the words, but she was beginning to understand, she thought.

She heard someone cough and looked up to find Fie standing over them. He gave Priest a look, jerking his head to the side. Priest looked surprised, but he closed the book and stood, moving away to the entrance of the small tent they'd created. Fie took his place on her right and Drax appeared at her left. Her head swung from one to the other, her belly fluttering as they stared at her.

Neither of them said a word as Fie untied the thick cloak, letting it fall from her shoulders to the rocks where she sat. He unbuttoned her tunic, opening it.

She finally found her voice. 'What are you—'

Drax hushed her, his very warm hands cupping her cold cheeks.

'But—' She looked at Priest who still stood close by.

'Don't worry about him,' Fie said. 'Let him watch if he likes.'

Her eyes widened, but when she looked for him again, he was gone.

Fie removed her tunic and Eve found that she was already anticipating their touches. She desperately wanted something that she didn't understand, but knew it was only them who could provide this phantom thing. Her heart was racing, and her body shook, not just from the cold.

'Is this the bond?' she whispered.

Drax shook his head. 'No. What you feel is your fae side. We are driven by a yearning for our true mates. You're finally awakening to it.'

Fie bared her breasts to them, touching them gently, her nipples hardening in the cold. She shivered and Drax pulled her billowing cloak over them, he and Fie crowding closer to her to warm her with their bodies.

Fie began to kiss her neck and her eyes closed on a sigh as his hands drifted into her hair, pulling her head to the side as he licked and bit and sucked gently. She felt a hand slide into her breeches, cupping her most intimate place and she started but Fie was there, whispering in her ear to calm her.

Her breeches were undone, giving Drax access to her, his fingers moving through the folds between her legs. He found the bud of her pleasure and pinched it. Eve arched up with a moan and they both chuckled.

'Do you like that female?' Drax murmured.

She nodded.

Her trousers were pulled down her legs and her boots removed, and she found herself pressed into a bed roll, warmed by both Fie and Drax's bodies as they toyed with hers. They made her writhe and moan as their fingers touched every sensitive part of her, played her like an instrument.

∼

Drax

DRAX HELD their thrashing female for Fie, ensuring she was warm, protecting her from the worst of the elements while Fie slid himself into her hot, wet heat. He was the leader now. He could take her first. It was his right and, although Drax felt a small pang of jealousy, he knew that they'd made the right decision by giving him command of the unit. Things between him and Priest had changed. No longer were they at each other's throats. Their Brother still didn't treat Eve as his mate, but his attitude towards her was slowly changing.

Drax chuckled, for what they were doing with Eve was as much a punishment to Priest as the beating they'd given him in Kitore. His Brother might not want to admit that he wanted her as well, but they knew that he did. It was only a matter of time before he succumbed. At the moment, he was nowhere to be seen and Drax snorted. No doubt he was close enough to hear their female though.

Fie pulled out slowly and thrust in again hard, making her moan under him, her back arching.

'You love this, don't you, female?' he whispered in her ear, holding her down tighter and feeling the surge of her excitement.

Their female liked rough games but only with them. Her mates.

Fie set a slow pace purposely so that she would not reach

her peak too soon. She wriggled under him in frustration, wanting more but still not yet understanding quite what it was that she yearned for.

'Would you like my cock as well, female?' Drax whispered.

Her eyes darted to his, slightly wary but also incredibly aroused at the prospect. He loved being able to feel her this way thanks to the bond they shared.

He pulled his already hard staff from his breeches and Fie grinned, pulling out and pushing into her hard, making her squeal.

Drax pumped his cock in his hand, watching their female's tits bounce as Fie rutted her. Her eyes were on his. They flicked down to where he fisted himself and back up to his face. He gave her a look of challenge, and her eyes narrowed slightly as she opened her mouth.

Unable to pretend patience, he surged forward, and she began to lick him, sucking on the end of his hard rod, making him grit his teeth, his eyes rolling back in pleasure at how hot and wet her little mouth was. He pushed into her, and she took as much of him as she could, pulling back when it was too much, and she gagged on his length. Drax let her set her own pace, at least until she got used to the size of him. Her tongue swirled around him, and she suckled, moving him in and out, using her hand at the base of him. It didn't take long for his coiled body to finally release, grunting as he filled her mouth with his seed.

Eve hadn't yet found her pleasure. Fie spread her legs and her nether lips wider so that they could both see all of her. Bending down, Drax began to lick her. With a cry, she gripped onto him, her fingers digging into his hair as he reciprocated what she had just done for him, laving at her, sucking on her, blowing cool air onto her. She came suddenly, violently, her body bowing as she screamed inaudible words into the air.

Fie ground out a curse as her body clamped down around his cock, getting one final thrust in before throwing his head back with a howl.

All three of them collapsed onto the small bedroll together breathing heavily, Eve's body shuddering not with cold now, but with aftereffects of pleasure. They redressed her quickly, for sadly it was much too cold to keep her bare. They put their bedrolls together to keep her warm though neither of them felt the cold as she did.

'Did you enjoy that?' Fie asked.

When she nodded timidly, Drax decided that the next time he wouldn't be letting Fie go first regardless of whether or not he was the leader. Drax would claim that tight, wet pussy for himself.

She sighed between them, and they cuddled her closer, watching as her eyes began to close and she dozed in the center of them.

Fie gave a low chuckle. 'Looks like we tired her out. Do you think Priest heard?'

Drax grinned in response. 'Aye. It won't be long before he claims her properly as well.'

Fie frowned. 'She doesn't like him.'

'She fears him,' Drax whispered, 'because of what he must do to make her conjure. He fears her because of how he feels when he must make her conjure.'

'But surely that's all finished now. We don't need—'

'Don't we?' Drax interrupted, giving Fie a look. 'If we find the children up at this fucking temple, do you think we'll be leading them from the mounts on foot in all this?' He gestured to the door of their makeshift tent and to the storm beyond, his lips forming a grim line. 'It shouldn't have been done that way. I should have stopped him at the very beginning... but I thought it would be worth it.'

'Wasn't it? We got to the Underhill.'

'Look at the shadows in our female's eyes, Brother, and you tell me.' Drax shook his head. 'And then Priest decided to break the bond when she was at her most vulnerable. It will take time for her to trust him, just as it did for her to trust me after the Camp.' He caught Fie's eye. 'We've all hurt her. In truth, you and I are no different from Priest. Gods only know how we came by our true mate. None of us deserve her.'

Fie looked down at Eve. 'We treat her as our Fourth and as our mate now. What if Priest continues not to?'

Drax followed Fie's gaze to their sleeping female. 'Then we find a new unit member as we discussed in Kitore.'

Fie's eyes widened for a moment, looking like the younger fae male that he was. Then, he seemed to remember that he was in command here and his gaze hardened.

'We do what we must to ensure our mate is safe.' He frowned. 'What will happen if ... if she becomes with child.'

'We will have to keep it from the Council,' Drax murmured very, very quietly. Speaking treason against the Council was dangerous no matter what realm you were in. 'We cannot allow her to be taken from us. We can keep her safe better than anyone else. We've seen that from the Underhill.'

Fie nodded. 'We make sure Priest knows as well.'

'Aye.'

Drax lay back, listening to the wind howling. The storm was finally starting to abate, but it was getting dark so there was no point in carrying on now. He and Fie stayed with Eve, Priest returning in the night to sleep in the warmth.

When they woke the next morning, it was silent with a calm stillness that new snow always brought. The wind had died down to nothing and they packed up the camp. They carried on with the journey, taking the narrow passes slowly though at least the new snows gave them traction on the ice-covered stones of the paths they traversed, making them marginally safer.

It was high noon before Priest pointed up at the next peak. There, nestled in the rock, was the carved edifice of the ancient temple they were searching for. They'd have to make their way down and through the valley below, which they couldn't see because it was beneath the misty clouds that circled the peaks.

Come, let's find a way down,' Fie said, leading the way with Priest following.

Drax glanced at Eve who was behind him. She was quiet. She usually was, but today he felt a confusion in her that he hadn't before.

'What's wrong?' he murmured. 'You're unsettled.'

She looked at him in surprise. 'I keep forgetting you can do that.'

'Do what?' he asked.

'Know my thoughts.'

He grinned. 'It's not your mind I know. It's your heart.'

She snorted. 'That's even worse. Why can I not feel yours in the same way?'

Drax shrugged. 'Perhaps you can, you simply don't know how to sense it. It is part of a fae bond for all parties to know each other so intimately so, I ask you again, female, what is it that's upsetting you?'

She glanced at him and then at Fie.

'Nothing,' she said.

Drax leaned back on his horse. 'Is it because you enjoyed what we did yesterday together?'

She looked away and he knew that he'd hit the nail on the head. 'I never did anything like that before you,' she murmured. 'The night I met you … when you all came into my room, I was afraid Jays would give me to you all. I thought it would be … I didn't think I'd ever enjoy it with *one* man, much less with more than that.'

'We are not like the human men you have known.' Drax took her hand and was glad when she didn't pull it away immediately. 'I know that in the beginning we were not kind to you.'

He grimaced. It was time to speak of something he didn't want to, but this conversation was necessary.

'At the Camp, when I … when I bound you and claimed you, I know that—'

Eve put a hand up to stay his words. 'Camp laws are Camp laws. I know what would have happened to me had you not done it. It was the lesser of two evils.'

'You are our Fourth and our mate. You will never again be treated as anything less,' he promised her, 'and anyone who tries will die, either by your hand or ours.'

She looked out over the cliffs. 'When will we arrive at the temple?' she asked, changing the subject.

'By tomorrow I'd say.' He hesitated. 'There's something I should warn you about. I'm guessing Priest hasn't told you.'

'Told me what? What is it?'

He could feel her disquiet and cursed himself, but she should know what was coming. It was wrong to keep her ignorant.

'Are you yet able to reach your magick?'

Eve shook her head. 'Not by myself.'

'Almost a hundred and seventy children under fourteen went missing from the Underhill.'

Her eyes widened. 'So many?'

'Those children are the only fae children. Do you understand? All of them. We told you we're a dying race.'

'Why is that?' Eve asked.

'No one knows,' Drax replied. 'Finer minds than mine have been put to the task. But no one's been able to make heads or tails of it. All we know is that far fewer babes are being conceived in families and far fewer fae females are being born. That was why we were surprised when we found you. The fae Council doesn't know of your existence or you'd never have been left here. You would have been taken to the Underhill.'

'Even being half human?' she asked.

'Aye, even halflings are important to us now.' He grimaced. 'Not that you're not … that humans aren't … I mean?'

She gave a small laugh, surprising him.

'It's all right. I understand. It's far easier for humans to increase their numbers.'

Drax nodded. 'Do you understand what I'm trying to tell you?'

She stopped her horse. 'Speak plainly.'

He drew his horse up beside hers. 'If they're in that temple, we can't very well take them down those passes, Eve.'

He felt her become anxious.

'I'll need to make a portal,' she said faintly.

She said nothing more, urging her horse onward.

They caught up to the others who were waiting for them to begin the descent into the valley below where, with some luck, they'd find an entrance to the temple.

Drax prayed to the gods that the fae children were there or else they were at a dead end once more, but a part of him also hoped they didn't find them here. He didn't want to watch Priest's methods of making Eve conjure. Terrifying her with her past did more harm than good.

Running a hand over the frosty hair growth on his face, Drax sighed. Perhaps he shouldn't have told her that they might need her to make a bridge. She was already worried.

They began the steep decline into the hidden valley below, not sure what they'd find, but hoping this mission would soon be over.

∼

Priest

As they journeyed down past the clouds, they realized that the valley was full of thermal vents coming up from deep in the rock. Heat blasted from the earth, making the surrounding air as warm as summer. There was no snow at all. Plants grew where there should have been none, green and lush and rivalling even the Underhill. Priest had never seen such a place and, as they descended, it became so warm and humid that they had to take off their ermine lined cloaks, even their tunics.

The female was down to her chemise and Priest couldn't take his eyes off of her shapely curves. Being part fae had its perks. She'd filled out quickly now that she was being given proper meals. He stifled a groan as he thought about the night before in the storm. The sounds she'd made with Fie and Drax had made him want so badly to join them. He'd had to leave the tent or risk just that and he wasn't ready to share her with them. Not yet.

He didn't know when things had changed. But they had. He wanted her. He could admit that to himself. He'd wanted her since their time in the Dark Realm together. He might have needed to seal their bond, but it had hardly been a chore. She should hate him for what he'd done, but she didn't. He could feel how she was when she was around him.

It would take some time to navigate their way through the valley and reach the next mountain. He couldn't wait. He loosened his shirt, his body uncoiling as that fae part of him took over and he smiled in anticipation, knowing how he would do it.

'We should stop and rest,' Priest said, hoping his Brothers wouldn't sense his ulterior motives.

There was a pool of clear water close by. It appeared untainted by whatever the vents were spewing out that smelled vaguely of brimstone. Eve got off her horse and Priest announced that he was going to hunt. He looked at her.

'Why not come with me?' he asked.

She hesitated just as he'd known she would for she was very wary of him still and he couldn't say that he blamed her. A tiny voice said that it would be easier if he enthralled her, that he could make her forget it afterwards. But he disregarded that wayward thought as soon as he had it, disgusted with himself. He would have their Fourth properly. He wanted to have her begging for it, needing him as he needed her.

She walked with him out into the forest.

'How do we do it?' she asked, and he grinned at her question.

She really thought they were out here to hunt for game, she didn't realize yet that he would be hunting her.

'There's a fae custom,' he said smoothly, letting his glamor recede from him.

'A fae custom?' she echoed, her guileless eyes finding his as he looked her up and down.

She turned away from him, not understanding where his thoughts were going, but not before she noticed his appearance had changed and her heart began to beat faster. He felt something else from her as well and it wasn't fear. Their mate liked what she saw.

'Aye,' he said, emboldened by her reaction. 'It's a hunt, a chase of sorts, but you are the prey.'

Her eyes snapped back to him, a trace of fear in her eyes, but something else as well.

'Prey?' she asked.

'Aye,' he said again. 'Let's play a game. If you can make it back to the others without me catching you, you're safe.'

'And if I don't?' Her voice wavered.

He looked her up and down again, cocking a brow and licking his bottom lip.

She looked shocked, their little Fourth, and he couldn't help but imagine her on the forest floor beneath him, squealing in pleasure as he rammed himself into her.

'I'll give you a head start,' he said, closing his eyes.

She stayed on the path, frozen in front of him.

'Run little halfling. Time's running out.'

She let out a breath and then he heard her turn tail and run like a rabbit through the brush. He grinned to himself. He'd give her a small head start, but they'd been walking in circles. She had no idea which direction the camp was in, and he was counting on it.

He walked after her at an unhurried pace, knowing that he would be able to track her easily, and that she would tire long before he did with her shorter stride and her panicked gait.

'Run, run, run, little rabbit.' he called, and his superior ears picked up the sound of her gasp.

He veered off to the left, silently stalking through the forest. He could smell her. She was close. She was hiding. His nostrils flared, as he smelled her arousal as well as her body's scent. Even if he hadn't been able to smell her bloodline, there was no doubt what Eve was now. A fae female would practically be a puddle after a chase with her *mate* as well.

Priest was shocked at his thoughts, but not surprised. He hadn't been lying when he'd announced that he didn't believe in fated mates, but gods knew he'd never met another female like her.

What were the odds? As a Brother, to have a Fourth was rare enough, but to have one that was also a fae mate, not just to him, but the rest of the unit as well ... He'd never even heard of such a thing happening before.

He leapt at a bush but found her already gone. Chuckling to himself, he continued through the undergrowth, sniffing the air. She was so close. He threw a stone into the thicket ahead and darted around a tree, coming up behind her as she was peering in the other direction.

He grabbed her with a laugh, and she screamed as he turned her, pushing her back into the tree trunk, smashing his lips into hers and cutting off her cry. He didn't waste any time, pushing her to the mossy ground, straddling her and holding her wrists above her head. She struggled, of course, not one to go down without a fight.

'Let me go,' she cried as he ground his pelvis into hers.

'A deal's a deal with a fae,' he whispered in her ear, licking a trail down to her collarbone. He could sense a tiny bit of fear, but it was nothing compared to her other feelings coming from her. She was as ready for this as he was.

He ripped off her chemise and used it to bind her wrists. He placed them on the ground above her head, but he didn't restrain her with the bond. He didn't want her afraid, after all.

'Be a good girl and leave them there.'

Her body trembled at his words as his hands moved down to cup her breasts, playing with her nipples until they were hard, but she didn't move her arms. In the humid air, he kissed her navel, dragging his long, elongated canines down the sensitive flesh of her abdomen as he unbuckled her belt and pulled down her breeches.

She stretched out under him with a whimper, and he

smiled against her skin, stilling for a moment, and basking in the feel of her, the smell of her. His nostrils flared and he scented it. Under the heady sweetness of her arousal was the undeniable scent of ... something he'd never experienced before. Their female was ripe for breeding.

Letting out an animalistic growl, he flipped her over to her front, dragging her to her hands and knees.

Taking her plait, he hauled her up against his chest as he felt how ready she was between her thighs.

'You're mine, female,' he breathed into her ear and gave a dark chuckle as her wetness coated his fingers at his words.

She arched back, her body pulsating, and she moaned into his neck.

'You want this don't you female,' he muttered. 'You need me to fill your tight cunt with my seed. Your body yearns to be bred as it yearns for the very air you breathe.'

He thought he heard her say 'yes', but then she bit her lip, clamping her mouth shut. Priest grinned at his mulish female, shuddering with the strain of taking this more slowly than his fae side wanted.

'I'll get it out of you yet,' he promised as he took out his hard length.

No longer able to hold back, he pushed her head down to the ground so that her arse was in the air, and he slid himself smoothly and deeply into her, reveling in her cry of pleasure.

She was so tight, he almost spent himself there and then but resisted, gripping her hips, and pulling back only to thrust in harder, propelling her forwards. He played with the pucker of her arse as he moved, taking moisture from her other channel, and easing his thumb into her as well. She reared up with a shocked cry, trying to twist around, but he had her pinned with his other hand on the back of her neck.

He grinned. He knew that neither of his Brothers had had

the chance to play with her here yet. He would be the first of them, he vowed.

He leant forward, sensing her increasing unease, and needing to sooth her.

'Don't worry, Eve,' he said. 'I'll not fuck you here until you beg me to.'

He moved his thumb inside her, wiggled it and felt her clench around him.

'Mmmm. And you will soon, I think.'

Keeping hold of her, Priest began to fuck their female as he'd wanted to for so long, unable to fathom why he'd waited.

She was making noises under him, whimpers and moans, mewls and sharp cries as he wrung sensations from her the likes of which she'd only felt at the hands of his Brothers. She clawed at the ground, making marks in the moss with her bound hands.

'Don't worry,' he whispered in her ear. 'I'll give you everything you need, and more.'

He sent a pulse of magick through her that made her tense under him, and she gasped, her eyes flying open to lock onto his.

'I thought you'd enjoy that,' he murmured, doing it again and enjoying her cries of pleasure as his magick worked her into a frenzy as well as the rest of him was.

He set a pace that made the center of her pleasure vibrate frantically as he pressed his finger over it.

She began to make even more noise, moaning and crying out with each thrust of his cock, her body squirming and shaking as if it didn't know what to do, how to comprehend the pleasure that he was giving her until, finally, her entire being tensed and she screamed his name into the air.

He finally let himself go, his seed spilling deep into her fertile womb, the enjoyment and satisfaction running through him incomparable to anything before it. He gripped her hips and allowed himself to feel the sensations that rolled through him with the force of an avalanche, finally pulling himself from her and collapsing on the ground, breathing hard.

He opened his eyes to find her face next to his, staring at him with unfocused eyes and he couldn't help the grin that alighted his face at the sight of his very well-pleasured female, knowing that there was a very high probability that she would find herself with child after this.

He wondered how she'd take the news.

~

Fie

Priest and Eve returned from the hunt and Priest, somewhat smugly, informed them that it had been fruitless. Fie rolled his eyes. As if he and Drax hadn't heard their Fourth's cries, felt her emotions, as if they didn't notice her lack of eye contact, flushed cheeks and the faint, lingering scent of sex in the air.

He and Drax shared a look, but they didn't say a word. They were glad that Priest was finally warming to Eve though Fie was surprised that their Brother had shared something so intimate as a chase with her. That particular ritual was reserved for mates only and Priest had scoffed at the word only yesterday.

They began the ride through the valley in the direction they had caught sight of the temple, high in the cliffs.

'There must be an entrance somewhere at the base of the mountain,' Fie said absently, looking at the clouds that whirled above.

Drax nodded. 'Undoubtedly. We just need to find it.'

Fie frowned as he looked at Eve. When she and Priest had first come back from their *romp*, she'd been sated and relaxed, though a little bit embarrassed, but now trepidation and nervousness was coming off her in waves as they got closer and closer to their destination.

'What's wrong with Eve?' he asked Drax quietly so she wouldn't hear him, trying not to snarl at his Brother.

Fie didn't like it when their female was distressed. The bond between them was clearly becoming stronger as her fae side asserted itself.

'I told her the truth,' Drax said. 'She's no quivering waif. She would rather know what might have to be done.'

Fie let out a breath. 'You shouldn't have said anything until we know more.'

'Our female is a Fourth, not a subordinate,' Drax countered. 'We should always ensure she knows as much as we do.'

'Very well,' Fie conceded. 'Let's get this over with and gods help us if the children aren't there.'

All of them looking grim, they made their way through the densely packed forest. The trees up here were the largest Fie had ever seen and it made little sense as no sunshine seemed to filter through the cloud bank that whirled slowly above.

They reached the base of the cliff and looked up at the sheer face that rose up in front of them.

'What might this door look like?' Eve asked, peering at the dull, grey rock in front of them.

Priest shrugged. 'It won't be easily seen, but there will be one down here.'

'How can you be so sure?' she asked.

'Because this temple mirrors others that exist in the Dark Realms,' Priest said. 'There will be a door here somewhere.'

'Fan out,' Fie ordered, 'but make sure you can see the others.'

Fie dismounted, leading his horse towards the crag, keeping his eyes sharp and using his hands to feel for anything in the unnatural surface. The rock was unmarred, its surface solid and smooth as glass though it held no reflection.

'This is magick.'

Priest nodded. 'Dark Realm.'

'Are you certain?'

Priest nodded. 'The scent is faint, very old, but it's definitely Dark Realm.

Priest turned to Eve 'Magick sometimes has a scent about it,' he said. 'Can you smell it?'

She took a sniff. 'Like copper.'

Priest nodded, looking pleased.

'It's stronger here,' he said, walking the line where the cliff rose from the ground and hovering his hands over it.

They heard a clank and the sound of something dragging and even Priest jumped back.

'What the fuck did you do?' Drax snarled.

'Nothing!' Priest said. 'I didn't even touch it.'

A section of rock in front of them began to move, sliding away seamlessly to form a dark hole. The door. Stairs led upwards into pitch black, dust covering them and the empty webs of long dead spiders hung down.

'Come,' Priest said.

He whispered a word and an orb of light appeared in his palm.

Fie was surprised. Priest didn't usually expend the energy for mundane conjures when there were other ways. He was in a hurry, already entering the mountain, moving slowly up the stairs.

'Wait. What about the horses?' Eve asked, giving her mount a friendly stroke on his velvety nose.

'We'll have to come back for them in the spring,' Drax said. 'I doubt they'll venture up into the colder passes with all the greenery down here to eat. We'll leave them with our amulets and they'll be safe enough until we return.'

They took the supplies they needed from the horses' backs, leaving everything they didn't by the base of the cliff. The saddles and bridles they stowed in the alcove there the steps began so that they'd be able to find them when they were able to return.

After quickly plaiting their amulets into their manes, they left the horses to roam free and followed after Priest up steps as smooth as the stone of the cliff outside. Each one looked as square as the day it was carved although that must be a very long time ago. The staircase wound upwards as far as they could see in the dim light and long before they reached the top, even Fie was beginning to feel fatigued by the climb.

But finally, they ended, opening out into a small landing. At the end was a closed door.

Fie handed Eve a dagger.

'Take it,' he said.

She grabbed the hilt with a nod of thanks, holding it at her side and hiding it in the folds of her cloak.

He drew his own short sword and heard the others do the same.

Drax approached the door and tried the latch.

He shook his head and Fie stepped forward, putting away his sword and getting out his case of lock picks. Grateful for his youth in the family business, he made short work of the door, opening it gently, peering out into a nondescript corridor.

He heard the unmistakable shuffle of footsteps and closed

the door a bit, leaving a tiny sliver to spy through and grimacing as it creaked. Priest conjured silence just in time as two soldiers dressed in black with red stripes on their tunics marched passed, neither of them even glancing their way.

'What do you see?' Drax asked impatiently.

Fie answered over his shoulder. 'Library guards from Kitore.'

Drax growled. 'If they're Nixus's men, then they do not yet know that he's dead. It wasn't all that long ago that it happened after all.'

Fie gestured to Priest and Drax, opening the door wide enough for them to slip through. 'Take them,' he said. 'Bring one back here alive.'

Priest and Drax disappeared and, a moment later, they heard a muffled thud. Two men were dragged through the door and Fie closed it again.

Priest launched the first one down the stairs without hesitation, the sound of the body's succession down to the bottom oddly muted.

Drax took the first one by his tunic, hit him once and shook him. 'Where are the fae children?'

'Ain't no children here,' the soldier growled, his ruddy complexion even redder from Drax's blow.

Drax drew back his fist to hit him again.

'Enough,' Priest muttered. His voice changed as he imbued it with power. 'You will answer.'

Fie watched as the soldier's eyes became unfocused and Drax let him go.

'Where are the fae children?' asked Priest.

'Downstairs in the square eating their daily meal.'

'What are your orders?'

'We wait for our relief contingent from the Library ... but they should have been here days ago.'

'Have you had any birds?' Drax asked him.

The man didn't answer.

Priest rolled his eyes. 'Have you had any birds?'

The man shook his head. 'No. But there have been storms all through the passes for weeks. We didn't expect any to get through.'

'As you suspected,' Fie said to Drax, 'they don't know.'

Priest's eyes narrowed on the soldier. 'If you hear nothing, what are your orders then?'

'We're to wait until mid-winter. If no one comes, the First Scholar ordered us to kill the fae whelps and return to Kitore.'

'Nixus, that fucking prick,' Drax snarled.

'How many soldiers are here?'

'Twelve.'

'Twelve?' Fie asked. 'That can't be right. There should be a hundred and sixty-seven children. How could so few men have brought them all here?'

Priest asked the question.

'There were many more of us in the beginning, but an illness killed over fifty.'

'And the children?'

'None of them caught it.'

'How have you kept the children here with so few of you?' Priest asked.

'There are some thirty priests here as well and ...'

'And what? You will speak!'

'And the children are fed herbs in their food to keep them docile.'

Fie had heard enough. He nodded to Drax who tore his knife across the man's throat and threw him down the stairs to join his friend.

'Ten left,' he growled.

Five stood. 'We kill them all. The priests as well if they give us trouble.'

'Four will be walking around. The others will be in the guard room,' Drax said, peering out into the corridor. 'All is clear.'

'We take the ones on patrol first. Eve with Priest. Drax with me.'

They walked out into the hall, Priest and Eve going right and he and Drax turning left.

'You should have kept the female with you,' Drax murmured, but Fie shook his head.

'Perhaps he'll be able to get through to her before she needs to open a portal. Perhaps then, he won't have to ...'

Drax nodded. 'Aye, perhaps.'

They exited the hall and found themselves on a high, open-air walkway. Stone arches overlooked the main square below and, as they heard more footsteps, he and Drax realized that another two soldiers were walking around the top of the cloister. Hiding behind a couple of the thick columns that made up the archways, they waited for them to come closer.

Fie looked down into the square itself and his heart leapt as he saw many children, some playing, others sitting. They were there. They were alive.

'Thank the gods,' he whispered, leaning his forehead on the cold stone, and closing his eyes in relief for a heartbeat.

And then he darted out of his hiding place, slitting a guard's throat, watching Drax run another through with his sword. They put the bodies out of sight behind the columns.

'Eight more to go. Let's leave the other two to Priest and Eve and find the guard room. We'll take care of them quickly enough if they're anything like these two useless cunts.'

Drax nodded and they left the cloister, walking through to another winding hall. They strode around a corner and found a priest, his eyes widening as soon as he saw them. Before he could yell for help, Fie had leapt forward and swung his sword, cleaving the man's head from his shoulders. Blood spurted out from his neck as he fell to his knees and his head rolled down the corridor, bumping into the wall.

'Noticeable,' Drax said, observing the mess, and Fie grimaced.

'We better finish this quickly then.'

They kept going, beginning to hear the muffled sounds of men talking and laughing as they neared the lower levels of the fortress, close to the main gates where a guard room would be in any other keep. They took a small staircase down and were met with a closed door, laughter and talking coming from the other side.

Drax took the latch in hand and Fie nodded, fingers groping for the dagger at his belt and finding it missing. He'd given it to Eve upstairs.

'We need to get that female her own weapons,' he murmured.

Drax grinned, pulling his dagger from his boot and tossing it to Fie.

He threw the door open and Fie sprang across the threshold, killing one short soldier outright as his knife ran headlong into his chest. He killed two more after that and Drax, right behind him, slew another pair. He ran one of the men through and stabbed another in the throat. One was left. He cowered in a corner. His sword clattered to the ground and his breeches became saturated with piss.

Drax stared at him in blatant disgust.

'Please let me live,' he begged.

Drax merely shook his head, throwing his knife and embedding it in the man's heart without mercy. They would have shown the children none, after all. Mid-winter was only days away. They'd got here in the nick of time.

The soldier fell to the ground and Drax dragged his

weapon from the other man's flesh, wiping it clean on the Library guard's uniform.

'Coward,' he muttered and spat on the man's corpse.

'If Priest and Eve did what they were meant to, all the guards are dead,' Fie said. 'The priests aren't fighters. They'll hide once they know the soldiers are gone. Let's go down to the square. Remember to remove your glamour so that the children are not afraid.'

Drax immediately became taller, leaner, broader and his eyes turned violet. As he showed his true face, Fie did the same. They walked slowly and quietly down to the main square and, as soon as they walked in, the children began to turn their heads towards them. Subdued chatter broke out and Fie raised his hands for quiet.

'Rogue?' he called.

'Fie?'

A boy ran forwards to him and threw himself into his brother's arms, hugging him tightly. Fie embraced him back, finally relaxing in a way that he hadn't since he'd heard his brother was gone.

'Are you all right?' he asked, and his brother nodded. 'Is anyone hurt?'

'No, but they put something in our food to keep us calm. Pricks didn't know I saw 'em, but they all had slow hands. I fished it out of the pot before last mealtime so everyone's coming 'round,' Rogue said.

Fie chuckled. 'You've done well.'

'Are you here to take us home?' a small girl nearby asked.

'In due course,' Fie said. 'Be strong and stay close.'

On the other side of the square, he saw Priest hugging a young woman.

Eve was behind him, feeling happy that they'd found their kin, but afraid as well though she was trying to steel herself. Fie felt his heart break because he knew what Priest was going to have to do. He tried to catch his Brother's eye, but Priest avoided his gaze.

∼

Priest

PRIEST EMBRACED HIS SISTER. Taking her face in his hands, he kissed her forehead. He could scarcely believe that he'd found her at last. He held her close again and then looked past her to Eve, who was standing not far away. The link between them flared to life and he could feel that she was glad for them. But she was also afraid for the same reason and his happiness at finding his sister alive was tainted because soon he would have to do what he'd promised himself he wouldn't ever do again. He was going to have to make her conjure a portal unless she could do it herself.

He set his sister aside, squeezing her shoulders. 'We're here to take you to the fae realms,' he murmured to her. 'Let them all know that they need to be ready to leave as soon as we give the word.'

He went to Eve.

'Close your eyes,' he said without preamble.

She tensed, but she did as he asked. He put his hands on her shoulders, tracing down her arms and then up again to calm her.

'Imagine you're in a tunnel,' he said, letting out a slow breath, 'walking in the light. It guides your way. It comes from your body. It begins to get brighter and brighter as you move towards the door at the end. You can see more light piercing the keyhole. It's brighter than you, brighter than the sun. The key is in your hand. It's metal. Heavy. Can you feel it?'

'Yes.'

'Put the key in the lock. Turn it and open the door. As you do, the bright light flows into you making you brighter still. You are full of magick, full of power. You need that to create your bridge.'

'I can feel it,' she breathed. 'It's all around me.'

'That's it,' he said. 'Focus on it. You need to take us to the same Dark Realm that we went to before. Remember that great portal that we went through?'

She nodded

'Do it now.'

She closed her eyes, her body tensing as she tried to find what she needed.

She opened them a moment later. 'I thought I could do it,' she said brokenly.

'I found the power, but I can't wield it.'

She looked him in the eye. 'I'm sorry. Do it.'

Priest's eyes sought his sister, speaking with some of the other children in the square. He turned them back on Eve, his gaze searching hers as he breathed out, putting his head to hers. He didn't say that he was sorry. He didn't wait any longer. He couldn't or he wouldn't be able to do what was necessary. He only hoped that she could forgive him *again*.

He put his hands around her throat and began to press. Whispering in her ear, he took on the Bull's voice and felt her terror spike when she heard the timber she knew so well.

'Get on your knees,' he said, hating himself. 'I'm going to let your friends watch next time we fight. I'm going to beat you and, when I'm finished with you, I'm going to tell Talik that I'm not going to fight for him again unless he lets all the men in the crowd come to your tiny room and fu—'

The sizzling in the air stopped his words and a bridge erupted into the room, large enough for all of them.

He saw his Brothers herding everyone through, and he kept a hold of Eve's throat just hard enough that she stayed afraid, hoping she could hold it open for long enough to get everyone out of here.

She was locked in a memory that he had put her in, her body shaking, her lip trembling. He didn't know what she was thinking about now other than she must be trapped in a flashback. Tears flowed from her eyes and down her cheeks and only when the last of the young ones had gone through did Priest let go of her, drawing her through the portal she had made.

Drax and Fie were right behind them and they found themselves in a market, the same one that he and Eve had been in before. The larger portal there was open and the children, without any prompting, were already travelling through that one as well.

Priest swung Eve into his arms. He carried her through the larger tunnel and out the other side ... straight into the vibrant and colorful main hall of the highest fae court.

The floor was in disarray, children running across the polished marble towards family members, others looking around hoping to see someone they knew. People were laughing and crying. The Council Five were trying to bring order, but no one was listening.

Fie drew himself up and walked towards the high dais where the Council members sat behind a long table of black wood. Three females. Two males. These five fae held the highest influence, one of them Lord Gerling, Eve's father.

Priest didn't say a word to the others, but he held back hoping to the gods that her sire didn't get close enough to realize who she was. If he smelled her ...

'As usual, you make a grand entrance,' the oldest, dourest councilor, Isbeth, said, causing some around them to titter. 'But I suppose we can overlook it, considering who you've brought with you.'

To Priest's shock, he saw Councilor Isbeth smile as she

looked at two of the smallest children they'd brought with them who were currently being hugged by her daughters. They'd saved her grandchildren, he realized, filing it away. One never knew when a favor would be needed, and it was good to keep a mental ledger of such things.

'We certainly had our doubts,' Lord Gerling sneered at them, peering down as if they were the dirt on his shining boots, 'but all the fae rejoice in your success. Wherever did you find them?'

The ease with which Fie stepped forward made Priest admit that his Brother was well suited to being their leader, certainly more than he'd have given him credit for. They knew it was Gerling who'd done this, but they had no proof and no idea why he'd turn against his own.

'Nixus, the First Scholar of Kitore, had hidden them in a far corner of the Light Realm.'

'Did you not bring the human to face the consequences of his actions?' one of the other female councilors questioned, her beady eyes narrowing on them.

'I'm afraid he was killed some weeks ago, Councilor,' Fie answered smoothly.

'We commend you,' Isbeth said. 'The payment promised shall be yours.'

Fie, Priest and Drax bowed their heads in thanks, but it was all for show. Anything less was unthinkable in the circumstances. Though they didn't need the coin, to refuse it was an insult.

'And who is this you bring with you?' Gerling asked, his eyes fixed on Eve who still hung limp in Priest's arms. Priest relaxed his arms surreptitiously, trying not to look overly protective.

'Simply a human female we found with the children. We'll get what we can out of her and send a report on our findings.'

Gerling's eyes narrowed a fraction. 'If she's what you say, she should be taken down for interrogation in my own dungeons.'

Priest kept his calm, but only because there was no other avenue open, not here in the presence of the entire Council.

'She's merely a peasant girl,' Fie said with a wave of his hand, 'not directly involved. She simply might know a detail or two.'

Gerling straightened, his posture daring them to gainsay him. 'All the more reason to begin soon before her feeble human mind forgets anything important. I'll do it myself.'

The other councilors nodded their heads in agreement; all except Isbeth. She simply regarded them, her expression giving them no inkling of her thoughts.

'This was a grievous crime against the fae,' the other male said, 'and the outcome could have been much different. If this human knows anything more, Lord Gerling will get it out of her.'

A fae guard came forward and it took everything in Priest not to fight. Committing treason wouldn't help their Fourth, their mate. They'd never escape with their lives.

'Give the human to him,' Fie muttered and Priest realized that his grip on Eve had tightened.

Fie chuckled. 'You can have another human if you desire one, Brother,' he said more loudly.

Some of the fae around them chuckled.

Clenching his jaw, Priest forced himself to laugh and let Eve go as the guard stepped forward to take their female. He watched as Eve was carried away through a door over the guard's shoulder as if she was nothing more than a sack of grain. No doubt she was being taken to the dungeons.

Fie, Drax, and Priest bowed to the Council. They'd be expected to melt into the crowd now, the children no longer their concerns.

Priest's sister appeared by his side.

'Thank you for coming for me.' She took his hand and squeezed it covertly. 'I found mother and father at the back,' she murmured. 'They're grateful to you for what you've done, but they … they won't come and tell you themselves. I'm sorry.'

Priest gave her a rueful smile. 'It's not your fault, Muriah. I've made my choices and they've made theirs. Go before you're seen speaking to a Dark Brother and your future is ruined.'

She snorted, but, with a final squeeze goodbye, she disappeared before her conversation with a lowly mercenary could be remarked upon.

He saw Fie speaking with one of his extended family, his little brother standing in front of him while he made arrangements for the boy to be taken care of at least until the Council decided what was to be done with the children now that the Underhill was practically impregnable.

Priest wasn't worried about Muriah. She would have left the Underhill soon anyway. The next time he saw her she'd probably have a mate and be amongst the many fae of the court. She was safe. That was all that mattered … but their Fourth was very much not and there was little they could do.

They were led to some nondescript, luxurious chambers to rest and refresh themselves, but for once Priest didn't truly take in the comforts around him except to ensure no one was concealed therein to spy.

As soon as they were all inside and alone, Priest spoke the words, conjuring a silence around them so that no one could hear what they were saying outside the room.

Drax began to pace. 'What are we going to do? Fuck! She's in the Council's dungeon. How are we to get her out of there?'

'We shouldn't have brought her here.'

'You'd have rather left her in the temple in the middle of nowhere?'

'Better there than here.'

'Enough,' Priest hissed, silencing both his Brothers. 'Arguing does nothing for our Fourth. In truth, the dungeon isn't our concern. If Gerling is seeing to her personally, he'll smell his familial ties as soon as he enters her cell.'

'What will he do with her?' Fie asked. 'He hates halflings. Will he …'

Drax shook his head slightly. 'Political alliance or debt payment. She's worth more to him now she's grown. He'll have her married off to some fae lord he owes something to or wants something from.'

'We need the Council on our side. Isbeth is our best bet. She's grateful for the return of her grandchildren so we're entitled to a special request,' Priest said. 'She might be persuaded to help.'

Fie nodded. 'Set up a meeting,' he ordered. 'Quickly.'

Priest walked out into the hall, summoning a fae guard standing close by.

'We need a private meeting with Councilor Isbeth,' he said.

The guard inclined his head, 'I'll make the request but they're usually busy so I wouldn't get your hopes up,' he muttered, pulling a cord.

A human servant appeared a moment later, smiling shyly at the guard, but cowering away from Priest.

Priest frowned, not liking in the least that the female was afraid of him. How far he'd come since they'd found Eve.

The guard spoke to her quietly and she soon calmed down, scurrying away to do his bidding.

'Did you enthrall her?' Priest asked conversationally, watching the retreating human with interest.

'Never.' The guard gave him a pointed look, his eyes also

training on the human girl as she walked down the hall. 'Not all of us agree with how the humans are treated.'

Priest inclined his head, returning to their room to find both Brothers pacing.

'Calm yourselves. Eat something. You'll be no good to her if you aren't hale and strong.'

Fie sighed, sinking into a chair while Drax made a point of picking up an apple and biting into it.

Priest followed his own advice, taking one as well. 'We might have a chance if we tell Isbeth the truth,' he said, his mind turning.

'What do you mean?'

'I mean we tell her who Eve is, that she's our mate. That she has power. Gerling would never have given up his child if he thought she had magick. His error is our gain, and the current climate is on our side. As a mate to us all, there's more chance of getting her with child. Isbeth might be able to persuade the Council to let Eve stay with us instead of letting Gerling take her.'

His Brothers glanced at each other.

'And if she becomes pregnant?'

'The Council will know of her, but the most that will happen is she'll be forced into a sanctuary.' He threw up his hands. 'Wherever they send her, we'll go too.'

'Will they let us?' Fie asked.

'We'll make them,' Drax said grimly. 'It's a small price to pay to get her back.'

Moments later there was a knock on their door. They were summoned.

FIE WAS at the front as they walked into the Council's private rooms, he and Drax flanking their commander. But as they entered, Priest inwardly cursed as he saw three of the

Council sitting at the table instead of just one. Isbeth sat on one side, the other female in the middle and a male at the other end.

'We asked for this audience with Councilor Isbeth,' Fie said with a bow, 'to request the return of our Fourth ... and our mate.'

Three sets of eyes turned towards them.

'You did not say the human female was your Fourth and mate earlier,' the oldest council member, Lord Belarus, rasped.

'That was by design,' Drax said, speaking up from behind Fie with his head bowed. 'Our arrival here was sudden and largely unplanned. We weren't sure what welcome our female would receive at the court, so we decided to tread carefully.'

Fie drew himself up. 'We didn't presume that a council member would condescend to interrogate a human prisoner himself, but what's done is done. When can we expect our mate to be returned to us?'

Belarus inclined his head, looking directly at them though his cloudy eyes tended to blindness. 'Your mate has already been taken to one of Gerling's personal estates. He had business elsewhere so he will carry out her interrogation at his leisure.'

'You didn't tell me that, Belarus,' the councilwoman said, her sharp eyes boring into her colleague.

He merely shrugged. 'Didn't think it pertinent.'

Her eyes narrowed and Priest was suddenly glad he wasn't on this female's bad side.

'I'm afraid it's too late,' she said. 'If Lord Gerling has already taken her to one of his many private estates, you know as well as I that the Council itself has no jurisdiction there.' She gave a delicate yawn. 'You'll have to take up the matter with him directly, but I believe he's not meant to be due back at court for some days. You're welcome to petition at his borders but I doubt you'll get a response. I'm sorry we couldn't be more help. However, the Council thanks you for your service. Your payment will be delivered directly.'

She then looked down at her desk, shuffling some documents, and didn't say anything more. The door behind them opened. They had been dismissed.

They went back to their rooms and Fie immediately shouted his frustration.

'How could she be gone already? He must have known from the moment he saw her. He had this planned! Gods, he could have taken her anywhere.'

Priest ran a hand through his hair as Fie kept up his tirade, feeling empty. He couldn't even feel the bond as more than a fragile tendril and, gods help him, he missed the all-encompassing force of it.

Someone knocked at the door of their chamber and Fie quieted immediately. Priest drew a knife and opened the door a crack, surprised to see Councilor Isbeth herself in the hall.

He let her in immediately.

'Close the door,' she ordered, 'and conjure silence.'

Priest did as she said, nodding when he was sure no one could hear them.

'I couldn't speak freely in front of Belarus. He and Gerling always ally themselves with each other,' she said, sitting down and looking at the jug of wine that stood on the table.

Drax poured her a goblet and she took it without a word.

'Your mate is half fae.' It wasn't a question.

'How did you—' Fie began but she cut him off with an incredulous look.

'Because I'm no fool. What I want to know is why Gerling

is so interested in her. He rarely troubles himself with anyone's affairs but his own. For him to promise any sort of selfless assistance is unheard of. Do not lie to me. I will know.'

'She's Gerling's daughter. He had her taken to the Light Realm when she was a babe as payment for a debt.'

Isbeth scoffed. 'That sounds like Gerling, all right.' She shook her head. 'Goes on and on about not diluting our bloodlines with the humans to anyone who'll listen, but you best believe he uses them to sate his hungers. Fucking hypocrite.'

She put the goblet on the table. 'I will find out where he's gone, but it won't be easy. There's a party tonight to celebrate the return of the children.'

'Aye, we've received an invitation,' Fie acknowledged.

'Be there.'

'Why would you help us?' Priest asked, suspicious. No one here did anything for free.

'For two reasons. Our numbers decrease with every passing day. We need more births. The horde is chomping at our borders all the time and, if you're truly her mates, multiple fae offspring are almost certainly assured. Gerling's plans for her are unlikely to result in the same.'

'And the other reason?' Drax asked.

The Councilor stood. 'I grow tired of his constant intrigues and his rhetoric. He would have the fae die out before we 'contaminate' our families with new blood. I wish to spend time with my grandchildren.' She walked to the door. 'If you get a chance to kill him, take it.' Unlatching it, she turned back and surveyed them. 'This meeting never took place.'

Priest nodded, closing the door behind her.

'Are we really to waste our time at a party while our mate is in gods only know what sort of danger?' Fie growled, crumpling the invitation that had been delivered earlier in his fist.

For once Priest agreed with his Brother, but they had to find Eve if they were going to save her and, in the fae realms, information came at a price like everything else.

CHAPTER 12

EVE

She could feel soft sheets, smell flowers in the warm air and hear the crackle of a small fire. She stretched, making a noise of contentment. Someone coughed close by, and she froze.

Where was she? Still in the temple?

She cracked her eyes open and found herself in an unfamiliar room in a four-poster bed with a canopy above her. She found the source of the noise; a man sat quite close by in an overstuffed armchair. All around them was the casual opulence that she'd got used to in the Brothers house and it annoyed her very slightly that being reminded of them comforted her.

She didn't know the man in front of her, but he was looking at her as if he knew her. He was older with dark, sable hair that was greying at his temples. Though he was sitting, Eve could tell he was quite tall with a broad frame. His eyes were fae.

'I must say you've grown into a pretty girl.' His eyes moved over her, making her skin crawl. 'A very pretty girl.'

He seemed to consider. 'You clearly favor your human mother. No one in my bloodline has hair of such a light hue.'

'My mother?' Eve asked faintly, trying to put the pieces together, but her sluggish mind seemed unable to do so.

He snorted. 'I wouldn't bother asking much about her. I can't hardly even remember what the chit looked like.'

She closed her eyes and opened them again, trying to make her mind catch up. 'You're my father.'

'I prefer the term sire, but yes.' The man in front of her chuckled. 'Gods, I never expected to see you again. I assumed that bottom feeder Talik had worked you to death or some such. What name did your mother give you? It escapes me now.'

'Eve,' she said.

'Yes!' Her father snapped his fingers. 'That was it. Eve.'

He looked her over again, his eyes narrowing. 'Odd. I can smell the magick on you. I know with certainty that you can conjure, but as a babe there was nothing to prove you were mine at all. In truth I assumed one of the other human slaves had found his way into my harem and bred the bitch.'

Shaking his head, he gave her a rueful smile as if all of this was simply a silly misunderstanding. 'I'd never have given you up for such a small debt if I'd realized. Of course, we didn't know then that our birth rates were falling quite so drastically either.'

He leaned forwards and sniffed her, giving her a playful wink. 'But you smell fae enough to be of much more use to me than you were as a babe. You're going to continue in that same vein though. You're going to pay off a very large debt indeed.

'I'm a Fourth, a member of the Dark Army. I have mates,' she ground out, finally finding her voice.

He waved a hand. 'Where you're going, it won't matter. They'll never find you. That'll be apparent soon enough.'

With that he stood up and walked to the door.

'Don't try to escape,' he called over his shoulder. 'You'll find my home is a fortress ... and a maze. Food will be brought. I suggest you make yourself at home. This was your mother's room once upon a time, I recall.'

A key turned in the lock and she was left alone. Trying to remain calm, she slid from the bed, happy to find she was still wearing her clothes. She looked around the room as she took stock of her person. The knife that she'd had in the temple was gone, of course, and the pouches from her belt as well.

Eve moved around the room, checking in drawers, finding clothes and trinkets.

She wondered if any of these things had belonged to the human woman who had birthed her. There were no windows and the light seemed to come from the ceiling, a false sun in a painted mural.

She tried the door but, of course, to no avail. There was nothing else to do but sit and wait as her sire had said.

A young woman brought her a meal sometime later. She looked human, dressed in a short shift and nothing more, limping slightly as if one of her legs pained her.

She placed a tray on the table and turned to leave.

'Wait,' Eve said.

She didn't turn around.

'I'm not to speak to you,' she said in a whisper.

'But I need to—'

'Please!' she said. 'There are guards outside. If they hear my voice, I'll be punished.'

She cast her eyes down as she made her way slowly to the door. She knocked and it opened. She disappeared through it and Eve heard it lock again a moment later.

Eve ate the food the woman had brought. She wasn't hungry in the least, but it tasted pleasant enough even if she couldn't rightly say what it was. It was a welcome change from the rabbits and deer that she and the Brothers had been eating out in the wilds.

She felt a pang of loss when she thought of them. Would they come for her? They wouldn't leave her here, would they?

She'd just finished her meal when the door opened again. The human girl came shuffling in once more.

'What's your name?' Eve whispered.

'Sym,' she said. 'My name is Sym.'

'Can you help me get out of here?'

She looked up, fear flashing in her eyes. 'No. Human slaves don't leave this place.'

'I'm not a human slave,' Eve countered.

Sym raised a brow. 'It doesn't matter what you are. You're in the same lot as the rest of us. They'll use you up until there's nothing left.'

She took the tray to the door and knocked as she had before. This time, after it opened, two burly guards stood at the threshold.

'You're to come with us,' they said, one of them pushing Sym out of the way as casually as he'd bat at a fly.

She slumped into the wall, barely keeping a hold on the tray she carried. But she didn't look up nor say a word as she righted herself and shuffled down the hallway in the opposite direction.

'Don't go far, human,' one of the guards called softly after her. 'I'll be making use of you when my rounds are done.'

His friend chuckled. 'Why do you always want that one, maimed as she is?'

The first one winked. 'I like the way she struggles. Besides, I heard she was bred once and, if I can get a babe from her, my status will be elevated with the Council enough that I won't have to work for this cunt anymore.'

Eve didn't try to hide her disgust and contempt at their words, but neither of them seemed bothered in the least by her opinion.

They didn't speak anymore but were much more respectful of her than they had been of Sym, keeping their distance from her as they led her down a large corridor that was oddly sparse in comparison to what she now considered to be fae standards.

She soon realized why as they turned a corner and the luxury began; carpeted floors, rugs, furs, tapestries, murals, fine furniture, and beautiful, useless baubles. Where she had been must be where the human slaves were housed.

She was brought into a large hall where her father sat at the head of a very long table, food piled upon it.

'Ah, there you are,' he said pleasantly. 'Come. Sit with me.'

She did as he said, taking a seat next to him.

'Look at this,' he said, brandishing a letter.

She glanced at it but made no move to take it.

'I can't read,' she said mulishly, and he looked surprised.

'Well, that won't do at all,' he muttered to himself.

A short, thin man stepped forward.

'Have him brought,' her father said, not deigning to look up.

The man bowed, leaving the room.

Eve didn't have time to ask who was being brought before the doors were opened and Talik of all men was brought in. He was in heavy chains, his head hanging low. He'd been beaten, dried blood crusting his nose and mouth.

He was brought close, and his eyes widened as he saw Eve.

'Tell them,' he begged her. 'Tell them I didn't harm you.'

Her eyes narrowed at him. She didn't say a word. It might be petty, but she'd not save him. He may not have held the whip himself, but after everything he'd let the Bull do for all those years, he deserved nothing from her.

Her father stood and backhanded his prisoner across the face, the crack and Talik's cry of pain echoing through the room. He fell to the floor, chains rattling as the guards put him back on his feet, holding him steady.

'Pathetic. Because of you, I have a whelp who cannot even read.' Then he chuckled. 'After all I did to ensure I sired a child from a fae female, and all I can get is human babe.'

He gave a dramatic sigh as he wiped clean the hand that had touched the human with a nearby cloth.

'I can't send her to him like this. I'll be a laughingstock,' he said low, muttering to himself again as he sat down, his attention caught by some documents in front of him.

'Kill him,' he ordered, not bothering to look up as Talik was stabbed in the back. He even yawned behind his hand.

'Leave the knife in. I don't want blood all over my floors.'

Wide eyed, Eve watched as Talik's corpse was carried away. When she looked back at Gerling, he was regarding her.

'I'm afraid this is going to hurt, but it must be done. You can blame Talik for this along with his other misdeeds.'

She reared back in the chair as a sudden, intense pain seared through her skull. She screamed, holding her head that felt as if it was splitting open. Images began to flood into her consciousness, memories of lessons; long days and nights spent poring over books with letters and pictures, symbols that she began to recognize and understand, conjuring circles and magick.

By the time it was over, she found herself cowering on the floor, whimpering. The paper that her father had tried to hand before fluttered down next to her.

'What does it say?' he asked, his tone condescending.

Eve began to tell him again that she didn't know how to

read, wondering what game he played, but then she looked at it. The words made sense. She picked it up and held it closer to her face, her mouth opening on a gasp.

'Read the first line,' he commanded.

'My dearest Lord Gerling. I invite you to arrive at my borders on the second day before midwinter,' she said, unable to hide her shock.

She looked up at her father.

'It's taken. Good,' he said. 'That's today. We'll be leaving very soon. I expect you to behave with the decorum I have now imbued you with. Do you understand? I will not be shamed by you, blood or no.'

Eve's mouth fell open, for she did indeed remember lessons with tutors as a child where she learned fae etiquette, reading, writing ... magick; her father's memories.

She could use her magick. It was so simple.

'What did you do to me?' she asked.

'Gave you the education that I had,' he said with a wave of his hand. 'Most of it you won't need, but it will at least stop me from being labeled the fool should you find yourself moving in fae circles. Now,' he stood. 'You'll be taken back to your room to await our departure to your betrothed.'

'Betrothed?' she asked, taken aback.

He rolled his eyes. 'You're not very quick witted, are you? Still, I never promised him an intelligent daughter, only a breedable one.'

He turned back to his papers. 'Take her back to her room and prepare the carriage.'

Her sire didn't look up again. 'Don't embarrass me, or I'll make you wish I'd killed your whore mother before she birthed you.'

The guards escorted her out and, as soon as the door to the hall closed, Eve ran. She was quick, and the guards behind had not been ready for her to bolt, so she was able to elude them as she ran down the hallways. She found herself back in the human wing, and raced past her room, confused as she was sure she'd gone in the opposite direction.

As she went down the long corridor, the rooms became smaller. Some were without doors, some were merely cells with irons bars on the outsides until she got to a dead end. She was trapped. There was no way out. She turned, but the guards were there, strolling down the hall and she understood what her father had meant by his home being a maze. There was no way out unless he wished it.

She could conjure!

She grasped hold of the magick inside her, the light Priest had helped her to see made tangible by her will.

But nothing happened. It fizzled into nothing. She almost cried in frustration. Why couldn't she do it?

'If you're attempting a conjure, it won't work here,' one of the guards said.

The other laughed at her as they advanced. 'Come on. You might as well be trying to escape from one of these locked cells, female.'

They each took hold of her and began to take her back to her room. As they walked, Eve was able to see more clearly into the cells. Some held men, huddled on the floor. In others there were women dressed in rags, one or two languished on beds wearing nothing at all, seemingly in stupors for they didn't even realize that anyone was passing as they stared up at nothing, their expressions vacant.

'What's wrong with them?' she couldn't help asking aloud, not expecting an answer.

But one of the fae guards replied. 'Your father likes to enthrall them before he fucks them.' He grinned in a way that made her want to shrink back. 'Me, I like 'em with a little spirit, isn't that right, girl?' he called to the woman who was sitting in her tiny room on a cot. It was Sym, the servant who'd brought Eve her meal.

The guard looked at his friend in askance and the other one shook his head with a grin. 'Go on then. Get the slave with child if you can.'

The first guard sauntered into Sym's doorless room. 'You know what to do.'

Sym didn't look up at him as she pulled her shift from her shoulders, letting it pool at her feet. The guard winked at Eve.

'You see? I don't need to make her do what I want. She knows what happens when she doesn't please.'

The guard still in the hall with Eve rolled his eyes. 'Don't be late for rounds. I'm not covering for you this time.'

He took Eve by the arm, and steered her down the corridor to her room, the look on his face as he eyed her one she'd seen many times on the Bull.

She looked down, heart beginning to beat faster. Could she beat back a full-fae male if she needed to? Was she strong enough?

'I believe I'm making Lord Gerling's daughter nervous,' he murmured, putting his hand on her rump, and squeezing.

Her eyes narrowed, but she did nothing. He wanted her reaction. She'd give him none.

'You'll be expected to breed, you know,' he said softly. 'If you don't, gods only know what Ceres will do to you. He's known for his cruelty.' His hand wandered. 'I could help. My seed is stronger than some pampered lord.'

Resisting the urge to batter the male who was more than twice her size, Eve opened the door to her room herself.

'Lay another hand on me and I tell Gerling,' she hissed. 'I'd wager he'd let me choose your punishment simply to amuse himself and, by the gods, I'll see your cock cleaved from between your legs.'

He took a step back, paling, and she watched him swallow hard. 'I beg your forgiveness. It was a misunderstanding.'

With a snort, she walked into the room and heard the lock turn. She sat on the bed, thinking of the girl just down the hall, wishing she could help her. But she couldn't even save herself. What good was she to anyone else here?

How was she going to get out of this? Escaping this magicked fortress was clearly impossible. She would have to wait until she got to her final destination. Perhaps she would be able to use her newfound skills to flee whomever her father was selling her to. She had memories of how to conjure her particular brand of magick and she could see now why Priest's efforts to instruct her had failed. It wasn't the same. He'd been trying to unlock something that was a secret of her father's family. Now that she knew what it was, she could draw on her power effortlessly. It was just that Gerling had some conjure in place to stop bridges opening in his home. It was bad luck, but it made sense. A fortress wasn't a fortress if anyone could just go in and out as they pleased … but perhaps on the journey to wherever she was going to be taken next …

She lay back on the bed to wait, planning how she was going to escape this cursed place and very glad that her father had underestimated his halfling daughter.

∼

Drax

'Are you ready?' Priest asked, straightening his formal black tunic as he looked in the mirror.

Behind him Fie swore. 'We should be going after our Fourth, not attending parties.'

Drax ran a hand through his hair, he agreed with Fie

wholeheartedly, but this was a fae realm and things had to be done a certain way. He remembered now why he had left to join the Dark Army in the human realm. He'd never been able to countenance all of these fucking proprieties that served only to polish a shining veneer that hid the rot beneath. Keeping up appearances no longer made sense; not for a dying race like theirs. They should be putting their efforts into saving their kind.

'We must do what we have to,' he said. 'If we want to find out where she's been taken, we need to play Isbeth's game for now.'

'We need to get her back and make Gerling pay!' Fie growled.

Priest shot him a look. 'Do not let your emotions get the better of you. We all want Eve back, but we must be careful.'

'Aye,' Drax said, straightening the ceremonial dagger at his belt. 'We may be the heroes of the moment, but you know as well as I how quickly the tide can turn here. If we anger the wrong lord, the wrong member of the Council ...'

Fie's jaw tensed. 'I know. Let's go. We don't want to be late.'

Drax fell into step behind Fie as they left their rooms, going down the corridors laid with thick carpet and ignoring the slaves that hurried around trying to stay out of their way.

They reached the Grand Hall and Drax donned a mask of ennui making sure he looked his part. It wasn't hard. In truth, he was already bored of this realm and recalled their months stuck in Kitore with more contentment now than he'd felt at the time. And, yet, his mind was in turmoil, scarcely able to believe that Eve had been taken, that she would likely be sold in marriage knowing her father and his many debts.

Priest took a goblet from a tray that one of the servants was bringing around and Drax followed his lead.

They were here to dance to Isbeth's tune. Nothing more.

He took a sip from his goblet, tasting the finest wines to be had in the realms. He expected nothing less in the highest of the fae courts.

'The Council isn't here yet,' Fie murmured glancing around the room at the many wealthy fae in attendance.

'Of course they'd be late to their own fucking party,' Priest muttered.

'Silence,' Drax whispered from behind his cup. 'That's dangerous talk as you well know.'

They mostly stayed in each other's company for the evening as they skirted around the dancing couples, watching their brethren indulge in too much wine and the most entertaining delights the Dark Realms had to offer. The night wore on, no one from the Council appearing.

Finally, Isbeth arrived alone, making her way slowly over to them as she mingled.

'Our most sincere thanks once more for finding the treasures that might have been lost to us forever,' she said smoothly as if they hadn't been awaiting her pleasure for hours.

'We did nothing more than anyone else would do,' Fie said somewhat stiffly.

Isbeth gave a small smile. 'There is a token the Council would like to give you to show our personal gratitude. It's in the library awaiting your earliest convenience,' she said, so quietly that they almost couldn't hear her.

Drax gave a shallow bow. 'Our thanks, Councilor.'

'Good evening,' she said, meandering away to another group without preamble, but still making it look as if she was in no hurry to leave them.

As soon as they were able, Drax, Fie, and Priest made their way slowly to one of the doors that led onto the balconies where they'd be able to climb down. From the gardens, they could move freely around the back of the estate to where the library was without anyone knowing where they'd gone.

They slipped outside into the warm air, avoiding the lights twinkling through the gardens, but it was early enough that no one was yet out here. They were alone as they traversed the stone steps, keeping to the shadows, their footsteps making nary a sound as they made their way to the side of the house.

Drax opened a window, and they stole into the library. They didn't have to wait long as the inner door opened almost immediately, and a shadowy figure entered and approached them.

'The Councilor sent me,' said a female slave, stepping into the light.

She held a folded parchment out to Fie. 'I was instructed to give this to you,' she said, keeping her eyes low. 'She also says that Lord Gerling has entered talks with Lord Ceres to give your Fourth to him.'

'In marriage?' Priest asked.

'As a slave,' she answered.

'Fuck,' Drax muttered. 'How can he get away with this?'

'The same way he always does,' Priest said. 'Our thanks. You may go.'

He waved a hand and the woman left without a word, giving a small bow, and looking thankful that she'd been dismissed.

Drax turned to his Brothers. 'Why would he give her as a slave? This doesn't make sense. There's more at play here than we understand or he wouldn't be giving her away so flippantly and not to Ceres.'

'Who is Lord Ceres?' Fie asked.

'A powerful figure,' Priest answered, 'though he rarely attends the courts himself. He sends emissaries. He's wealthy beyond measure. The only reason he's not part of the Council is because he has no wish to be. He has influence through the Dark Realms and controls many of the trade routes as well.'

'Why haven't I heard of him?'

Drax shrugged. 'He is not often mentioned by name. He works through stewards and others who are employed by him.'

'What does he want with Eve?'

Priest frowned. 'Gods only know, but I'd guarantee it's nothing good. What does the parchment say?'

Fie unfolded it. 'It looks like she's still in this realm. Far from here though.'

Drax nodded. 'I thought I could feel her very vaguely earlier, but, as you say, she is far from here.'

'But how can we get there from here without anyone noticing?' Fie asked.

'We can't,' Priest said. 'The only way we can do that is if we take a portal out of this realm and then go back on ourselves. I suggest we do it soon. If we can get to Gerling's estate before Eve is traded, then we might be able to break her out.'

'Aye,' Drax agreed. 'That's our best hope. Ceres could take her anywhere.'

Priest nodded grimly. 'We'd never find her. At least if we know where she is, we can bide our time until the right moment.'

'Gerling will be having us watched. He'll know if we take a portal straight there.'

Fie opened the window again and threw a leg out. 'We go back to another Dark Realm. Doesn't matter which. We kill our trackers and then go from there. Agreed?'

The others nodded and Drax felt a moment of pride at how far Fie had come since he'd first joined their unit.

'Go back to our room and gather our things,' Fie said to them. 'We'll take the smaller portal from the courtyard. At least then our leaving won't be marked to everyone in the court.'

They left the library, Drax and Priest making a brief stop at their chambers to collect their packs. They walked down to a small door past the kitchens that led out into a tiny courtyard where Fie waited for them. There was a portal here that not everyone knew existed.

'I can't see it without my amulet. Are you sure it's there?' Fie asked.

Drax nodded. 'It's by the path there. Always open. You just have to go to it.'

They stepped through and, in the most seamless journey that Drax had ever encountered, they found themselves in a quiet village. It was dark and there was no one around to see them arrive, the residents all in their beds for the night.

'Come,' Priest murmured, slipping into the shadows, and drawing his sword. 'It won't take long.'

Priest was right. A moment later, three men appeared in absolute silence, looking for them and Drax smiled grimly in the dark, glad to be finally taking action.

He and his Brothers waited until their prey was close enough before they sprang out of the darkness and killed all three outright, dragging their corpses out of sight.

They didn't waste any time, going back through the portal to the fae realms. This time they emerged in the north, close to where Gerling's estates lay in a small village. His fortress could be seen high on the hill, large and foreboding, silhouetted against the sunset.

'I can feel her,' Fie said. 'She's still here. We aren't too late.'

Drax sighed with relief as he felt the bond flare to life. Fie was right. Eve was close by. 'Let's find somewhere to lay low until we know more of what's happening.'

They took a room at a small inn at the edge of the village, the casement looking out over Gerling's home.

Fie went down to the tap rooms to learn what was going on up at the house and Drax had no doubt he'd come back with a plethora of information in the form of local gossip for them.

Drax stared out at the fortress, wondering if Eve was all right. She was alive. At least they knew that much.

'We're coming for you,' he whispered.

He was afraid. What if they couldn't get her back? What if she was sold to Ceres and they couldn't find her? He didn't know what brand of magick Ceres possessed but, considering his influence, Drax could guess he'd give Eve more than a run for her money especially as she still couldn't control hers properly. She was a lamb to the slaughter.

Drax put his head in his hands.

'We should have made certain that she could take care of herself around other fae,' he said to Priest.

His Brother gave a sigh. 'It's my fault. I terrified her into using her magick because it was simpler and faster instead of teaching her properly. I practically ensured she couldn't access her magic for herself.'

He sat down heavily on the bed. Drax put a hand on Priest's shoulder.

'We're all to blame,' he said. 'From the moment we met her, we were blinded by her lineage, both human and fae. If she'd been anyone else, we'd have seen that she was our mate from the beginning. We wouldn't have treated her like an enemy.'

Priest squeezed his hand. 'When we get her back, we'll make up for the pain we caused her. She'll never feel such things again.'

Drax closed his eyes, turning away. 'Can we make such promises? Fie perhaps. He came from a loving family, but you and I ... we're Dark Brothers. I never knew my father. My mother's family didn't bother with me after she was taken and yours—'

'Mine are a bunch of cunts save my sister,' Priest finished with a snort. 'We can learn to be good mates. We must or it won't matter if we save her. We'll lose her anyway.'

Fie came back in and they fell silent. 'Gerling is expected to be leaving his estate within the hour.'

'So soon?' Drax said.

Fie nodded. 'Good thing we got here when we did, but it may already be too late. We won't have time to infiltrate Gerling's fortress.'

Drax swore, but Priest looked out at the estate on the hill, his eyes narrowing as he thought. 'He'll have to come back through the village with her. Gerling allows no portal magick within his walls. We follow them through the bridge and take her. We'll await them in the square.'

They left the inn, finding a quiet spot in view of the portal in the main square to wait. Drax was coiled and ready. They would not let Eve be taken where they could not follow. They would save her from her father and from Ceres.

CHAPTER 13

EVE

As soon as they took her out into the open, she tried to call on her magick to open a portal, but it still wouldn't work. Whatever stopped her from conjuring extended to outside his fortress as well it seemed.

She gritted her teeth as she stepped inside the carriage. How long would she have to meekly go along with this farce before she could escape and find her Brothers?

Her father sat opposite her, dressed in even finer clothes than she'd seen him in previously. He'd sent her clothes to wear as well. She was now dressed in a silken sapphire gown with matching, impractical slippers.

'Who is Lord Ceres? What does he want with me?' she asked.

His piercing eyes took her in. 'He is a fae male of great standing and wealth. If you please him, the rewards will likely surpass any dreams you've ever had. Anger him and your punishment will surpass your worst nightmares. As to what he wants,' Gerling shrugged, 'I have no idea. In truth I was surprised when he requested you in return for the absolution of my debt to him. Still, fae females are all but barren now. He probably hopes for offspring with conjuring abilities.'

He leant back. 'I suggest you rest. It will take several hours to reach our destination,' he said, following his own advice and closing his eyes.

Eve stared out the locked window, watching as they entered the village. She raised her magick, trying again to see if she could conjure, but she couldn't.

Gerling cracked an eye open. 'I wouldn't bother. The carriage inhibits most forms of conjuring just as my home does. And before you go for the door to run the human way, know that you'll never escape the guards. They have access to their magicks. You won't get two steps down the road.'

Eve sat back, letting out a breath. The window of opportunity to escape and survive was rapidly closing as they entered the village down in the valley that she'd seen from the top of the hill. The carriage halted and the guards on horseback drew in closer as lightning began to strike the ground around them, making her tense.

Gerling chuckled. 'There's nothing to fear. The carriage and those near enough are protected from the energy bursts.'

Eve didn't relax at his words though, craning her neck to see the great glowing tunnel as it enveloped them. She doubted she'd ever get used to traveling this way.

The light of the bridge disappeared a moment later, leaving them in pitch black darkness, but the procession still moved forward as if this was commonplace.

Eve stared out of the window, but she could see nothing at all. There was only black outside the carriage. It was a void.

'What is this place?' she asked.

'Some say the first of the Dark Realms to come into being,' her father muttered, awe, fear, and jealously in his voice. 'There is only darkness here in this vast place Ceres calls home. No one can come here without an invitation.'

He conjured a small orb of light that hung in the air between them and then fell silent. Their pace continued, constant and unending, for so long that Eve began to doze in her seat despite her fears.

Then the carriage jolted to a stop, and she was wide awake in an instant. The door opened and her father alighted first.

'Come,' he said, taking her hand and helping her down the steps as if he hadn't basically brought his own daughter to sell in matrimony.

Still unable to see anything around them, she stayed close to him, much closer than she would have normally. His soldiers surrounded them, and they made their way on foot in silence. The only sounds were their boots crunching over what Eve hoped was simply gravel.

The men stopped and a door appeared in front of them, glowing with symbols that she didn't recognize.

The guards in front of them parted and Gerling took her arm, opening the door and pulling her through with him into a dome-ceilinged stone building. A grand staircase coiled up in front of them, the sides of the hall opened into other rooms and alcoves via simple stone archways. There was no furniture, no decor of any kind.

Gerling led her up the stairs to a lone, wooden door at the top and pushed her over the threshold. Inside was yet another sparsely furnished room that her father looked around with distaste.

'One could easily mistake you for a lesser lord, Ceres,' he scorned.

Eve caught sight of a large male sitting in a chair in front of a small desk across the room. Was this Ceres?

'Luckily, I don't give a fuck what one thinks,' the male

countered with a languid smile, his eyes falling on her. 'So, this is the daughter that you enslave to me,' he said, confirming his identity.

Eve's eyes widened. Her father had said marriage before, but he didn't gainsay Ceres as their host stood up and walked towards them.

'Very small for a fae,' he commented, his eyes flicking up and down her body impersonally, 'but if she truly has your blood in her veins, she'll do nicely.'

'She does and you can have her. Do with her what you will,' Gerling said, 'but that concludes our business. My debt to you is repaid in full.'

'Done,' Ceres said with a finality that chilled Eve to the core, 'but there's one more matter to discuss before you depart.'

'And what's that?' Gerling sneered.

'Your incompetence.'

Her father spluttered in anger. 'My what?'

'It was your alliance with the First Scholar that left my plans in ruins and allowed my wayward property to escape me to the Light Realm, a place I *still* cannot set foot in because of you.'

'It wasn't my fault Nixus took the magick for himself and then lost it! That was his foolishness, not mine!'

'Unfortunately for you, he's already dead and the only one left to sate my fury is you.'

'You can't do anything to me without the retribution from the Council Five!' Gerling sneered, but his eyes widened, his bravado rabidly being replaced by fear.

A bridge opened behind him, and Eve jumped back as her father screamed, trying to scramble away as a black tentacle reached through the opening and wrapped itself around his neck, hauling him off his feet and pulling him through the breach. He kicked and struggled, his eyes pleading, but Ceres had already forgotten him.

Eve simply stared as the portal disappeared. Gerling was gone. She looked up at the imposing fae in front of her. Was he about to do the same to her?

'What do you want from me?' she asked, finding her voice somehow.

'It's not a question of want, female. It's a question of need.'

'I don't understand,' she said drawing back as if that not being too close to him would save her from whatever he was going to do.

'It's so simple that even a creature like yourself will understand, halfling.'

He towered over her looking equal parts benevolent and wicked as he grabbed her chin and forced her to meet his own fathomless eyes.

'You *are* a little thing, aren't you?' he mused aloud. 'How amusing that such a tiny being is the only creature in all the realms who has the power to help me.'

'I don't understand,' she said again, and he chuckled.

'Of course you don't,' he called over his shoulder, 'but the fact is that you are the only one who can get me to the Light Realm. My many agents have failed to bring back my property, so I must go myself. You will open the portal for me.'

'But you just …' Eve gestured to where Gerling had been pulled through the portal that Ceres himself had made. 'Or even my Father could have—'

'No, my sweet girl. You aren't thinking,' he said, punctuating his words as if he was speaking to a child while he sat back at his desk. 'I cannot go to the Light Realm … A binding pact made long ago that is enforced by the oldest magicks. Ergo, I cannot make a portal there nor travel through one from the Dark Realms. Your father, being fully fae, was Dark Realm through and through. He could create such a bridge, but I would not have been able to pass through it as more than a shadow. I need you. With your father's brand of magick and your mother's ties to the Light Realm, I'll be able to cut through the barriers that keep me from that place.'

His gaze fastened on someone behind her. 'Take her to one of the cells until I'm ready for her.'

Strong hands grabbed her, turning her, but whatever held her could not be seen. She struggled, giving a cry, but an invisible hand over her mouth silenced her.

Ceres smiled as she was dragged backwards, her slippers gaining no purchase on the smooth floor.

'Finally, after so long, it's almost finished,' she heard him murmur.

∽

Fie

THE PORTAL BEGAN to close and he, Priest, and Drax had to run for it, barely getting through before it shut completely. They stayed behind the other soldiers, their heads down, hiding behind their armor as they pretended to be Gerling's men and hoped they were close enough not to get hit by any stray bolts from the breach as they were now without their amulets.

Eve was in the carriage with her father, but gods only knew where the bridge had brought them. None of them had ever been to such a dark realm as this one, but they'd all heard the stories of those who got lost in their inky depths.

'Stay with them,' he whispered.

They kept up with the carriage, staying as close as they dared while keeping in the formation of the other troops. All around them was blacker than the darkest night and though some of Gerling's men had torches, the light didn't permeate more than a step or two ahead. They couldn't even see the ground though it crunched like rock and Fie was unable to examine it further without giving them away.

They trekked by the side of the carriage as they marched over the pitch-black terrain. They could hear noises, howls and screeches, rustlings. Some echoed from the distance, others were much too close for comfort, but none of the guards deviated from their course, and nothing came for them.

Fie assumed that the carriage or even Gerling himself was magicked in some way to either be invisible to the Dark Realm's occupants, or perhaps they were protected by an object as their amulets usually protected he and his Brothers.

The carriage drew to a halt and the soldiers' steps ceased. He watched as Eve, dressed in the finest fae fashion, was helped down and set on her feet. Gerling wasted no time. He drew her forward and said a word. A doorway opened. He pulled her through, and it closed behind them. Only then did the men begin marching again, going forward, and leading the carriage away.

Fie, Drax, and Priest held back, waiting for the men to disappear into the darkness and hoping no one looked back. Standing exactly where the door had been, Fie nodded at Priest who, without being prompted, said the word that they'd heard Gerling utter.

The door appeared and Fie threw his torch away from them, only to see another creature's many, many gleaming eyes watching them just off the path, silent and unseen, just for a second before the flame of the torch flickered and died.

'Fuck!' he exclaimed, pushing his Brothers through the door, and sealing it behind him.

'Did you see that?'

Priest and Drax grinned at each other.

'Finally saw one of the beasts of the ink realms, did you?

There was a time that you couldn't even *be* a Dark Brother until you'd fought one and survived.'

They both chuckled, drawing their swords and moving forward, leaving Fie gaping. He belatedly drew his own weapon and followed after them.

They found themselves in a sparse but well-lit hall. It was made of stone and looked older than the ancient temple where they'd found the fae children.

'Where are we?' Fie whispered and Priest looked around, considering.

'I think it's a fold.'

'Like the Underhill?'

'Yes, but smaller. A perfect place to hide.'

'What fae can create such a thing?' Drax asked.

Priest looked back at his Brothers. 'There aren't any fae that could make this. Only a god has the power.'

'Are you saying Ceres is a god?'

Priest shrugged. 'If he is, we best find Eve and get the fuck out of here.'

They crept up the large staircase and were met with a door.

Fie put his ear to it, hearing Eve's voice accompanied by a much deeper one that did not sound like Gerling. The voices went quiet and, after a few moments, when he heard nothing else, he nodded to the others.

Drax opened the door with a very soft click. Behind it was another sparse room with a desk and a small chair. They went in cautiously, but there was no one there. Corridors bled into each other, leading to other parts of the fold. The windows showed only black.

'Do you feel her?' Fie asked, and all three of them looked towards one of the many halls. She was down there.

'Let's get this done before we're found,' Drax muttered.

Not wasting any more time, they went down the hall and

immediately saw her huddled in a tiny cell built into the end wall only just big enough to sit in. There was nothing else down the corridor at all. Only the cell.

She stood as she saw them. 'How did you find me?'

She seemed surprised that they'd come for her.

Fie picked the lock and the door of the cell opened.

'This is too easy,' Priest muttered.

'Where is Gerling?' Drax asked.

'There's no time. I'll tell you everything later. We need to get out of here now. Ceres is—'

'Did you really think you'd escape so easily?' a voice said from behind them. 'You fae are entertaining, I'll give you that.'

Fie turned to find the largest male he'd ever seen. He put his sword up and the male waved aa hand through the air in almost an afterthought.

Fie was thrown through the air and into the wall, falling to the floor with a thump.

He groaned, edging up the stones to get to his feet.

Priest stepped forward and said a word in the old tongue. A wind began to whip through the corridor, pushing Ceres back a few steps, but all he did was give a chuckle.

'Run!' Fie yelled but wondered where they could actually run *to* that a god couldn't find them.

But Eve grabbed Priest, who was closest to her, instead, and a portal appeared in front of them. Fie ran for it as she and the others were pulled through, hurling himself over the threshold and into the tunnel headfirst.

He found himself on the floor, staring up at a ceiling he recognized. They were back in their house in Kitore.

'You can control your conjures,' Priest wheezed as he sat up.

'An unintended gift from my father,' Eve replied, standing

and brushing herself off. 'Ceres can't follow us here. That's what he needed me for; my Light Realm blood and my father's magick, so that he could get around some magickal pact.'

Drax clenched his fists. 'Fucking Gerling. I'll bet he's back in his fortress already, untouchable as always.'

'No,' Eve said. 'He's dead. Ceres killed him.' She looked down, her brow knitting. 'Gerling was the one who allied himself with the First Scholar who took the children. He helped the Library's men attack the Underhill.'

Fie ran a hand through his hair. 'I knew it! I fucking knew it was him! He was the one who let Kitore's soldiers in to kill the warriors. It could be no other! When it was done, he probably appeared like a savior and told the females to take the children to Kitore for safety. He was fae, on the Council. They would have thought he was trying to help them and then they got to Kitore and were imprisoned, their children taken from them ...'

'And Nixus murdered them all as he siphoned their magick from them,' Priest finished, looking sick to his stomach.

'How could one of our own do such a thing?' Fie asked.

'I'm sorry,' Eve said. 'I'm so sorry for what he did.'

'No. Never blame yourself for his actions,' Fie said, drawing her to him and staring into her eyes. 'We did enough of that when we met you and we're all sorry for it. We were fools and none of this was your fault. You're nothing like him, Eve.'

Eve's eyes flicked to Drax. 'He was the one though, wasn't he? He took your mother from you.'

Drax's jaw tightened. 'Yes.'

'My father began all of this,' she said. 'And, on top of that, he was doing Ceres' bidding as well. I understand why you'd hate me. All of you. Please don't pretend otherwise. Break the bond and you'll never have to set eyes on me again.' She looked down. 'I promise.'

Fie glanced at the others, panic making his mouth suddenly go dry. 'Is that what you want?' he rasped.

'No, but—'

'You're our Fourth,' Drax said, 'and, more than that, you're our mate. We love you, Eve. You're never escaping us ever again.'

∼

Eve

'Where are we going? You know you'll have to tell me if you want me to take us there via a bridge, don't you?' Eve laughed.

'You'll see,' Priest said, a gleam in his eye as he pulled her along through the rooms to the main entrance hall.

He was different now, she thought. Over the past days, he'd become lighter and happier. He joked with her and the others, surprised her with trinkets and treats. He and Drax hadn't argued once since she'd brought them back to Kitore either.

They all seemed happy to be in the city and weren't making any plans to leave anytime soon. They took her out in it almost every day, entertained her and showed her everything as if they were helping her make up for all the years she'd been a captive. And they never let her go out alone, which she blustered about, but secretly found endearing. They were all such different men than they had been in those first days. They cared for her. They were the family she had always dreamed of.

The only thing they hadn't done was touch her. None of them had since the chase with Priest in the mountains. She found that she missed their caresses. She missed the feel of their bodies against hers. But she wasn't sure how to tell them what she wanted from them. A small part of her feared that they had tired of her, that they no longer wanted her that way. It was just a stray doubt, but it was enough that even thinking about broaching the subject with any of the Brothers made her want to bury her head in the sand so, like a coward, that was what she'd been doing.

'Come,' Priest said. 'They're waiting for us.'

Eve giggled, giving into his carefree manner and couldn't help her wide smile as he looked back at her with a grin.

They passed through the kitchens and out into the small courtyard behind the house, its high walls making it a secluded spot that wasn't overlooked by prying eyes.

Fie and Drax were there and, as she walked outside, she saw that they'd drawn a fighting ring on the ground.

Her brow furrowed in question even as her body began to ready itself at the mere sight of it after her many years of combat.

'What is this?' she asked, half in excitement and half in fear.

None of the men said anything, each of them hesitating.

'We thought—' Priest began.

'You said before that you needed the fights,' Drax interrupted, looking at Priest meaningfully. 'We wanted you to know that if you do want to compete in the rings, we won't stop you so long as none of the fights are to the death.'

'And we thought you might like to spar with us sometimes,' Fie said, almost looking shy as he said it.

Eve walked around the pit they'd made, identical in size to the ones in every town and city.

She couldn't help the smile as she unbuttoned her tunic.

'Which one of you will be first?' she asked, throwing it on a stone bench nearby.

They all looked at each other.

'We thought you might like to take all of us.'

'All of you?' she asked, her boldness waning just a tad as she wondered at Drax's choice of words.

'Are you sure about this?' Fie asked Priest quietly.

He didn't think she could hear him, but her fae senses were getting better all the time.

'I've fought her more than once,' Priest breathed,' and I know how excited it made her.'

'Unless you don't think you can win,' Priest said more loudly to her. 'After all, you've never beaten one of us, have you, Eve?'

Her eyes narrowed at his challenge, and she walked to the middle of the circle, readying herself.

Priest said a word that Eve now knew meant 'silence' in the oldest of the fae tongues, so that none of the neighbors would hear anything, she expected.

All three of them shucked their tunics, roiling up their shirt sleeves and getting rid of their weapons.

They advanced on her and her breathing quickened, her skin prickling. She shivered, but it wasn't in fear. This felt so different than it had before when she used to enter the rings. She was anticipating it, excited by the three fae males who, she'd noticed, had let their glamors down.

They came closer and she felt like a bird trapped in a cage, but she stood her ground, a smile breaking free as she hit Drax square in the jaw and he staggered back.

'Our Fourth has gotten stronger,' he commented, rubbing where she'd struck him.

They closed in, all three of them coming for her at once. She was able to beat them back, but Priest lunged at her. Fie took advantage of her diverted attention, getting behind her and pinning her arms back. She used them as leverage to kick Priest in the chest.

He fell back with a laugh, and she grinned. This fight was unlike any other she'd ever been in, and she was loving every moment of it.

She found herself held in place by Fie and no matter how much she struggled, he had her arms in a lock she couldn't get out of.

Drax and Priest came for her together this time, each grabbing a leg as she tried the same move again.

They crowded in front of her. Their heights and their broad bodies that might once have intimidated her in the ring now made her feel something completely different.

'You see?' Priest smirked, glancing at the two others, his nostrils flaring. 'I told you, she would enjoy it.'

His knuckles grazed down her cheek and he gripped her throat. Her breathing hitched, her eyes widening for a moment as she was assailed by memories of him doing the same to make her conjure, of the Bull in the pits.

Regret passed over his features and his hand caressed her neck gently instead of squeezing. Leaning into her, he put his cheek against hers.

'It's us,' he murmured. 'You have nothing to fear, my love.'

And she nodded jerkily. It wouldn't be like it had been when she lost to the Bull. Never again. He brushed his lips against hers and she could tell that he was hungry for more. Her shirt was unlaced and ripped away, leaving her in her chemise and breeches, shivering slightly, but not from fear nor from cold. Excitement flowed through her veins, making her bold.

She bit her lip, wondering what they would do next while she was at their mercies, but then she felt Fie's arms slacken and she grinned at Priest, kissing him, and catching his lip between her teeth. She nipped hard and he jerked back with a sound of disbelief as she twisted from their grasps.

Looking back, she gave them a wink, her grin widening as she opened a small portal in front of her. She jumped through and it closed immediately. She appeared in the house. She could see them from the back door, cursing at themselves and each other. She laughed loudly as she ran through the kitchens.

She heard them giving chase as she ran up the stairs to Fie's chamber. She sank down and rolled under his grand bed, stilling her breathing as she heard their footsteps pounding through the house as they searched for her.

The door to Fie's room was flung open, and three sets of boots stomped in.

'We know you're in here, Fourth,' sang Drax. 'We can smell how wet our little games have made you.'

'Come out, come out, little rabbit,' Priest muttered.

Eve struggled to contain the excited giggles that bubbled up from her throat, but knew she'd failed when a meaty hand grabbed her booted ankle and dragged her out from underneath.

She shrieked as she was pinned down on her back, beginning to struggle. She almost couldn't help herself. She'd not go down without a fight.

But then Fie's voice said in her ear, 'You will not move.'

She gasped as she looked at him, arousal warring with apprehension. He hadn't used compulsion on her before, but she couldn't not do as he told her.

Priest and Drax didn't waste any more time, pulling off her boots and the rest of her clothes.

'Spread your legs for us. Let's see that pretty cunt.'

She glared at Fie as she did as he ordered, whimpering as one of their fingers delved into her channel immediately.

Priest gave a dark chuckle. 'You're making a puddle on the floor, female,' he muttered.

Drax felt her, licking his finger with a groan as he stared at her. Fie reached down her body as well, each of them taking a turn to touch her, feeling how wet and slick she was.

Priest stretched her nether lips wide and probed her channel with something cold and solid. She tensed, swallowing hard and giving Fie a worried look.

He hushed her. 'We will not hurt you,' he said, staring into her eyes and cupping her cheek with his hand and then he winked. 'You'll like it.'

The thing was removed, and then she felt it pressing at her back passage. She squirmed as it entered her easily at first, her gaze flitting to their faces as they all watched what Priest was doing between her legs. She gave a grunt as it slid further in, the pressure making her uncomfortable.

'Get up,' Fie ordered, helping her to her feet and the compulsion disappeared.

Her fingers fluttered to her arse, but Fie pulled them away, kissing her neck, holding her wrists gently above her head.

'Do what you're told. Be a good girl for us,' Priest said as they undressed, 'and we won't have to give you any more orders.'

Fie, now as bare as she was, sat in the middle of the bed, drawing her down with him and placing her facing away from him in his lap. Drax knelt between her bent knees, kissing her lips as Fie sucked on her neck, each of them taking a breast in their hand. Drax kneaded gently while Fie twisted hard, the sensations of their hands, lips, fingers, and that *other thing* already beginning to overwhelm her.

Fie entered her first and she gave a loud gasp. With the thing in her arse as well, she'd never felt so full. He began to thrust gently, moving her up and down easily on his length. In front of her, Drax gave a growl.

'I was meant to have her first this time.'

Fie chuckled. 'Share her with me then.'

Drax surged forward and, as Fie drew out, he pushed into her instead, their cocks alternating.

Eve couldn't help the moan that passed her lips, and then they were both inside her at once, both of them holding her in place tightly, stretching her tight channel. Her mouth opened on a breath she couldn't take, her lungs freezing as the feeling of them both inside her was too much for her, making her body tighten, climb higher and higher.

Priest appeared next to her, thrusting into her mouth. She felt his magick coiling inside of her, making her gasp, her hips rolling.

Her breath came in fits and starts. But she couldn't reach her pleasure for their pace was too slow. They kept her balanced on the edge of a cliff she longed to fall down.

Eve made a sound of frustration, wishing they would go faster and Fie hushed her again.

'All in good time, Eve,' he ground out breathlessly, licking a trail from her ear down to her shoulder and scaping his teeth against her.

'Turn her.'

They switched places, Drax on his back on the bed, Eve facing him. Fie pushed into her open mouth and she tasted herself on him.

Priest pulled her hips up into the air as Drax moved under her pushing up into her, his movements still maddeningly slow and gentle. Priest eased the thing out of her body, and she squealed as he replaced it with the head of his cock.

She twisted her neck and looked at him, fear in her eyes even though she trusted him. He rubbed her back.

'I promise I'll not hurt you,' he said as he eased himself inside her to the hilt, stretching her even more.

She whimpered and moaned, crying out as they all shared her. Priest thrust harder and she was urged forward, forcing Drax deeper into her.

Fie grasped her hair, throwing back his head with a long groan as she felt his seed flow down her throat.

He pulled out of her, caressing her cheek and kissed her mouth, his tongue invading her.

Drax and Priest picked up the pace, both of them holding her securely in place for their pleasure and hers. Drax gave a roar, holding her down on his cock, Priest following soon after. And he reached his hand around, doing something with his magick on the bud between legs. She screamed, her back bowing as her body went taut, her legs shaking as her pleasure was finally allowed to crest. Her screams echoed through the house, the aftermath making her body shudder as she whimpered and moaned, her channels grasping at the cocks still inside her.

LATER THAT AFTERNOON while Fie lounged in the bath close by, Eve lay between Drax and Priest in the bed, her body sated and pleasurably sore. The Brothers both drew their fingers over her in lazy patterns as they dozed together.

Drax leaned down and kissed her.

'I knew you were our mate the day we left the Camp,' he admitted quietly as he stroked the underside of her breast and nuzzled at her neck.

'How?' she asked, surprised.

'It was the dream you told me of at the Camp. All fae females have visions of their true mates before they meet them. As soon as you described it, I knew you were destined for us.'

'I *knew* you knew what it meant despite what you pretended,' she accused, hitting his arm playfully and grinning at him.

Eve turned her head to look at Priest next to her and then at Fie in the bath, his head resting on the wide brim with his eyes closed. She was scarcely able to believe that these men were hers, that they wanted her. For so long she'd been a shadow, living on so little with nothing and no one. But now she had more than she'd ever dreamed.

'Can we return to Gerling's fortress?' she asked, thinking about his human slaves and, more specifically, Sym.

She had to do something to help.

At their silences, she opened her eyes to find a look passing between Priest and Drax.

'We were going to wait to tell you …'

'Despite his many attempts, Gerling sired no other children besides you.'

'So?' she asked them.

'You're his heir, Eve.'

Her eyes widened. 'Me? But I'm a halfling. No one even knows of my existence.'

'That won't matter,' Priest said. 'One sniff of your blood is all it will take to convince the naysayers. The law is clear. Gerling's estates and possessions, his wealth. Everything is yours and … something else as well.'

'What else could he possibly have?'

'His seat on the Council will go to you too.'

'If you want it.'

'But I …' Eve sat up, her mind working, thinking about Sym, about Drax's mother and the other human slaves. 'If I have a seat on the Council, I'll have influence, won't I? I can change laws, perhaps even have the human slaves freed.'

Drax nodded, caressing her face as Priest drew her body closer to him, sandwiching her between them.

'Whatever you want or need, Eve. We're here for you as your unit and as your mates.'

The End

Not ready to leave Eve and her Brothers just yet? Want find out what happens next, before Seized to Sacrifice (Book 6) begins?

Use the URL below for your exclusive bonus scene: https://BookHip.com/RCVWBWL

(If you already receive my newsletter, just put in the email you used and you'll still be able to get the link.)

If you enjoyed this book, **it would be amazing if you were able to leave a review on Amazon, Goodreads, and/or Bookbub.**

Reviews are so, so helpful to authors (especially new ones like me!) to get us noticed and, I'm not gonna lie, I love reading them!

Also, keep reading for the exclusive beginning of *Seized to Sacrifice,* Book 6 in the Dark Brothers series, coming out in February 2022!

JOIN MY MAILING LIST

Sign up to my newsletter and receive an exclusive epilogue to find out what happens after Eve and her Brothers go back to her father's house!

Members also receive exclusive content, free books, access to giveaways and contests as well as the latest information on new books and projects that I'm working on!

Use the URL below:
  https://BookHip.com/RCVWBWL

It's completely free to sign up, you will never be spammed by me and it's very easy to unsubscribe.

AND keep reading for an exclusive sneak preview of Trapped to Tame, Book 5 of the Dark Brothers Series.

SEIZED TO SACRIFICE (SNEAK PREVIEW)

She has no memory of her past. They remember her crimes far too well. Can love save them, or will everything they care about be destroyed?

Pre-order Seized to Sacrifice (Release date Feb 2022) at www.kyraalessy.com/seized2sacrifice

Rye

It couldn't be her.

He focused his eyes on the figure, but the sun was in just the wrong spot, and he couldn't see properly across the square. A cart stopped in front of him, obscuring his line of vision and he cursed aloud.

It couldn't be her. Not after all this time.

He was going to turn away. He meant to. He had finished his business for the day, and it would dark soon. He should return home while the roads were easiest to navigate.

But as he turned with his horse to leave, he grimaced and swung back. He couldn't let it lie. He had to know.

The town was still heaving as it always was when the bridge was open. Now that it was one of the only ones left, people came from all around the realm to trade here.

Leaving his mount, Ryder skirted around the stalls of Dark Realm goods, the human pedlers calling out their merchandises in booming voices that added to the frenzied atmosphere. There was an air of desperation. Everyone knew the portal would close soon and, with things being how they were, gods only knew when it might reopen.

He edged around the short wall of the stone well, those who knew him as one of the local lords letting him through the throng with nods or murmured words of greeting.

He reached the row of cages that held their human wares and was gratified to see that many were empty despite the auction not having begun yet. Moving down the row, he peered into each one, trying to see which of them had been the female he'd seen. But all of them were men, ragged and thin ... until he got to the final pen.

She was huddled in the corner, her white knuckles gripping the iron bars. Her deep red hair, what he'd noticed from the other side of the square, hung limply around her face in clumps. Her dress had clearly once been white, but was dirty and torn now, stained from a recent wound on her temple. Blood was smudged down her cheek and neck and he canted his head as he stared at her, his heart hammering in his chest.

He must have made a sound because her eyes, eyes he hadn't see in so long, found his, vibrant blue. His breath caught, knowing her instantly, but there was no spark in her expression. She didn't recognise him.

His lip curled. How quickly had the bitch forgotten them?

The slaver came up behind him.

'Auction starts soon if you want 'er,' he said.

He was a plump, jovial man that Rye had seen around. One wouldn't instinctively know he was a flesh merchant by looking at him, but by the way she flinched back, Rye wondered who the man really was behind his jolly smile.

'How much do you think you'll make?' Rye asked, his eyes returning to her, moving over her more carefully.

He saw the signs of the lash on her shoulder and his jaw tightened. Had this man been the source of her head wound too?

'Fifteen, maybe, as she's the only female I have today,' he said, stroking his whiskered cheek with the backs of his knuckles as he thought.

'Where did you come by her?' Rye asked, his eyes not leaving her as if he was afraid she'd up and disappear in front of his eyes.

The slaver's face lost some of its cheer at the question. ''Round abouts,' he said, not giving anything away.

''I'll give you thrice that if you sell her to me now.' Rye pulled out his coin purse.

The slaver didn't even bother to haggle, knowing he'd not get more. 'Done.'

He unlocked the cage and made a grab for her, pulling the woman out by her hair. She squealed, clinging to the bars, and the slaver jerked her close, grunting something in her ear that made her let go immediately, the fight leaving her.

She was thrust at Rye.

'She'll make a good slave if you know how to handle her,' he laughed, not noticing Rye's thunderous expression as he saw more whip marks on her back.

The slaver's eyes followed Rye's and he shrugged.

'Sometimes they need to learn their place quick.'

Rye gave a curt nod and, after thrusting the coin purse at the slaver, he made his way back to his horse, pulling the now subdued woman along after him. He tied her hands together. She didn't fight, didn't even look at him, as they made their way slowly from the town and out into the forest paths.

His Brothers were going to be surprised, he thought as he looked down at her. Finally, revenge for what she'd done to them would be theirs.

Read the last dark adventure in this amazing series today!
More info at www.kyraalessy.com/seized2sacrifice

ACKNOWLEDGEMENTS

For Patch.

Who was 10 months old at the time Trapped to Tame was released.

Who became a teenager while I was writing this book and constantly bothered the living shit out of me every time I sat down to write because he wanted to play … or whine at me for no reason … or have my coffee froth.

Who bit my toes and my clothes when I didn't give him attention while I was trying to edit a book to a deadline that had already passed.

Who woke me in the dead of night (every night) by jumping on my head for cuddles.

If there are major problems in this book, blame Patch, the 40lb cocker (Yeah, right! There's no way this beast is a not a sprocker at the very least!) spaniel who thinks he's a lapdog.

Patchy, I love you, you adorable asshole.

Also, stop licking other dogs' junk and letting them pee on your head.

ABOUT THE AUTHOR

Kyra was almost 20 when she read her first romance. From Norsemen to Regency and Romcom to Dubcon, tales of love and adventure filled a void in her she didn't know existed. She's always been a writer, but its only now that she's started to tell stories in the genre she loves most.

Kyra LOVES interacting with her readers so please join us in the Portal to the Dark Realm, her private Facebook group, because she is literally ALWAYS online unless she's asleep – much to her husband's annoyance!

Take a look at her website for info on how to stay updated on release dates, exclusive content and other general awesomeness from the Dark Brothers' world – where the road to happily ever after might be rough, but its well worth the journey!

- facebook.com/kyraalessy
- twitter.com/evylempryss
- instagram.com/kyraalessy
- goodreads.com/evylempryss

Printed in Great Britain
by Amazon